DAUGHTERS OF TUSCANY

SIOBHAN DAIKO

Boldwood

First published in Great Britain in 2024 by Boldwood Books Ltd.

Copyright © Siobhan Daiko, 2024

Cover Design by Head Design Ltd.

Cover Photography: Shutterstock and iStock

A CIP catalogue record for this book is available from the British Library.

Paperback ISBN 978-1-83751-882-1

Large Print ISBN 978-1-83751-881-4

Hardback ISBN 978-1-83751-880-7

Ebook ISBN 978-1-83751-883-8

Kindle ISBN 978-1-83751-884-5

Audio CD ISBN 978-1-83751-875-3

MP3 CD ISBN 978-1-83751-876-0

Digital audio download ISBN 978-1-83751-877-7

Boldwood Books Ltd
23 Bowerdean Street
London SW6 3TN
www.boldwoodbooks.com

For Prisca

1

Emma tapped her heels against the dark bay flanks of her Maremmano mare, Bella, urging her into a trot up the steep unmetalled road. Dust furled as she squinted in the warm May sunshine. The afternoon had turned hot, and she squeezed Bella's reins to slow her down to a walk. On her right rose the massive, ivy-covered red-brick walls which enclosed the front gardens of the ochre-coloured Villa Bivio. Nearly nineteen years ago, she'd come into the world there; it was her beloved home.

The wide valley spread below: slopes of cultivated land verdant with wheat, olives and vines nestled below forested hills on one side and the clay knolls known as *crete sinesi* on the other. Hard to believe the estate had been virtually a desert when her parents had bought it back in 1920. It had suffered for centuries from a lack of water. But Papà had soon presided over an organisation of landowners and had begun working on water management projects to irrigate the land. He'd arrested the soil erosion, then turned his attention to reforestation, roadbuilding and planting. The Bivio was highly productive now, a far cry from the dismal place it had once been, and their tenant farmers consequently lived a much better life.

Emma eyed the zig-zag road opposite, lined with tall black-green cypress trees. She remembered Papà telling her the story of its origins. After her parents had bought the estate, the land at the top of the hill had been levelled and new farmhouses had been built. They'd needed a road, so Papà had decided to create a track inspired by thirteenth- and fourteenth-century Sienese and Florentine painters. It truly was beautiful, and Emma had ridden up it earlier to enjoy the fresh air.

Her gaze swept beyond the valley towards Monte Amiata, an extinct volcano whose magnificence dominated the distant landscape. It always reminded her of the pictures she'd seen of Mount Fuji in Japan. She gave an involuntary shiver. Not quite a year and a half ago, Japan had gone to war with the Allies. The entire world was at war, it seemed. Papà said that the recent Axis defeat in North Africa had paved the way for an imminent invasion of Europe. He believed that British and American armies would soon land in Italy, perhaps even on the Tuscan coast.

Emma shivered again. Allied planes had been bombing big cities like Naples in daylight hours for months, but now their raids had become ever more horrific. Just a couple of weeks ago, a squadron of twenty-six Liberators had flown over nearby Grosseto. Having dropped their bombs on the airport, they'd then proceeded to fly low over the little town. Because of the suddenness of the attack, the sirens hadn't sounded until the planes were overhead. People dressed in their Easter Sunday best were thronging the streets. The Liberators machine-gunned them, then went on to attack children riding a merry-go-round and even fired on people trying to escape into a wheatfield. The aircraft had wheeled back over Grosseto, machine-gunning a group gathered by the door of the church.

Emma swallowed the bitter taste in her mouth. It made her ashamed of the British and American blood she'd inherited from her mother, and fearful for the future.

Bella gave a whinny, jolting Emma back to the task at hand. She dismounted at the gates to the *fattoria* home farm at the rear of the villa and smoothed her horse's sweaty neck.

'Thanks for a lovely ride, beautiful.' She kissed Bella's velvety soft nose and smiled as an equine whisker tickled her chin.

Bella blew out a sweet, hay-scented breath.

Emma walked her in circles until she'd cooled down, then led her into the stable block at the far end of the courtyard. She brushed the dried sweat off Bella's coat and made sure she had a hay net and plenty of water.

A whinny came from the adjoining stall and Zorro, the estate's black Maremmano stallion, popped his head over the half-door.

'*Ciao, bello,*' Emma said, going up to him.

He nuzzled her long plait of red hair, shook his head, and rubbed his forehead against her chest.

She scratched his poll, her fingers threading through his thick forelock. 'Are you missing Marco as much as I am?'

Marco Landi was the son of the *fattore*, the estate manager. He was two years older than Emma and she loved him like a brother. They'd grown up together, both of them without siblings. Marco had the patience of a saint, as far as she was concerned. It was he who'd taught her about the ways of the countryfolk and she loved going out for long rides with him around the 5,500 acres of her parents' property.

Zorro nuzzled her again. Both he and Bella were mostly used for pulling the farm carts to take produce to market when the white oxen were otherwise busy. But Papà allowed Emma and Marco to ride them as well, on the condition they took good care of them. She gave a sigh. Last month, Marco had been conscripted into the Air Force. He'd had to interrupt his architecture studies at the university in Florence and was an officer cadet stationed at Pian del Lago near Siena now. What would happen to him if the Allies landed? Most of the sons of the estate's farmers, who were old enough to have been drafted, were in the armed forces as well. What would happen to them?

The echo of footfalls interrupted Emma's thoughts. Orazio, Marco's father, the estate manager, was approaching.

'Your papà has telephoned, Emma. He's at the fortress. The British POWs are due shortly and he would like me to drive you up there to meet them.'

Emma smiled at the *fattore*. When she'd turned sixteen, he'd begun to refer to her as '*signorina*'. She'd reprimanded him, told him in no uncertain terms that she was 'Emma' like she'd always been. He'd then insisted that she call him 'Orazio' in return.

'I'll go and change out of my jodhpurs,' she said. 'I'll only be a couple of minutes.'

She'd been ambivalent about meeting the POWs after the bombing of Grosseto. But the men in question clearly weren't to blame; they'd been imprisoned well before that atrocity, in the big camp at Laterina near Arezzo. Papà had used his contacts to be assigned a group of fifty to work on the estate, given that they'd been left short-handed by the conscription of practically all their able-bodied young men.

Now that the Allied prisoners were about to arrive, Emma couldn't help feeling curious. Papà had driven to meet them at the Chianciano railway station, to oversee the loading of their kit onto oxcarts. He'd then gone ahead in his car while they marched the eight kilometres to the estate's fortress – an old fortified settlement about a kilometre away, which also housed two keepers and their families, as well as the parish priest of the church within its walls.

Emma was glad that Papà would reassure the keepers' wives,

who were preparing to barricade themselves inside their apartments for fear of the enemy, check on everything and wait for the prisoners to arrive.

* * *

After changing into a pair of slacks and a clean blouse, Emma re-plaited her dark burgundy braid. She touched the gold cross on the necklace her late mama had given her, which she wore every day to remind herself of the woman who'd been a distant figure in her life. It was hard for her to reconcile the mother who was never around with the young Anglo-American woman who'd fallen in love with Marchese Camillo Ginori while staying with family friends in Florence. Mama had been so smitten with him that she'd invested her capital with his to buy the Bivio estate soon after they were married. They'd had Emma almost straight away, but Mama had soon grown bored with life in the depths of the Tuscan countryside. A wealthy heiress, she'd spent most of her time abroad. Emma had been home from her English boarding school for the summer holidays when Mama's latest lover had driven his car off the road while under the influence of alcohol, on a winding road above Monte Carlo, killing both of them. Not long afterwards, Hitler invaded Poland and Emma had never returned to her school. Papà arranged for a tutor to come twice weekly from Siena, and she was preparing her university entrance exams with the *professore* now.

Emma left her bedroom and went down the steep stone staircase which led to the central hall of the villa, lit by a skylight. A door opened onto the wing that linked the sixteenth-century house with the *fattoria*. Just beyond stood the building in which the olives were pressed and the estate's oil made and stored, as well as the granaries, the laundry room, the woodshed and, a little farther off, the carpenter's shop, the blacksmith's and the stables. The villa and the *fattoria* formed, according to old Tuscan tradition, a single, closely connected little world and Emma loved it more than any other place on earth.

Orazio was waiting for her in the yard where the oxcarts brought in the wheat, olives and grapes from the estate's farms. They got into a small three-wheeler lorry and, ten minutes later, after heading up a steep dirt track leading through the woodland behind the *fattoria*, they'd reached the medieval fortress.

Imposing stone walls towered above them, topped by a bell tower, and Emma remembered that an old lady used to live there. Papà bought the property nine years ago, after the woman passed away, and added its 2,000 acres of land to the Bivio estate.

Orazio parked the lorry and she walked with him through the open big metal door of the entrance portal.

The courtyard inside teemed with men and Emma's ears rang with the sound of British and Italian voices.

'There you are, Emma.' Papà bounded up. 'This is Lieutenant Russo.' He introduced the short, dark-haired man who'd approached with him. 'He speaks English and is in charge of the prisoners, has a guard of ten men from Sicily.'

Papà indicated a group of swarthy-looking soldiers, who were milling around, smoking. Orazio had inserted his way into the midst of them, probably to assert his authority as far as the estate was concerned.

Emma shook hands with the lieutenant.

'And this is Corporal Smith, the prisoners' representative.' Papà presented a tall blond fellow, who'd made an appearance next to him.

Corporal Smith saluted. 'Pleased to meet you, miss.'

'Likewise.' Emma forced a smile.

Papà took her hand. 'I'll show you around.'

She hadn't been inside the fortress since it had been prepared for the POWs.

'Lead the way,' she said, her heart swelling with love for her father. He stood head and shoulders above everyone else, not only physically, but also metaphorically. In his late forties, he still had the energy of a much younger man despite his hair thinning and greying at the temples. The whole world loved and respected him, for he'd done so much for the local community. He wasn't entirely saintly, though. Emma suspected there were women in Rome and Florence who were more than 'just friends'. He and Mama seemed to have had that kind of relationship. Emma had been away at school and hadn't known too much about it until Mama had died. Even now, Papà would disappear for long weekends from time to time, giving the excuse of 'business meetings'. Emma refrained from probing. His love for her was unconditional and what he did in his own time was his own business.

She followed him through a doorway into three big interconnecting rooms, one of which had once been the stables. In addition, there was a dining room, kitchen, and washroom with twelve basins and two showers, all freshly whitewashed and perfectly clean, if primitive. Beds for the prisoners – double-tiered bunks with straw-filled sacks for mattresses – had been provided by the Italian army, apparently, as well as cooking utensils and food that was to be prepared for them by a cook.

She went up to a barred window and tugged at it.

A sandy-haired young man with a close-cropped beard approached. 'If you're doing that for us, miss, don't bother.' He spoke in a Scottish accent. 'Me and the lads have fallen on our feet here, we think.' He laughed. 'We were bored out of our minds in Laterina and can't wait to get our hands dirty in your fields.'

Emma stood back, looked him up and down. 'Do you speak any Italian?'

He shook his head. 'No. But we're all keen to learn.'

'Good. Have you any experience working the land?'

'We were all involved in gardening one way or the other back home. If we'd been farmers we would've stayed behind to feed the nation.' A smile lit his blue eyes. 'Any chance we could have a bit of a field where we can knock a ball about?'

'I'll ask my father but I'm sure that can be arranged.'

She did so as soon as she was in the Fiat 1500 with Papà, motoring down the steep road back to the villa.

'What do you think our farmers will make of the prisoners?' she asked him after he'd agreed to the sandy-haired young man's request. 'I mean, they won't be able to communicate with them, will they?'

'They're not here to socialise, *mia cara*. They're here to work. It will soon be time for the reaping and then the threshing of our wheat.'

Emma nodded. Life at Bivio was ruled by the seasons.

'Any news from Marco?' Her thoughts were never far from the person she considered to be her best friend.

'Oh, yes. I forgot to tell you. He telephoned earlier to say he'll have some leave next month and will be back to help with the harvest.'

'Wonderful!'

She couldn't wait to see him. Couldn't wait to go for long rides with him. Couldn't wait to simply be with him and bask in his friendship.

2

A whoosh of heat warmed Rosa's face as the mouth-watering aroma of freshly baked bread filled her nostrils. She retrieved two round loaves from the outside oven, put them on a wooden tray and, in the style of a true countrywoman, placed the tray on top of her head. Keeping her body erect, her hips swaying in forward movements, she made her way up the wide stone staircase at the side of the farmhouse. Her family – the Vaninis – like all Tuscan farmers, lived on the upper floor above the storerooms and an arched recess where the farm's carts were kept.

The late-afternoon sun hung low in the sky, illuminating the golden fields of wheat blanketing the gentle slopes below. A crow cawed from the nearest of the cypress trees lining the dirt track; it flew down towards the Orcia, the river whose waters had been harnessed by the *padrone*, Marchese Camillo Ginori, about twenty years ago.

Rosa breathed in the luscious aroma of the bread again. When she was little, she'd marvelled when her brother, Maurizio, had told her that, in the cities, people baked all summer in their kitchens. Not so in the Tuscan countryside, where the extreme heat made it necessary for folk to bake in red-brick ovens built outdoors. Earlier, Rosa had used brushwood to create a quick, violent fire; the moment it had burnt itself out, she'd pushed the ashes to one side, and had slid the loaves in on a long wooden shovel before dislodging them with a flick of the wrist.

She'd reached the top step, so she lowered the tray from her head, wiped sweat from her brow with the end of her apron, and tucked a wayward curl of dark brown hair into her headscarf. She exhaled a deep breath. Maurizio had been conscripted into the army a year ago when he'd turned nineteen, and had been sent to fight in Russia. They'd had no news of him since and the entire family was bereft, not least Babbo.

Rosa pushed open the heavy oak door and stepped inside. Her two younger brothers – Giulio and Alberto, aged twelve and ten, still far too young for the draft, thank God – were sprawled on the polished brick floor, playing a game they'd invented with some pebbles. Giulio looked up and gave Rosa a cheeky grin.

She smiled at him, then glanced at her three-year-old daughter, Dora, who was sitting with Rosa's sisters – Teresa and Ines, eight and six – at the kitchen table. Ribbons in their hair and pinafores over their clothes, they were leafing their way through a picture book which had been a gift from the marchese's daughter, Emma. (She made a point of visiting the different *poderi* and bringing presents for the children, much to everyone's delight.)

'Mammina,' Dora cried. '*Ho fame.*' I'm hungry. 'Can I have some bread?'

'I'll go and slice you some now, *cocca.*'

Rosa's heart filled with pride. Dora was as bright as a button, curious about everything. She attended the *asilo* kindergarten attached to the primary school which had been set up by the marchese some years ago. Oxcarts collected her and Rosa's siblings every morning and brought them home in the afternoons along with all the other school-aged children on the estate. It was the summer break now, though: three months off so the *ragazzi* could help on the *poderi*. Everyone pitched in, for that was the way of things. Farmers had big families for that reason.

Rosa took the bread through to the far side of the kitchen, where Mamma, Nonna and Lucrezia, Rosa's sixteen-year-old sister, were preparing supper while listening to a light entertainment programme on the radio.

'You took your time,' Lucrezia muttered. 'Mamma and Nonna are making me do all the hard work.'

'Not likely,' Rosa retorted. And it wasn't. Lucrezia got away with blue murder. The prettiest by far of all the sisters, with thick almost-black wavy hair and flashing dark eyes, Lucrezia had Babbo wound around her little finger. She would go to him with petty complaints and he always took her side.

Babbo was sitting in the corner of the room, cigarette in hand and a glass of red wine from his own vineyard in front of him. He looked tired. It was hard work running the *podere* without Maurizio's help. If only Babbo's brother, Zio Virgilio, hadn't emigrated to America over twenty years ago in search of a better life. Babbo and Mamma were married shortly afterwards, and it had been expected that Mamma move in with the Vaninis. (Babbo didn't have any other brothers; his six sisters had all left once they'd found their own husbands.) That too was the tradition. Women went to live with their husband's family.

The familiar smell of *aglione* – garlic-infused tomato *sugo* – permeated the air. Rosa placed the loaves on a counter and sliced a few pieces to keep the bambini going until the meal was ready. She handed them to the hungry children, then returned to the cooking area. The old hearth, with its enormous chimney where Nonna would sit on winter evenings, sometimes with a broody hen in a basket beside her, still housed the old range. A modern

electric stove stood next to it, one of the many provided by the
marchese to his farms. He'd also installed running water and
indoor bathrooms, making life a lot easier for them all.

Rosa picked up a rolling pin to join in making the *pici* noodles,
taking her place between Lucrezia, Mamma and Nonna at the
flour and semolina-dusted work surface. They were humming
along to a song on the radio, 'Chitarra Romana', and Rosa
hummed with them while they rolled out the dough.

As she worked, Rosa's thoughts drifted. She'd never imagined
her life turning out like it had. She thought she'd escaped the
drudgery of the farm almost four years ago, when she'd married
Francesco, a waiter in a Chianciano hotel. A year older than her,
he'd been conscripted to fight in North Africa, leaving her pregnant. Sadly, she couldn't manage on her own in their Chianciano
apartment. The alternative, moving in with Francesco's parents –
whom she barely knew – didn't bear thinking about. So she'd
come home to have her baby and wait for her husband to return.
Except Francesco had died in Libya in February 1941, killed by the
Allies.

Rosa exhaled a deep breath. British prisoners of war were due
to come to the *podere* tomorrow to help with the harvest. She
would rather boil her head than have anything to do with them.

The Vaninis had no choice in the matter, she reminded herself.
They were a typical Tuscan peasant family. Sharecroppers. As
throughout much of the region, the Bivio was run on the *mezzadria*
system whereby the *padrone* kept the houses in repair and
provided half of everything needed to cultivate and improve the
land, while the *mezzadro* paid him back in kind, handing over 50
per cent of all that was produced. No one complained, for the
Bivio wasn't your average estate. The marchese had been an excep-
tional *padrone* right from the start. Babbo told stories about how,
when he was a young man, their pale grey Maremmano oxen used

to pull the ploughs that tilled the soil. The marchese had subsequently raised money to purchase tractors and then a threshing machine for the estate.

Rosa remembered how desperately poor they'd been when she was little. She was always hungry then. Now, although they lived a simple life, they produced enough food to be self-sufficient. But anxiety niggled at the back of her mind. Everyone was talking about an imminent invasion by the Allies. She hoped Tuscany wouldn't become a battleground.

Her chest tightened. What would happen to her family then? She felt sick with worry for Dora. It only made it worse that those *maledetti* Allied prisoners were due to arrive first thing tomorrow. How she wished they could manage the harvest without them.

With a sigh, Rosa went to help Nonna, Mamma and Lucrezia add the *pici* to the big saucepan of boiling water. She gritted her teeth. She would stay clear of the *inglesi*, come what may. They were the enemy, even if they had been taken prisoner.

A week later, Rosa was descending the stone staircase, balancing another tray on her head: salami and seasoned tomatoes which would be a mid-morning snack for the workers. Her shoulders tensed. She'd managed to avoid face-to-face contact with the POWs until now. A group of six plus a guard had been arriving every day in one of the estate's oxcarts. Alongside Babbo, they'd been cutting the wheat with scythes, placing it on the ground and then tying it into sheaves. When all the wheat had been cut, they'd carried the bundles to the open space in front of the farmhouse and had built an enormous pale-yellow stack ready for threshing.

They'd been hard at it since dawn, when Marco – the *fattore's* son, home on leave for a few days – had arrived with a tractor towing the estate's threshing machine.

Babbo had given the prisoners different tasks. Three of them had been ordered to climb on top of the wheat and, with their pitchforks, throw bundles into the thresher, which then spat out the grains of wheat from below. Lucrezia, Giulio and Alberto were collecting them in sacks. The other three prisoners were unloading and stacking the bales of straw that came out the other end.

Rosa couldn't resist a smile. To protect themselves from dust produced by the threshing, they had tied knots at the four corners of their handkerchiefs and placed them on top of their heads.

She placed the tray of food on the wooden trestle table set up in the shade of an olive tree. The POWs' guard was sitting there watching the goings-on with a pistol in his belt and a cigarette in his hand.

'*Bon jornu.*' He wished Rosa good morning in Sicilian.

Before she could respond, Mamma appeared with a bottle of *vin santo*, sweet wine.

'Time for a break,' she shouted.

Babbo put down the *staio*, the wooden container with which he and Marco were measuring the threshed wheat. The *fattore* would soon arrange collection of the produce to be handed over to the estate. After grinding the grains into flour, one and a half quintals per person was allowed to be kept and the rest needed to be handed over to the government stores: the *ammassi*.

Marco – who spoke good English, apparently – went to invite the prisoners to enjoy the food and drink.

Within minutes, Rosa found herself surrounded by 'the enemy'.

Her chest tightening, she turned on her heel and made her way up the outside staircase to get on with preparing the harvest celebration lunch. At the top of the steps, curiosity got the better of her. She paused to take a good look at the POWs milling around the table below. Dressed in shorts, their sleeves rolled up, there seemed to be nothing remarkable about them. All six were fair-haired, their skin tanned from being out in the sun, and they were all similar in height, slightly taller than Babbo and Marco. Only one of them stood out. He appeared more well-built than the others and, before she knew what she was doing, she found herself admiring his tall, muscular form.

Disgusted at herself, she turned her gaze away.

The valley spread out below, dust-coloured now that the wheat had been brought in. Soon the weather would turn ever hotter, and it would become a land without mercy, a land without shade. Even if she sat under an olive tree there would be no respite, for its leaves would become like little flickering tongues of fire and the cry of the cicadas above would split her ears with their high-pitched song.

'Mammina!' Dora was tugging at her skirt. 'Me, Ines and Teresa have been helping Nonna make the *pici*, but we're tired now.'

Rosa bent and lifted her daughter into her arms. She kissed her plump cheek and, with love in her heart, carried her back inside.

* * *

When Babbo's share of the sacks of grain had been loaded onto the prisoners' shoulders and had been emptied into the granary beneath the house, it was time for the harvest celebration lunch. The marchese had arrived in a three-wheeler lorry with his daughter and the *fattore*.

Rosa carried the last tray of food down to the forecourt, where

Giulio and Alberto were having fun jumping into the mountain of *lòcca*, the dust that had come out of the threshing machine.

Try as she might, she couldn't help a quick glance at the prisoners. They'd stripped off their shirts and were sluicing themselves down in the open with water drawn up from the well. The fresh, clean scent of Marseille soap mingled with the aroma of wheat and straw. The muscular fellow turned and beamed a smile at Rosa. She hurriedly tore her gaze away.

Mamma called everyone to the long trestle table, where she was ladling out clear meat broth. Rosa took her place next to Dora, well away from the POWs and their guard. Babbo had insisted that they join in.

'They've worked well,' he'd said. 'They should be rewarded.'

Rosa watched them surreptitiously while they tucked into the celebration banquet.

Smoke-cured hams were followed by piled up dishes of *pici* with *aglione*. Then came two kinds of meat: a great gander, *l'ocio*, fattened for weeks beforehand, as well as tender stewed rabbit. Deliciously sweet tomatoes, aubergines, red peppers and new potatoes accompanied the main course, which was washed down with flask upon flask of red wine. Even the children were allowed to have some, watered down to keep it from going to their heads.

When all the plates had been emptied, Rosa and her sisters cleared them and returned with platters of pecorino sheep's cheese, which had been made by Mamma and Nonna. After handing them around the table, they went back to the kitchen to fetch the *dolce*, the dessert. *Cantucci alle mandorle,* small almond-flavoured biscuits, made without yeast or fat and baked twice for a satisfyingly hard bite. These would be dunked in *vin santo*, the ubiquitous sweet wine.

Marchese Ginori proposed a toast, and everyone responded, '*Salute!*' Here's to good health.

The muscular man met Rosa's gaze as she placed a plate of *cantucci* in front of him.

'*Come ti chiami*?' What's your name?

Surprised that he could speak any Italian, she told him.

'*Mi chiamo* Tom Johnstone,' he said in reply.

Flustered, she turned on her heel.

Out of the blue, the prisoners started singing 'Happy Birthday'. Although the words were in English, it was the same tune as the Italian version, and it turned out that the birthday boy was Tom. The entire table joined in except Rosa. Her stomach rolled with misery. Today was also her late husband's birthday. How could she have forgotten? Francesco should be here, enjoying the festivities, not an Englishman called Tom.

'Mammina, can I have a peach?' Dora tugged at her sleeve. 'I don't like *cantucci*.'

The biscuits were too hard for her, and the *vin santo* too alcoholic.

'Come, *cocca*.' Rosa held out her hand. 'Let's go and pick you one.'

The fruit orchard grew on the same level as the farmhouse next to the vegetable garden, and there were ripened apricots as well as the first small peaches of the season.

Rosa picked a red-gold peach and sat herself down in the shade with Dora cuddled on her lap. Warm sun beat down on the pale slopes below, now despoiled of their riches. Only the olives and vineyards were still green. It would be the grape vintage next on the calendar, but not until September before the rains returned, and the making of their olive oil would take place before Christmas.

Footfalls sounded, startling Rosa.

Her heart missed a beat.

Tom Johnstone was approaching.

She held Dora close.

He lowered himself down.

'*Fa caldo.*' It's hot. He wiped his brow.

She asked him how he'd learnt to speak Italian. But he clearly didn't understand her question.

'*Io. Italiano. Un poco.*' Me. Italian. A little. He brought his thumb towards his index finger.

'*Come ti chiami?*' Dora chipped in to ask his name.

He told her, and it seemed he was about to attempt further conversation, but more footfalls sounded as Emma was walking towards them.

'Your grandmother went upstairs to listen to the radio,' she said. 'She came back down and told us that the Allies have landed in Sicily.' Emma repeated what she'd said to Tom, in English, her expression darkening.

A sick feeling spread through Rosa. 'What will happen now?'

Emma remained silent, obviously at a loss for words.

But Tom sprang to his feet, his face wreathed in smiles.

Of course he'd be smiling; he's the enemy, Rosa reminded herself.

She watched him run back to the table to share the news with his fellow prisoners and her heart filled with misgiving.

3

It was a beautiful September day – the extreme heat of summer had passed – and Emma had gone with her father to Siena. They found a parking space in Market Square and walked to the Piazza del Duomo, graced by the glorious white marble façade of the thirteenth-century cathedral.

Papà lengthened his stride. 'I suppose I'd better make tracks.'

He had an appointment to introduce himself to the new prefect, the man in charge of governing the province.

'I'll meet you at the Cannon d'Oro,' Emma said. A modest restaurant where she and Papà ate lunch whenever they visited the city.

'At one o'clock, *cara*. Good luck with your shopping!'

She was on a quest to buy gifts for the children on the estate as well as stationery for herself. Her chest squeezed with excitement. She'd recently passed the university entrance exams and would be studying law in Siena next month.

Outside the Palazzo Reale, a three-storey ochre-coloured building with barred windows on the ground floor, she kissed her father on both cheeks.

'*A dopo.*' See you later.

After watching him go through the enormous iron door leading into the Prefettura, she made her way to the Piazza del Campo. Every year, she and her father would attend the *palio*, Siena's annual horse race around the square. Sadness slowed her steps. There hadn't been a proper *palio* since Italy had gone to war with the Allies in 1940. A war which the majority of Italians hadn't wanted. A war foisted on them by Hitler.

She spent a couple of hours searching the shops for gifts and stationery. Stock was low in most of them and some were almost empty. Wearily, she made her purchases, placed them in her rucksack, then headed for the Cannon d'Oro at the top of the town.

Inside, she glanced around. Her father hadn't arrived yet, so she walked across the terracotta-tiled floor to their regular table under an arch in the corner.

A waiter approached and she ordered a glass of water. She checked her wristwatch. Ten past one. Papà was late. She picked up a fork and fidgeted with it. Her father was meticulous about being on time. A feather of anxiety tickled her spine. A month ago, he'd received a letter from the fascist militia in Siena, ordering him to gift them a motorcar. He still hadn't replied. Political arrests were happening all over the country, but surely not to Papà? Emma's hand trembled, but she told herself not to be silly. Her father hadn't done anything wrong. She should be more worried about the Germans than about the local fascists.

She thought about the Allied successful invasion of Sicily. The Axis air defence had been negligible and no reinforcements had arrived from Germany. The *tedeschi* had abandoned their Italian ally as they had done in Africa and Russia. Not long afterwards, news came that Mussolini had been deposed, betrayed by his own men. Emma and her father had been shocked by Churchill's statement: 'If the Italians have neither the will nor the courage to free themselves from Germany, we shall continue to make war upon them from every quarter, by and, air and sea... Italy will be covered with scars and bruises from end to end.'

How completely and utterly heartless!

Allied planes then began dropping leaflets on Italian towns and cities:

Out with the Germans... or fire and steel will be used against you.

Since then, more and more Germans had been turning up in the Val d'Orcia, close to home. Tanks on manoeuvres. Gunners camped beneath Radicofani. Papà said German armoured divisions had also crossed the Brenner pass from Austria.

It was all too tragic.

Rumours abounded that Italy wanted to make peace with the Allies, but the Italian government didn't appear to have any clear plan of action with respect to Germany. The prime minister was shilly-shallying, apparently hoping the *tedeschi* would leave the country of their own accord.

Fat chance of that.

In mid-August, the Germans who'd camped below Radicofani suddenly left. Not to return to Germany, unfortunately, but to head south. Soon afterwards, the first Allied bombs had fallen on the Val d'Orcia near an isolated farmhouse, wounding three people. Presumably dropped by planes lightening their load on their way back to their base. The same day, Messina had capitulated. The Sicilian campaign was over. Would a campaign on the Italian mainland happen next?

Emma and her father had sat and waited with an ever-increasing dread of invasion and diminishing hopes of peace. Italy would become a combat zone and that broke Emma's heart. The

Allies' exhortations to the people to rid themselves of the Germans was like urging a sheep to rid itself of a wolf.

Five days ago, on 3 September, she and Papà were listening to the BBC when it was announced that British and Canadian troops of the Eighth Army had landed in Reggio Calabria, the toe of Italy. The news was subsequently confirmed on Italian radio: a great Allied convoy had been sighted off the Bay of Naples. Emma's pulse had thudded. A landing was imminent.

'Sorry I'm late.' Papà's melodic voice interrupted her fearful thoughts. 'That pompous new prefect kept me waiting for an age.' He pulled out a chair. 'Did you have a successful shopping trip, *mia cara*?'

She reached across the table and squeezed his fingers.

'I think I bought every last picture book in Siena.'

'Good.' A smile gleamed in his eyes. 'The children will be delighted.'

* * *

Emma and her father enjoyed a tasty lunch of *gnudi*: ricotta, parmesan and spinach rolled into balls, served with melted butter, crispy fried sage and a dusting of pecorino cheese, all the while chatting about the estate children and various jobs that needed to be undertaken, steering clear of war talk – a pleasant respite that Emma appreciated.

Replete, they made their way through the medieval streets to the car and set off for home.

About thirty kilometres south of Siena, on the outskirts of the pretty fourteenth-century walled village of Buonconvento, they reached the same roadblock where their travel permits had been checked that morning by stern-faced soldiers. Emma's father brought his Fiat 1500 to a halt.

The soldiers were grinning from ear to ear now.

A private took Papà's papers from him and gave them a cursory glance. 'Soon we won't be checking people's permits any more.'

'Oh? Why's that?'

The soldier's grin widened.

'Haven't you heard? Our captain just told us an armistice has been signed with the Allies.'

Grimly, Papà thanked him and drove on.

'Do you think it's just a rumour?' Emma asked, taking in her father's serious expression.

'It's been on the cards for some time, sweetheart. But I'm worried Badoglio, our prime minister, has been too hasty and has rushed into this without having a proper plan.'

Emma's shoulders drooped.

'You mean a plan about the Germans, don't you?'

'I expect they'll occupy all our main cities and will counterattack the Allies in the south. Maybe even form a line of defence across the Apennines.'

'What will Italy do?' She could hear the panic in her voice.

'Badoglio should have closed the Brenner immediately after taking over from Mussolini. Instead, he allowed massive numbers of Germans into the country. Italy – and the Allies – will just have to deal with them, my darling.'

They lapsed into silence, each lost in their own thoughts. Emma couldn't help worrying about Marco. Would he have to fight the Germans? He was still undergoing training, but that wouldn't last for ever. She missed him terribly and longed to see him again. He hadn't been home since July, and he'd been so busy helping with the harvest they'd barely spent any time together. It would be the *vendemmia* soon; if he was given leave to help pick the grapes, she wouldn't see much of him then either.

* * *

After a restless night listening to the laughter and merrymaking echoing from the valley – the farmers had lit bonfires and were rejoicing in the belief peace had come – Emma woke to the news that the Allies had, indeed, landed south of Naples.

She sat glued to the radio in the sitting room for much of the day. At lunchtime, she heard that Bologna, Padova and Verona had already been occupied by the Germans. In the evening, a friend phoned her father and informed him that the king and Badoglio had left Rome.

'I can't believe it,' Papà said. 'How can they abandon us to the *tedeschi*?'

Emma worried even more about Marco then and said as much to her father.

'What will happen to him?'

'It's a desperate situation, *mia cara*. We can only hope and pray he'll be all right.'

The telephone rang and her father went to answer it.

'That was the main POW camp in Laterina,' he said after hanging up. 'They want us to tell the lieutenant and his soldiers to protect our prisoners from any German attempts to seize them. I'll go up to the fortress now. Wait here, Emma, and stay tuned to the radio.'

She did as he requested, trying to keep her spirits up. The situation seemed surreal, as if she were going through a bizarre nightmare. Except it was actually happening and she wouldn't wake up and find life had gone back to normal. The radio kept repeating Badoglio's proclamation, that he'd signed the armistice to 'save the nation from further and graver misfortune'.

How short-sighted of him with the tedeschi already at our doors.

Papà returned momentarily and sat himself down in his armchair next to the radio.

'I found the lieutenant and his soldiers making preparations to run away,' he said. 'So I told our prisoners they were free to go, but they'd be unwise to set off along the roads, where they'd run straight into the Germans.' He extracted a cigarette from his silver case and lit it. 'I suggested that as soon as the Allies land further north, we'll let them know and they can make their way across country to join their own forces.'

'What did they say to that?'

'They agreed it would be best to wait. I've promised them a map so they can become familiar with the lie of the land. I also recommended that they lock the main fortress door and post a sentry. Then I showed them the tower staircase at the back which they can take to escape if necessary.' He chuckled. 'As I was leaving, four of them came back from the *fattoria*, carrying a demijohn of wine, so I left them to celebrate their "freedom" in peace.'

'Peace?' Emma sighed. 'If only...'

* * *

'I've just heard on the radio that there are German troops in Chiusi,' Papà announced at breakfast the next morning. 'They're in control of the railway and are requisitioning cars left, right and centre.'

Emma gasped. Chiusi was only seventeen kilometres away.

'Oh, dear Lord.'

'Sorry to bring more bad news.' Papà sighed. 'But the phone lines to Rome and the north have been cut.'

'What'll we do now?' Emma's voice trembled.

'I'd like you to help me and our workers hide as much wheat, potatoes, cheese, wine, etcetera, as we can. Also to bury a store of petrol and take the wheels off our cars.'

It was hard work. She spent the entire morning carrying supplies with her father down to the huge cellars beneath the villa, helped by their staff. Orazio and his assistants then bricked up the stored items behind makeshift walls.

Later, Emma walked up to the fortress with Papà. They found the prisoners spending the day in a nearby creek to escape the attention of any Germans who might be passing. Papà told the POWs that he would arrange for them to be moved tomorrow to an isolated farmhouse.

'Thank you, sir,' the Scottish fellow called Tom said. 'We don't want to go to Germany if we can help it.'

'Any chance you can arm us?' the English corporal in charge of the POWs asked.

'With what?' Papà's mouth twisted. 'We'll do our best to hide you, but that's it, I'm afraid.'

'Fair enough.' The corporal saluted. '*Grazie.*'

'At least they were grateful,' her father muttered to Emma as they headed down the road. He seemed about to add to his statement, when a figure stepped out from the treeline.

Emma stopped dead in her tracks.

'Marco! What are you doing here?'

He was dressed in plain clothes, his handsome face creased with fatigue, his eyebrows drawn together.

Papà gave him a stern look.

'Please explain yourself.'

'I haven't deserted, don't worry. As soon as Badoglio made his pronouncement, our commandant gave us the sauve qui peut order "*si salvi chi può*". He'd changed into *Borghese* civilian clothing and we all followed suit. Germans were already in the vicinity with their Tiger tanks. All we had were muskets.' He indicated the weapon slung over his shoulder. 'There was nothing to be done but to get away as quickly as possible.'

Emma gazed into his forest-green eyes.

'How did you get here?'

'I walked.' He ran a hand through his wavy dark brown hair. 'Met some Tuscan soldiers in plain clothes on the way. They'd escaped from Verona and Bologna and told me all our officers and the men who can do so are on the run. Those who are caught are being put into transit camps by the *tedeschi* and will soon be sent north to labour camps.'

'How dreadful.' Papà touched his hand to Marco's arm. 'We'd better get you somewhere safe, young man.'

'I was hoping I could go home.'

'It's the obvious place where the authorities will look for you. There's plenty of room in the villa. You can stay with us.'

'I'll go and tell your parents,' Emma added.

She fell into step beside him. She couldn't stop smiling. Marco was safe; it was truly a miracle. The first of many, she hoped.

4

Rosa was helping with the *vendemmia*, the grape harvest, in the vineyard on the southern slope of the *podere*. Gripping her secateurs and snipping away at the purplish-red bunches, she worked alongside Lucrezia, her little brothers, and the ten British men the *padrone* had sent to help them.

Sweat stung Rosa's eyes in the warm autumn sunshine. The ideal moment for picking always came during a long period of sun which followed rain; it had rained last week, although thankfully only a little. (Too much rain would have caused the grapes to rot on the stalk.) Babbo always waited for the moon to be on the wane before setting the date to start, and now the perfectly ripe grapes were luscious with juice. Babbo had been up at dawn to taste the fruit. The time had come; it would be a good vintage, he'd said.

Rosa inhaled the intensely sweet scent. Her hands were so sticky she was almost prepared to waste her drinking water on rinsing them. But thirst overcame her desire to be clean and she took a sip from her water bottle instead.

Her basket was soon full and she carried it to one of the chest-nut-wood tubs known as *bigonci*, located at intervals along the interlaced rows of vines. *Mamma mia*, her pannier was heavy and grape juice trickled down her neck and into her blouse.

She emptied her basket and went back to the task at hand. While she worked, her mind turned to recent events. What a terrible situation had come to pass. The whole of Italy north of Rome was under German martial law. Trains, telephones and the post were subject to Nazi control. No one was allowed to send private letters and telephone conversations were listened into. Everywhere, there were Italian soldiers on the run, left to fend for themselves by the king and Prime Minister Badoglio, both of whom had fled to Brindisi and were now protected by the Allies. And, as if that weren't bad enough, Hitler had sent his paratroopers to spring Mussolini from where he'd been imprisoned in a central Apennine hotel. The German-controlled Radio Roma couldn't stop crowing about his release.

Rosa eyed the Scotsman, Tom Johnstone, who was working on the terrace below hers. He seemed to know what he was doing as he snipped at the stems of the vine. She couldn't resist allowing her gaze to linger on him momentarily. He truly was a fine figure of a man.

Without warning, he turned and looked at her and his attractive face broke into a smile.

She glanced away in embarrassment. Whatever had she been thinking of, staring at him like that?

After the armistice, Babbo had said there could be no question of concealing the British men on the estate for long. Too many people knew of their presence, including the shopkeepers of Montepulciano where the *fattore* drew their rations. But Babbo had then related that Marchese Ginori had given the prisoners a choice: take their chances and try to make it to Allied lines or remain on the estate. Thirty-two of them had left in small groups, armed with compasses, maps and money provided by the *padrone*.

Before too long, though, Tom and four others had returned. They'd said there were Germans everywhere and they'd run out of food and water.

It was a strange situation. Babbo found out that the captain of the Montepulciano Carabinieri had phoned the marchese to enquire about the prisoners. After he'd explained that he needed their labour, the captain had told him to keep quiet about it. So the British were still on the estate, although no longer staying in the fortress. They were sleeping in an empty farmhouse in the middle of the forest. The *padrone* provided food for them from his own stores.

Rosa's gaze fell on the bag by Tom's feet. When working on the farms, he and his companions always kept their kit with them and placed one man on the look-out so they could bolt if any Germans approached.

She wiped sweat from her brow and tucked a stray curl into the kerchief she wore like a nurse's cap on her head. Not because of the sun, but to keep earwigs out of her hair. She gazed up through the yellowed leaves to choose the right stalk, then took hold of a bunch and shook it to dislodge any wasps that might be feeding. Wasps were the curse of the *vendemmia*, and it was rare to get through the day without someone being attacked.

As if on cue, a scream came from Lucrezia.

'I've been stung,' she shrieked, dropping her basket.

Rosa set down her own pannier and went up to her sister.

'Let me see.'

A raised red welt puckered the skin above Lucrezia's thumb and tears coursed down her cheeks.

Rosa called out to her brother, Giulio.

'Can you take Lucrezia to Mamma so she can put some vinegar on the sting?'

Rosa would have gone herself, but Babbo had placed her in

charge of this section of the vineyard and she took her responsibilities seriously.

'Is she all right?' Tom Johnstone asked in halting Italian, coming up to where they were working.

'She always makes such a fuss about everything. She'll be fine.'

Rosa knew for a fact that Lucrezia didn't suffer from any allergies. Vinegar would take away the pain, she also knew from her own experience, having been stung often enough in the past.

Tom scratched his head, visibly not understanding her response.

'*Va bene.*' Okay. A smile lifted the corner of his mouth.

She couldn't help noticing the beguiling way in which he flicked his fair hair back from his attractively freckled forehead.

Don't look, Rosa.

He offered her a drink from his bottle of wine. It was traditional for the pickers to bring *vino* with them as well as a bottle of water and the Englishmen had obviously been told about the tradition. While working, you could drink a surprising amount without feeling any effect from the alcohol. It seemed to evaporate effortlessly from your body along with the sweat.

'*No grazie.*'

Italy might have switched sides in the war, but someone like Tom had killed Francesco. She was a widow and Dora was fatherless as a result. Accepting anything from him would feel like a betrayal.

At midday, cheers from Rosa's brothers announced the arrival of lunch. Everyone put down their baskets and secateurs and went over to the shade of the nearest olive tree, where Dora sat with Rosa's little sisters sharing the contents of a big pannier: bread, tomatoes, a bottle of oil, salami, mortadella sausage, and a paper twist of salt. Mamma and Lucrezia approached leading the donkey, Nino, who was carrying a container steaming with the main component of the meal – beans in a tomato sauce with *pinoli*, pine nuts – which they ladled onto tin plates.

Flasks of wine were passed round and, afterwards they bit into heavy, ripe figs and succulent pears, the juice dribbling down their chins.

Tom Johnstone had sat himself next to Dora, who was between him and Rosa.

He screwed up his blue eyes as he concentrated on Dora's chatter.

She was telling him about the game of hide-and-seek – *uno, due, tre, stella* – she'd been playing that morning with Ines and Teresa.

He spoke to her in English, his words just as incomprehensible to the child as hers had been to him. Dora didn't seem to mind, though. She dimpled a smile and carried on chatting.

'Back to work,' Babbo announced soon after.

And so, they returned to the vineyard where they laboured on into the afternoon, filling their baskets and emptying them into the *bigonci*.

Later, Orazio, the *fattore*, arrived with a long farm cart with hefty axles, drawn by a pair of stately white oxen who stood patiently flicking their ears to disperse flies.

When the *bigonci* had all been loaded by the men, the *fattore* set off back to the *fattoria*. The custom of treading the grapes beneath bare feet was a thing of the past. They would be squashed with stout wooden poles, and the mixture of stems, pulp and juice left to ferment in open vats for a couple of weeks before being put into *barili*, barrels, to complete fermentation during the winter. In true Tuscan style, nothing was wasted. Once the wine had been transferred to the *barili*, the remaining pulp of stalks, skins and pips – the *vinaccia* – would be refermented with some water added to make a light wine, known as a mezzo vino; or else it was distilled as grappa.

Rosa and her sisters now set to work to collect all the vine leaves lying about. These would be stored and used as fodder for the animals. Meanwhile, the men had started picking bunches of grapes that had been missed, which they then carried to be hung in the loggia on the ground floor of the farmhouse. Once the grapes on those branches – known as *pendici* – had dried, they would be added to the wine to increase its strength, flavour and colour in a second fermentation.

With a groan, Rosa remembered the final *vendemmia* before the war, the last occasion they were able to celebrate with friends and family.

She was newly engaged to Francesco at the time, and they believed they had their whole life together in front of them. After the plates, but not the glasses, had been cleared, an improvised band of guitar, accordion and fiddle had struck up and everyone began singing. Rosa had joined in with her favourite song, '*Vivere*' – 'Live'.

When the music changed, and dancing started by the light of the fire on the open side of the courtyard, Francesco had held Rosa close, whispering how much he loved her and longed for their marriage to take place.

Rosa's chest ached at the vivid memory. She was almost glad that such celebrations no longer occurred, for they would remind her too much of that time with Francesco. There was no one to celebrate with now anyway. The Englishmen would go back to their quarters when they finished work and the neighbours' sons were now conscripts on the run, hiding in the Val d'Orcia forests.

A tug on the hem of her dress interrupted her thoughts.

Dora's face was covered in pear juice.

'Mammina, my tummy hurts.'

Rosa bent and lifted her into her arms.

'Let's go to the kitchen, *cocca*. I'll make us a pot of mint tea.'

Tom Johnstone's gaze met hers as she walked past.

'*La bambina. Va bene*?' he asked. The little girl. Okay?

'*Mal di pancia*,' she said, pointing to her stomach.

She didn't wait for his reply and huffed to herself as she carried on walking.

The man was far too simpatico.

He might not be an official enemy, but he was still an adversary as far as she was concerned.

5

Emma glanced at Marco as they sat playing chess in the villa's library, walled with the leather-bound books so beloved by her father and herself. Marco was taking his time to make the next move and seemed distracted. Emma wasn't surprised. He'd been hiding from the *tedeschi* for three whole weeks now and yesterday, while she'd ridden out to take a birthday gift to a little girl on a remote farm, a German officer had shown up.

Marco had been helping unload wine barrels in the courtyard and experienced a narrow escape. The *tedesco* in question had roared through the back gates on a requisitioned Moto Guzzi motorcycle, spraying gravel as he swung it to a halt. Thank God Marco had been able to run and hide in the woodshed. Afterwards, when Emma had returned from her errand, he'd recounted everything to her.

'I had an unobstructed view through the slats. The *maledetto* Nazi asked for the *padrone* and my father went to fetch him. The German – tall, thin, blond – snapped his metal-heeled boots together and introduced himself as Kapitän Hofmann. He said he'd received orders to recapture all Allied prisoners in the district and arrange to send them to Germany. He went on to say that he'd be back in the morning with transportation.'

Marco went on to say that when the marchese protested that he needed the men to work on the land, which was essential as it was providing food for so many people, the captain had drawn himself up to his full height and said that the *padrone* was living in an invaded country, and that he couldn't expect enemy troops to roam about with freedom.

Emma sighed to herself. Last night Papà had gone to confer with Tom, the Scots guardsman, who held the rank of sergeant, and had taken charge of the prisoners after Corporal Smith had set off with a group of POWs following the armistice. When her father got back from the meeting, he told her that the Scotsman had come up with a ruse.

'A ruse? What do you mean?'

'They'll fake not knowing about the Germans coming to collect them in order to protect us.'

Tom had said that they owed Papà a huge debt of gratitude, that if they left now, the Nazis would realise they'd been tipped off.

Emma had listened open-mouthed while her father explained that all the men would go to work, digging a field in the valley below the villa, which was about half a kilometre from the road. Tom would perch on a hillock and, as soon as he saw the Germans, they'd all run for the hills.

Would the ruse work? And, if so, how would the Germans react?

She returned her attention to Marco.

He lifted his gaze from the chess board and shook his head in defeat.

'You've got me. Can't move my king nor protect him.'

'Check mate.' Emma held out her hand to shake his.

Emma's heart filled with affection. She'd spent more time with Marco in the past three weeks than she'd done in years.

She looked at her watch.

'The Germans are due at ten o'clock. It's nearly time. I'm on tenterhooks to see if the ruse will work.'

'Do you think the prisoners will make it through to the Allied lines?' Marco rubbed at his chin. 'I mean, Sorrento is a hell of a long way from here...'

'It is, but I suppose they're willing to risk the trek rather than being transported to Germany.' She kept to herself the realisation that she'd be devastated if any of the men were caught. If they all escaped, though, her father might fall under suspicion.

What a worry!

'Let's go out onto the *terrazza* so we can see what happens,' she said. 'Are you coming, Marco?'

'Si, si, Miss *stivali da commandante* bossy boots.'

She gave him a playful punch on the arm, and he returned the gesture with a laugh.

They went outside and waited. The British were all at work, readying the field for ploughing. Tom sat on a mound, keeping watch.

At last, an hour overdue, two open-top lorries escorted by a motorcycle appeared on the valley road.

Germans.

Armed with Tommy guns.

Six of them, including a man who, Marco pointed out, was the captain.

Papà went down with Orazio to meet them and warn them that the prisoners always kept a sharp look-out.

Orazio climbed onto the first lorry – it was he who'd show the Germans the way – and they set off down the hill.

Emma's father had returned to the terrace by the time the vehicle came to a halt. The Germans piled out; it would take them fifteen minutes or so to reach the British in the field.

But Tom and his men were already running for cover, dark shadows against the pale clay hillocks.

The *tedeschi* marched onto the field in single file.

They stopped dead.

Emma laughed out loud: the Germans were scurrying about like headless chickens.

'All they'll find will be spades and hoes left on the ground,' she said.

Before too long, the *tedeschi* began piling back onto the lorries.

A cloud of dust rose in the air as the motorcycle took the lead once more.

'They've left my father behind,' Marco muttered. '*Bastardi.* They could at least have given him a lift as far as the crossroad.'

'Let's hope they go back to Chiusi and leave us all in peace,' Emma said.

Her stomach clenched. *Oh, dear Lord.* Instead of turning right, they'd turned left and were heading in the direction of the villa.

'I'll go and find out what they want,' her father said.

Emma followed him, after making sure Marco would stay put.

By the time she and Papà had reached the courtyard, the lorries and the motorcycle had already pulled up.

A tall thin man, wearing a grey-green jacket, leapt from the bike and marched towards them. The silver eagle on his visor cap glinted in the sun.

'Herr Kapitän Hofmann,' Papà said. 'I told you the British always kept a sharp look-out.'

'I hope for your sake that you didn't warn them,' Hofmann retorted in heavily accented Italian. He smirked. 'Rather than return to Chiusi empty-handed, I've decided that we'll take your vehicle and horses.'

'No!' The word left Emma's mouth before she could stop it. 'Not our horses...'

A frown creased her father's brow. 'We need them for farm work. And there are no tyres on the car.'

'You have oxen to pull your carts, do you not? And a tractor as well as a small lorry and a pony trap, I believe? We could do with a couple more horses in our transport division...'

Emma stepped forward.

'Please,' she begged. 'Don't take our horses.'

The captain had the palest blue eyes she'd ever seen. He lifted an eyebrow.

'Who are you?'

'My name is Emma.' She stood her ground.

'She's my daughter,' Papà clarified.

Ignoring his response, the captain barked orders to his men.

Emma's blood pounded in her ears.

The Germans jumped off the lorries, then ran to the stables and garages.

How did they even know where they were?

The estate formed its own self-supporting little world. Surely they didn't have a traitor in their midst. Yet how did Hofmann know where to send his men?

A bitter taste filled Emma's mouth. From all accounts, occupied Italy had fallen into a state of civil war. Fascists and anti-fascists had taken sides against each other. Hatred against the fascists was growing everywhere because of the vile acts they perpetrated. She wouldn't put anything past them, even giving information to the Germans. A shudder of revulsion went through her.

'Get out of my way, *signorina*.' Hofmann's cold voice broke into her thoughts.

She planted her feet wide but her father grasped her by the shoulders and gently moved her to one side.

'It's for the best, *mia cara*,' he whispered.

'Poor Bella and Zorro. What will become of them?'

She watched helplessly while ramps were lowered from the first lorry and the horses were led towards them.

Bella allowed herself to be loaded, but Zorro didn't take kindly to being handled by strangers. He shied away, snorting. Showing the whites of his eyes, he reared up on his hindquarters. His front legs flailed then came down with a thump and he pranced sideways.

'Here, let me,' she said, stepping forward again. 'He's scared.'

Before Hofmann could say a word, she went up to the horse and smoothed his neck.

'*Sta buono, amore.*' Be good, love. '*Tutto andrà bene.*' All will be well.

Zorro nuzzled her long red plait of hair like he always did and she felt such a traitor handing him back to the German soldier.

At least the horse had calmed down enough to be loaded.

In the meantime, Papà's Fiat was being winched onto the second lorry.

Emma turned away, unable to watch a moment longer. Truth be told, she didn't want to give in to her misery in front of the Germans. Holding back a sob, she ran into the villa and straight into Marco's arms.

He held her while she wept hot tears.

'Those *stronzi*,' he said. 'I saw everything from the window. I can't take much more of this. I've got to do something other than hide.'

She squirmed out of his hold. 'What can you do? What can any of us do? We're like pathetic little ants being gobbled up by an anteater.'

'There's always hope, Emma. We must fight back. To do anything less would be like giving up. I, for one, couldn't bear that.'

* * *

A month later, Emma was walking up the rough track that led to Le Faggete: the isolated farmhouse where the British POWs had once been quartered. There'd been no news of them since that horrible day when Bella and Zorro had been stolen by the Germans. She only hoped the horses weren't being illtreated and that Tom and his comrades had made it to Naples, which had recently been occupied by the Americans.

Her feet skittered on the stony path and her calves ached from the steep climb. She gritted her teeth with determination. She was on a mission, and she'd fought long and hard with her father about it.

Out of the blue, the week before, Marco had come to say goodbye to her before setting off to assume leadership of the men concealed in the Bivio's forest.

'Why does it have to be you?' she'd said.

'I've had military training and my organisation skills are second to none. You know I've been wanting to get involved and fight back. You'll have to ask your father about the rest. My lips are sealed.'

He'd wrapped his arms around her, given her a brotherly hug.

'Be careful,' she'd said, her heart aching. She'd been on the verge of tears, but had swallowed them along with the lump in her throat.

'I'll see you soon,' he'd promised. 'We won't be far away and I'll drop by from time to time.'

She'd gone to Papà in the sitting room as soon as Marco had left. It was then that she'd learnt about the *Comitato di Liberazione Nazionale*, the Italian Resistance Organisation. Her father told her he'd joined the Chianciano branch of the multi-party secret entity, which was backed by the Allies and the king. Its members were united by their anti-fascist stance, and their main task was to direct the efforts of the partisan formations.

'Why have you become a member?' she'd asked, sitting in an armchair opposite the wood-burning open fire. The weather had turned chilly and she held her hands out to the warmth. 'Won't it be dangerous?'

'I know it's a cliché to say this, but desperate times call for desperate measures.'

'What do you expect to achieve?' She gave her father a sympathetic smile.

'You know that Mussolini has established a new army. Well, my darling, he has ordered all who were still in the Forces on 8 September to report for duty. Of course, not many will do so. As you're aware, those from our *poderi* are hiding in the forest. They've been joined by escaped prisoners from the Laterina camp. We need to organise them as some are starting to become a nuisance.'

'A nuisance?' She'd tilted her head.

'They're hungry and cold. Those who aren't local have been turning up at our farms demanding money and food.'

'And you think Marco will be able to lick them into shape?'

'I have every faith in him.'

She shook her head.

'Be that as it may. You shouldn't have sent him into such danger.'

'I didn't send him. He volunteered.'

A sigh escaped her.

Of course he'd volunteered.

'Tell me more about the Resistance, Papà. I'd like to know what Marco's involved with.'

Her father lit a cigarette and took a deep draw.

'It's early days yet. In Rome, I've heard that there are women who carry messages from one group to another, who find hiding places for Allied POWs, and even carry arms to the patriots. They call them *stafette*, and they are incredibly brave.'

That was the moment when the idea occurred to Emma. She, too, could be like those women. All she needed to do was to convince her father.

She'd badgered him for days; she wouldn't give up.

'It makes more sense for me to relay messages to Marco than for him to come down here and expose himself to any Germans or even fascist spies.'

She still couldn't fathom how the *tedeschi* knew the layout of the *fattoria*. Someone must have told them.

'I don't have anything to relate to Marco yet,' Papà said. 'And when I do, I'll go myself.'

'You could arouse suspicion heading up there. I mean, you never go for walks in the forest. You're always too busy.'

Finally, a couple of days later, her father received an encrypted phone call from Chianciano to communicate to the partisans the whereabouts of an arms cache where they would be able to pick up weapons.

Emma immediately wrung the information from him.

'I'm going,' he said. 'Don't follow me.'

But she did, of course. She'd stayed well back so he wouldn't notice.

At the edge of the treeline, she'd watched as he came across Giovanni, the *mezzadro* who farmed a nearby *podere*.

'Men keep on showing up demanding food,' the farmer said. 'We're running low on supplies.'

Emma sidled up to them.

'Ciao, Papà. Fancy meeting you here.'

'Fancy meeting *you*,' he'd come right back at her.

'Oh, I was just going for a walk,' she'd said innocently.

'So was I, but now I need to take Giovanni to Orazio and authorise a delivery from our stores.'

Emma had paused for thought.

How to get hold of the message?

An idea suggested itself to her and she'd forced a sneeze.

'The leaf mould is making me allergic.' She'd looked her father in the eye. 'Have you got a hankie?'

Earlier, in his study, she'd been looking for a book she'd mislaid and had caught him concealing a piece of paper in his handkerchief.

He'd reached into his pocket and had produced a creased hankie, which he handed to her.

'Take care,' he said.

'I will.'

She'd turned and resumed her walk.

As soon as she was out of sight, she'd unfolded the handkerchief.

The piece of paper with writing in code.

Her face had broken into a smile and, with a spring in her step, she'd set off back up the dusty white road.

6

It was a day of blinding cold sunshine, the sky limpid from the north wind off the Apennines, and Rosa, her father, and Lucrezia were perched high on ladders stripping olives from their twigs.

Rosa squinted through the sunlight filtering through the canopy. Like most of the olive groves on the Bivio estate, all the trees at *Podere Vanini* had been pruned to keep them roughly in the shape of an upturned umbrella so the sun would penetrate evenly. She smiled to herself, remembering the proverb, *Agli olivi, un pazzo sopra e un savio sotto.* 'A madman at the top of the olive tree and a wise man at its roots.' Babbo had dug manure into the soil at the base of every *ulivo*. Would that have conferred wisdom on him? If so, then were pickers like her crazy?

The ladder wobbled and, with a wry grin, she grasped a thick branch to keep from falling.

She glanced at her father, who was working on the incline below. The hillside was arranged in sloping terraces, each with a line of olive trees on the outside and a row of grape vines on the inside, with the grassy banks providing fodder for their livestock. Not one centimetre of the *podere*'s land had been wasted, and with good reason. Rosa gave a sigh. Babbo's share of the crops kept them from going hungry, but they were still as poor as church mice. The last occasion she'd had a few lire in her pocket had been when she'd worked as a kitchen maid in the Chianciano hotel, where she'd met Francesco.

She thought about him with sadness in her heart. When they were married, he'd insisted she occasionally treat herself to a pretty dress or some new shoes from the money they'd managed to save. Before then, while she'd been living at home, she'd had to hand over most of her pay to her father. She hadn't minded: it was how things were done. She now received a widow's pension from the government, a pittance, but it was better than nothing and her father was grateful that it helped cover some of their expenses.

Rosa grasped a thin branch and pulled the ripe olives off it. She hoped the harvest would be a good one. Her father had watched the development of flower and fruit closely throughout the spring, summer and autumn months before making the difficult decision about when to pick. The oil content of each olive grew substantially from October to December, but it was risky to leave things too late. A balance had to be struck between picking them from the tree too early and allowing them to drop to the ground. Windfalls would not be considered suitable for a virgin pressing. And the extra *vergine* oil was by far the best.

She dropped a handful of olives into the half-moon wicker basket strapped round the front of her waist. The 'first quality' oil came entirely from hand-picked fruit. Any that fell to the earth were used for 'second quality'. Those left to wither on the trees were 'third'.

The sound of children chatting broke into her thoughts. Dora was helping Rosa's younger siblings, who were being supervised by Nonna in the hard task of picking up the windfalls.

'My back's tired,' Dora complained.

'Nonsense,' Nonna retorted. 'Mine's not, and I'm seventy-five, which is a lot older than you.'

Rosa climbed down the ladder. Her basket was full, so she took advantage of the opportunity to have a quiet word with her daughter.

'We all need to work hard, *cocca*. I used to pick up the fallen olives when I was your age. If you bend from the knees, your back will be fine.'

Later, after the trees had been stripped and all the olives on the ground had been collected, Rosa helped her father separate the fruit – hand-picked and windfalls – into two big containers on the oxcart, which had already been hitched to a shaft that would be drawn by a pair of their pale grey Maremmano oxen. With their long curving horns and large, liquid dark eyes, the huge, slow, gentle beasts had been paired in a team since calfhood. Rosa inhaled their sweet musky smell. Babbo and the other Val d'Orcia farmers often thought of their oxen as almost human. The men even compared them to their own womenfolk. Rosa couldn't help an inward groan as she remembered yet another Tuscan proverb, which strongly advised against seeking a wife or an ox from afar: *Donne e buoi de' paesi tuoi*. 'Only choose women and oxen from your own neighbourhood.'

She didn't like being lumped together with an ox, much as she loved the creatures.

Dora tugged at Rosa's skirt as Babbo began to lead the oxen from the courtyard.

'Where's Nonno going?'

'He's taking the olives to the *fattoria*, darling.'

'Why?' Dora stared up at her.

'They need to be turned into oil.'

'How do they do that?'

'A big, round millstone worked by a blindfolded donkey, walking round and round, will grind them.'

'Won't the poor donkey get giddy?'

'He's wearing a blindfold for that reason.'

'Are you sure?'

'Absolutely. I've seen it with my own eyes.'

Before she was married, Rosa had once gone with Babbo to deliver their olives. The atmosphere inside the *frantoio* had been warm and dank in comparison to the clean chill outside. The olives were tipped onto trays, stones and all, and were soon crushed to a green-brown mass. This was scooped up with clean wooden shovels and the pulp put into circular containers made of rope. When several of these had been filled and piled one upon another under the great press, the extraction of the best-quality oil was ready to begin.

She'd never forget what happened next. A huge screw, with a block of wood to apply the pressure on these *gabbie*, or rope cages, containing the crushed olives, was then turned by a long thick piece of wood that acted as a tourniquet. Several strong men had to exert their full force to extract the oil, which streamed down through a hole in the floor into a large marble basin covered by a wooden lid to prevent any dust or dirt from entering. Rosa could almost smell the sweat of the men mixed with the pungent aroma of the oil as she thought about it.

After a sample of fresh oil was examined with great care and ceremony, Rosa had been encouraged to dip a piece of bread – *pan unto* – into the dark green liquid. She'd popped it into her mouth, savouring that delicious first taste and the slightly spicy flavour of the oil.

Buonissimo.

The whole process was then repeated with the windfall olives to produce the second quality. The third quality – a contradictory term in Rosa's opinion – would be used later to make soap, and the final pulp ended up as a sort of dark brown cake, which would be employed either as fertiliser or fuel.

Rosa gave a shiver. Winter was on the way and the first snow-falls with it. Babbo would be glad of the final pressing product to keep the family warm.

'Will Nonno bring back some oil with him today?' Dora asked, interrupting Rosa's musings.

'It will be stored in big Ali Baba terracotta jars in the cellars of the villa along with our wine.'

'Is that nice Englishman at the villa too?'

'No. Remember I told you he's gone to join up with other soldiers like him?'

'Why?' Dora asked, tugging at Rosa's skirt again.

'Because of the war, *cocca*.'

Rosa could still see Tom in her mind's eye. His fine face, his kind smile. She'd found herself thinking about him far too much of late, hoping he was safe. She breathed a sigh. It was a good thing he'd left last month. She'd been in danger of thawing towards him. The last time he and his fellow prisoners had come to the *podere* to help Babbo, she'd had to stop herself from trying to teach him some Italian. It would have been wrong of her, a complete betrayal of Francesco.

He'd have been horrified if he were alive and had found out.

* * *

'Mammina!' Dora came running into the kitchen a week later.

Rosa glanced up from the chopping board, where she was slicing onions for a pasta sauce.

'What's the matter?'

'I just saw that *inglese*.'

'Which *inglese*?' Rosa's stomach fluttered. Although Tom was Scottish, all British were referred to as *inglese*, English. Italians didn't differentiate between them.

'The nice one. Me, Teresa and Ines were playing hide-and-seek. We discovered him sleeping in the animal feed storeroom.'

'*Accidenti!*' My goodness. Rosa put down her knife and wiped her hands on her apron.

'Come along, Mammina.' Dora was already heading back out of the door. 'He's very hungry and he asked for you.'

Rosa picked up the nearest loaf of bread from the counter and followed her daughter down the outside stairs.

Tom was lying on a haystack at the rear of the room; he'd fallen back to sleep.

The poor man must be exhausted.

He was also filthy, his beard streaked with dirt, his clothes covered in mud.

Teresa and Ines stood to the side, goggling.

'Tom!' Dora called out before Rosa could shush her. 'Mammina has brought you some bread.'

He gave a start, blinked his eyes open. '*Buongiorno.*' Good morning.

'Dora said you were hungry.' Rosa held out the bread. 'Here, take it. Eat.'

He took the bread from her, and began to break off pieces and stuff them into his mouth.

'*Grazie*,' he said, thanking her.

His mispronunciation of the word brought a smile to her lips.

No, Rosa. Don't warm to him. He's a maledetto inglese.

She turned to Teresa.

'Go find Nonno and tell him that Tom is here, *amore*.'

Babbo needs to be made aware of the situation.

Tom carried on eating, barely chewing before taking the next mouthful. His entire focus was on the food.

When was the last time he'd eaten?

Rosa longed to ask him, longed to find out what had happened.

Something terrible to bring him back to Tuscany, no doubt.

'*Sei molto sporco,*' Dora piped up. You're very dirty.

'*Taci, Dora. Non essere scortese,*' Rosa muttered. Be quiet, Dora. Don't be rude.

'*Ma è vero.*' But it's true.

They were interrupted by the sound of Babbo and Teresa's footfalls as they came into the room.

'*Caspita!*' Babbo said. Good heavens.

Tom struggled to his feet. '*Buongiorno.*'

'Should I go and fetch the marchese?' Rosa looked her father in the eye. 'He'll know what to do.'

'I'll go.' Babbo shook his head. 'We must help this man. Maurizio could well be in the same situation in Russia and I pray every day that people are helping him.'

Her father left the storeroom before Rosa could comment.

She stared at Tom and he stared back at her.

'Would you like a drink?' she asked, making a drinking motion with her hand.

'*Grazie.*' He nodded.

'*Vieni.*' She beckoned. Come.

He followed her slowly up the stairs – he appeared so tired – and the little girls chattered like sparrows in their wake.

Nonna looked up from her seat by the fireplace. 'Who's this?'

Rosa gave a brief explanation, then went to pour a glass of water, which she handed to Tom.

He collapsed on a chair, and gulped down the drink. Tiny rivulets ran down his beard, darkening the dried-on mud.

'*Ho ancora fame.*' I'm still hungry. Again his accent drew a smile from her.

She went to the stove where a pot of bean stew was bubbling, filled a bowl and took it to him.

He smacked his lips and gobbled down the food, then made a washing movement with his hands.

She took him to the bathroom, handed him a bar of soap and a towel.

After leaving him to his own devices, she went to the room Maurizio had once shared with her brothers. There, she found an old pair of trousers, underwear, a shirt and a sweater. She knocked on the bathroom door, making sure to turn her eyes from Tom's emaciated body, the towel wrapped around his caved-in waist.

'Here you are,' she said, passing him the clothes.

He thanked her, his warm tone of voice making her chest tingle.

Her eyes met his and she glanced away quickly.

'Come to the kitchen when you are ready,' she said, flustered. 'My father should return soon.'

* * *

At the supper table later, after Marchese Ginori had spent half an hour closeted with Tom and Babbo, Rosa listened open-mouthed to her father recount what had happened to the *inglesi*.

They'd made it as far as Frascati, to the south of Rome. The two-hundred-kilometre trek had taken them two weeks of hiding by day and walking by night, using the maps the *padrone* had given them and the few phrases of Italian they'd learnt.

Unfortunately, the *tedeschi* were holding back the Allied

advance and the entire area was crawling with the enemy. Tom and his comrades were captured one morning, handed in by a fascist farmer, who'd found them sleeping in his barn, and was eager to claim a cash reward.

The group was immediately taken under armed guard to a train which would transport them to Germany. Tom, however, managed to separate himself from his comrades as they were being loaded onto a carriage. He'd lowered himself beneath the axles and remained motionless while the length of the train passed over him. He'd then made his way back to the Val d'Orcia, avoiding any human contact. Having already been betrayed once, he'd decided not to risk it again.

'It's no wonder he was starving,' Rosa said.

Tom was shovelling pasta into his mouth as if his life depended on it.

Babbo gave a small nod.

'The *padrone* said he can stay with us for the time being. Once he gets his strength back he can help me with the sowing.'

Babbo was late getting the wheat seeds into the ground this year. Rosa and her siblings helped him as much as they could, but having Tom around on the farm would surely be a godsend.

'What if the Germans find out about him?' Mamma asked, worry creasing her brow.

'They won't.' Babbo sounded confident. 'Our *podere* is one of the most remote and far from the valley road. We keep ourselves to ourselves. No one will know he's here.'

Rosa glanced at Tom. His eyelids were heavy and, with his belly full, he looked to be in danger of nodding off to sleep.

'Giulio, take the *inglese* to your room,' she said. 'He's terribly tired.'

Tom would be sharing with her brothers, just like she shared a room with her sisters.

He rose to his feet, looking distinctly odd in Maurizio's old clothes. The trousers were too baggy and didn't reach his ankles. The ceiling light lit his blue eyes and the dusting of freckles on his well-shaped nose. His beard was tinged with russet. If any Germans came across him, they'd know instantly he wasn't a local. No one around here had skin so pale or hair so fair. Rosa only hoped Babbo's confidence hadn't been misplaced.

She began to clear the dishes, nudging Lucrezia to lend her a hand.

After she'd done the washing-up, Rosa took Dora and her little sisters to clean their teeth, put on their nightdresses and say their prayers.

'Mammina, I like having the *inglese* here,' Dora said as Rosa tucked her into the big bed the little girls shared. 'He's so nice.'

Teresa and Ines echoed her sentiments.

Rosa made no comment. She kissed them all and wished them goodnight before returning to the kitchen.

Music was blaring from the radio, but Rosa barely heard it. Her mind was in a whirl. Everyone liked Tom, it seemed, except her. But was she lying to herself? She heaved a sigh of resignation. It wouldn't hurt to be kind to him. After all, Babbo had said he'd hoped Maurizio had found people who were treating him well. It wasn't Tom's fault that Francesco had been killed. If she wanted to blame anyone, she should be blaming Mussolini and Hitler. She chewed a piece of pecorino cheese and promised herself to try to be more understanding about the enigma that was Tom Johnstone.

7

It was the day before Christmas Eve, and Emma was standing on a ladder tying mistletoe to a beribboned curtain of bay leaves in the villa's front hall. She'd always loved *Natale*; it was her favourite time of the year.

Sadness filled her. This year she and her father would celebrate without the cousins from Rome and Anglo-American friends from Florence who generally visited. Having house guests would be impossible with the Germans breathing down their necks. She would miss the joyful banter around the table, the games of charades afterwards, and the feeling of being part of an extended family. Tarcisia, their cook, always made delicious *tortelli* stuffed with ricotta and wild herbs or mushrooms, followed by a *torta di verdura* – a rich quiche with pumpkin, leeks and spinach. The centrepiece of the meal would always be a capon, slow roasted with chestnuts. *Panforte* – a dessert made from nuts, candied fruits, honey and spices – and *ricciarelli* – soft almond cookies covered with icing sugar – would follow, washed down with *vin santo*, sweet wine. When Emma was little, the farmers' wives would walk for miles to bring a pre-fattened capon to the *fattoria*, but Papà had stopped the feudal practice, insisting they keep the birds for their own Christmas lunches instead.

Now, life at the Bivio had reverted to the way it had been centuries ago, as the outside world had become more and more cut off. With Emma's university education put on hold – her father had said it would have been too risky for her to stay in student accommodation on her own in Siena – she spent her time learning to spin and weave wool to make clothes for those who needed them. She also helped in the school and in the estate's clinic when she wasn't taking messages to Marco.

Her stomach fluttered as she thought about him, an unfamiliar sensation. What had got into her? He was her best friend and had never had that effect on her before. The war was doing strange things to everyone, she surmised. Seeing Marco in charge of a group of grown men, who clearly looked up to him, must have made her view him in a different light.

The flutters in her belly intensified; he would be joining the annual Christmas party that afternoon. He'd offered to dress up as Santa Claus, for the farm children who were under ten years old, a role usually performed by his father. But Orazio had come down with a nasty cold. Marco would be in disguise; no one would realise he wasn't Orazio. They were the same height and their voices were identical.

Emma hoped it wasn't a rash decision. She, her father, Marco's parents and the villa's household staff were the only people who knew Marco was there. God forbid anyone else found out. She remembered how the German captain seemed to know so much about the layout of the *fattoria*. Was there a spy in their midst? Children found it hard to keep secrets, in any case, so it was better they didn't know about Marco.

Emma climbed down from the ladder and put it away in the storeroom.

At least here in the countryside they weren't subjected to the reign of terror instituted by Mussolini's *repubblichini* in Florence. Her father had gone to the city on a short visit and, when he'd returned, he said that everyone he'd met had been extremely nervous. Apparently, the fascists were arresting and torturing people in what was known as a *villa triste* – a 'sad house', as the torture chambers were known. Passers-by would hear the victims' screams.

Those poor people.

The Bivio hadn't been entirely spared from strife, though. A month ago, all young men born in 1924 and 1925 had been ordered to report for duty to the Fascist Republican Army head-quarters in Chianciano. As a consequence, the nineteen- and twenty-year-old sons of the farmers had left home to join the partisans. Now their fathers were living with the threat of being detained. On the other side of Chianciano, a lorry full of German soldiers, led by the captain of the *repubblichini*, went to a farm and arrested the father of a missing recruit. As the truck was driving off, the boy ran out and begged to take his *babbo*'s place, a request that was granted but not before the boy's father had been beaten senseless. The families on the Bivio estate whose sons had dodged the draft were living in fear of a similar visit. Emma prayed fervently that the Allies would defeat the *tedeschi* soon, and that all this human suffering would come to an end.

She walked over to the Christmas tree in the centre of the hall: a tall pine, decorated with candles ready for lighting. Her nostrils filled with the rich camphor-like fragrance and she gazed at the pile of presents at its base. She'd worked hard making stuffed animals for the youngest children. Those a little older would receive special picture books. And the eldest more grown-up books they'd be able to read for themselves. *Babbo Natale* – Marco

– would hand out all the gifts. Emma couldn't wait for the party to start; it would cheer them all up.

A smile tugged at her mouth as Marco's voice echoed from the front doorway. She rushed to greet him, then stopped dead in her tracks.

'*Oh, mio Dio*. Oh, my goodness. You look wonderful.'

And he did. A pillow stuffed under the red woollen jacket gave him just the right paunch. A flowing white wool beard and wig, the latter of which was worn under the ubiquitous nightcap hat. The costume had been brought from America by Emma's maternal grandmother on a visit when she was only six. Grandma had been horrified to learn that children in Italy had hardly heard of Santa, and that they only received presents on Twelfth Night. The outfit had been a part of Emma's Christmases ever since; she couldn't imagine a celebration without Marco's father wearing it.

Would anyone realise it wasn't Orazio in disguise today? She couldn't help a quiver of worry tickling her spine.

'Our guests are arriving,' Papà announced as he came into the hall. 'Let's light the candles.'

He produced a cigarette lighter and lit three candles, two of which he handed to Emma and Marco, who proceeded to light the rest of them. Before too long, the tree was aglow, just like the eyes of the twenty children when they arrived. Accompanied by their mothers, they were taken to the frescoed formal dining room, where as good a spread as could be managed, given the circumstances, had been prepared by Tarcisia and her kitchen staff. The children sat on the floor, picnic-style, and, after ham and cheese rolls, *panforte* and *ricciarelli*, washed down with sheep's milk, Emma took them through to the hall, where Marco, deliberately covered in soot, emerged from the big fireplace and proceeded to hand around the gifts.

Emma's spirits soared, the faces of the awe-struck children

bringing tears of happiness to her eyes. They were so young and innocent. She would give anything for the war not to hurt them more than it had done already. Some had lost their fathers, some their brothers. And those who hadn't experienced such losses could yet do so. The Nazi-fascists wouldn't put up with there being partisans in the area for long. An image of the *villa triste* in Florence came into her mind and her flesh crawled.

Soon it was time for the children to go home, but not before those fathers who were too old for the draft had arrived for their traditional Christmas vermouth with the *padrone*.

They drank *brindisi* after *brindisi*, toasting and knocking back the drink until their wives took charge and ushered them outdoors.

Emma and Marco waved them all off in the courtyard, then went back inside.

'Where's Papà?' Emma asked, glancing around.

'I suspect he's had more than his fair share of alcohol and has gone to sleep it off.' Marco laughed. He paused under a sprig of mistletoe and glanced up. 'Can I have a Christmas kiss, Emma?' His eyes met hers and he tugged down his Santa beard.

'Of course,' she said, her cheeks burning.

Marco was a head taller than her. He tilted her chin and brought his mouth down to hers, brushing her lips in a kiss so soft and tender she wanted it to go on forever.

They'd never kissed like that before and she found herself unaccountably wanting more.

Wrapping her arms around his waist, she breathed in his familiar scent.

The harsh sound of a motorcycle engine interrupted them and they sprang back.

'Go, Marco! Now!' Emma's father had come down from his room.

Her heart set up a fearful beat. That sound could only mean one thing. Hofmann, or someone like him, had arrived.

Marco spun on his heel.

'I feel like a coward running away,' he said, turning to glance at her as he started to run.

'But you'll live to fight another day,' she said.

'Indeed,' Papà added. 'I'll go and find out what's what. Now go!'

Emma followed him outside. Her stomach churned. Hofmann had dismounted from the Moto Guzzi and was striding across the gravel.

'Good evening,' her father said. 'How can I help you?'

Hofmann's cold eyes swept over Emma, then moved to Papà.

'I'm looking for billets for our soldiers. And I've heard you have an empty fortress that might be just right for us.'

'But it's Christmas,' Emma stuttered.

'War goes on,' Hofmann sneered. 'Despite the season.'

Emma's father drew himself up to his full height.

'What my daughter is trying to say is that our church is within the fort's walls. The day after tomorrow we celebrate Christmas mass with our workers and their families.'

'Ah.' Hofmann tapped his chin. 'I was going to mention also that it has come to my attention that some of your farmers' sons have failed to report for duty. Their fathers can expect a visit from us soon.'

Icy dread sliced through Emma. She was speechless.

'I'll be back to inspect the fortress in the new year,' Hofmann said. 'In the meantime, *Frohe Weihnachten*.'

'*Buon Natale*,' Papà said, clearly refusing to respond in German as he wished him Happy Christmas in return.

'What can we do?' Emma asked her father when the roar of the motorcycle's engine had faded.

He shook his head.

'There's nothing to be done, *mia cara*. Just hope and pray for the Allies to get here fast.'

Two mornings later, Emma woke to a cold, crisp Christmas Day. But she was in no mood to celebrate. She barely touched her breakfast and her feet dragged as she walked up the hill to church with her father.

She sat in the front pew next to him, worrying about Hofmann's imminent visit. But, turning around to gaze at the congregation from the farms and the *fattoria*, a warm feeling spread through her as she thought about their kindness and hospitality to all the homeless passers-by, the British prisoners, Italian soldiers on the run. The spontaneous, unfailing charity and hospitality of the farmers struck a chord. Even now that the risks had increased, and the *nazifascisti* were supposed to be rounding up boys born in 1924 and 1925, no farm would refuse them shelter; they'd feed them, clothe them and do their utmost to protect them.

Emma's eyes fell on Rosa and her daughter. Papà had told her that Tom, the Scots guard, had returned to live with them and help on the land. Emma only hoped they wouldn't suffer any repercussions. But they weren't the only family in the valley helping ex-prisoners. The Bivio had become a place of refuge, a haven, and she was proud of the fact.

After the service, she stood next to her father and greeted everyone just like she'd always done. It occurred to her that she should put a brave face on. Once Hofmann had seen the fortress, he might decide it was unsuitable. After all, Germans had already requisitioned several hotels in Chianciano, which was a spa town, to use as hospitals. They might decide the rest of the hotels – empty because of the war – would make better billets instead.

A hollow expectation.

Back at the villa, she ate a lonely lunch with Papà. There was only one course – roasted capon – and Emma could scarcely swallow it.

In the evening, she sat with her father in his study to listen to the radio. News came through that Pisa and Pistoia had been bombed by the Allies.

On Christmas Day!

Papà got to his feet and went to the window. He drew back the curtain and gave a gasp. 'It's snowing, Emma. Come, take a look.'

She hurried to his side and stared out at the view. It must have been snowing for quite a while as the moonlit valley was already blanketed in white.

'It's as if nature is trying to cover up all the evil going on around us,' she said. 'It's so beautiful.'

And it truly was.

She stood with her father for a long while, her heart filling with sudden hopefulness.

Then the telephone rang.

The hope in her heart melted away as she listened to Papà's serious tone as he answered.

'What's happened?' Her voice quaked.

'That was the captain of the Chianciano *repubblichini*. Sandro must present himself in the morning or they will arrest his father.'

Sandro was the nineteen-year-old son of their gardener, Luigi Salvadori.

'Oh, no!' Emma gasped.

It had turned out to be the worst Christmas of her life.

She thought about Marco and it struck her that he and his comrades would be feeling the cold. Did they have enough warm clothes? Enough fuel? Tomorrow, she would try to make her way up to the partisans' hideout and take them the warm woollen socks that she'd knitted. She would put today behind her and look to the future. It would soon be 1944. The Allies would break through German lines and life would get back to normal. She touched a finger to her lips. Thought about Marco's kiss. Was he thinking about her like she was thinking about him?

She couldn't resist hoping that he was.

8

Rosa was scraping ice from the front step. Thank God Babbo had managed to plant the wheat for next year's harvest. He wouldn't have been able to do it without Tom's help, though. After massive amounts of food and rest, the *inglese* had recovered his strength in record time and was repaying the Vaninis' hospitality by working hard and helping with the children, who'd decided to call him 'Zio', uncle, and got on with him *come pappa e ciccia*, like a first and second course.

Dora's joyful laughter drifted up from the patio, where Tom was building a snowman with her, assisted by Rosa's youngest siblings. They were dressed in woollen hats, coats, scarves and gloves. It had snowed again last night, but the day had dawned crisp and clear. The entire valley had been blanketed since Christmas, which everyone thought was a blessing, for it had prevented the *nazifascisti* from rounding up the young men who'd failed to report for the draft. *At least for now.*

Tom's deep voice broke into Rosa's thoughts. He was speaking and understanding so much Italian now. The *padrone* had visited soon after Tom had returned a couple of months ago, and had brought him an English–Italian dictionary as well as a grammar book. In the evenings, once the little ones had gone to bed, he would sit with the family and listen to the radio, making notes and looking up the words he hadn't understood. Rosa couldn't help admiring Tom's efforts, and he was also teaching her daughter and siblings to speak a little English.

Babbo said he hoped that Maurizio had found people to help him like they were helping Tom. If so, maybe Maurizio too was picking up a new language.

'*Al Lavoro!*' Babbo had come onto the yard.

Rosa headed down the stairs. Today was the day when their pig would be slaughtered, and she would take the little girls for a walk in the snow to avoid them hearing the squealing and witnessing the death. She gave a shudder; she would never forget her first experience of a pig slaughter when she was a child; it had upset her for days.

All year long, the condemned animal had been fed on acorns and scraps, growing enormous from guzzling the family's slops that would otherwise have turned into piles of rotting rubbish. That morning it would be led out from its cosy stone-walled stall and onto the snow with its nose in a rope. Babbo would then slit its throat. It would squeal until it had heaved its final breaths.

Rosa exhaled a regretful sigh. The poor creature would take a while to die, and even when the blood stopped flowing its body would still move. The snow would be splattered with crimson, but Babbo, Tom, and her brothers would gather up the blood, trying not to waste a drop.

Yes, it was best that Dora, Ines and Teresa weren't around.

Inside the house, Mamma, Lucrezia and Nonna were already boiling water in a blackened cauldron on the open fire. Rosa breathed in the scent of the woodsmoke, which curled into the sky and clouded the frosty air. Babbo and Tom would help carry the cauldron down to the yard and then they would pour scalding water over the dead pig before scraping off the bristles, the soft ones, the hard spiky ones. *Porca miseria*, they'd curse – pig was such a hairy beast.

Once they'd cleaned its face and ears, they would string up its body in the cold storeroom. There they would slit it down the middle, slice the vitals into a bucket, knife out the lungs, the liver, the kidneys. Afterwards they would cut away the finest, purest fat – the suet – a solid cloud around the kidney.

Such a smelly job.

They'd take good care of all the fat, not just the suet, slice off hunks to make *lardo*, white with thin pink stripes, to be salted and peppered and herbed and sealed under a smooth stone for two weeks.

Finally, they would cut the pig into chunks. The animal would be just a jumble of shapes, a cathedral of ribs, loin, chops, *ossocollo*, neck bone, *coppa*, pork cup, pancetta, piles of fat and skin to make *cotechino*, the best flesh for mincing into sausages, intestines for the casings, and the well-washed, well-soaked gullet pipe ready to make a big thick *salame*. The huge pig would also provide four magnificent hams – to say nothing of all the stewing pork – to make the *fattore* happy. It would surely settle Babbo's accounts with the *padrone*. Not that the marchese ever demanded their settlement. Credit was always given when needed.

Rosa's limbs lightened as she stepped into the courtyard. She and her family would feast on the bones and the leftover pork for the next few days. She was looking forward to a change from *la cucina povera*, peasant food, which contained very little meat.

Rosa nodded a greeting to Tom. His smile made her chest tingle and she looked away in awkwardness. She was suddenly tongue-tied. *How silly!*

'Come,' she said to Dora and the others when she'd retrieved her equilibrium. 'Let's go for a walk.'

'Why?' Dora asked. 'I want to stay here with Tom.'

'*Vai con tua madre*,' he said. Go with your mother. '*Sii una brava ragazzina*.' Be a good little girl.

Dora nodded and placed her hand in Rosa's.

Just like that.

'*Grazie*, Tom.' Rosa felt her mouth crinkle into a smile. Dora was completely under his spell. It seemed she would do anything for him.

'You're so very welcome.' The English words were probably a pleasantry. Rosa wished she'd understood them.

Wearing thick sheepskin boots the same as the children's, Rosa led the little girls along the ridge in the direction of the forest. On the distant horizon, Monte Amiata shone white under the pale winter sun.

Dora blew out a breath that escaped in a cloud which made her giggle. Ines and Teresa did likewise and they soon turned it into a game to see whose 'clouds' were the biggest.

They kept away from the farmhouse for about an hour: long enough for the pig to have been killed but not enough time for all the hard work to have been completed. Rosa took the children straight up to the kitchen as Babbo and the others were still chopping up the animal. The heavy, slightly sickly smell from all the blood stuck in Rosa's throat.

* * *

At supper, they feasted on boiled bones, seasoned with rosemary, thyme and sage. Rosa gritted her teeth as Lucrezia sat herself next to Tom. She was flirting with him shamelessly and had been doing so for weeks – fluttering her eyelashes and poking her pink tongue from her mouth to lick the grease from her fingers. Rosa huffed. Thankfully, Tom appeared not to be taking the slightest bit of notice.

Why did she care? She was being ridiculous. The man was a foreigner who would return to his own country after the war. She didn't know what he thought of the situation in which he'd found himself. It was impossible to ask him. Although his Italian had improved, he was still far from being able to converse about feelings. He glanced up from his food and caught her eye. She looked away, blushing.

When everyone had eaten their fill, she rose to her feet to clear the dishes.

'*Posso aiutare*?' Tom asked. Can I help?

She told him it was women's work. '*E'lavoro di donne.*'

All the men she knew didn't help in the home, but it appeared that Tom's countrymen did, for he'd ignored Rosa's statement and was carrying plates to the sink. Even more astounding, he'd started to scrub them. She took the cloth from him and indicated that he should return to his seat.

Soon it was time to get Dora, Teresa and Ines ready for bed. That job always fell to Rosa: it was the least she could do to show her gratitude to her parents.

'Come on, *bambine*,' she said, lifting her daughter in her arms.

She took the girls to the bathroom to brush their teeth, then led them to the bedroom.

'Has the piggy gone to heaven?' Dora asked after Rosa had listened to her bedtime prayers.

'Of course.'

Was there a pig heaven?

Anything was possible in this crazy world.

She found the thought of the pig enjoying a heavenly field of clover to be comforting.

Dora was sandwiched between Ines and Teresa. With heavy eyelids, she put her thumb in her mouth and twirled a curl of hair. In seconds she'd fallen asleep.

Rosa bent to kiss her smooth forehead.

'*Buonanotte*,' she whispered. '*Sogni d'oro*.' Golden dreams.

Her little sisters repeated the words as Rosa made her way from the room.

Outside in the corridor, she gave a start.

Tom was standing there.

She took a step backwards.

'*Cosa vuoi*, Tom?' What do you want?

'*Niente e tutto*.' Nothing and everything. His smile set her heart racing.

He moved forwards and she did likewise.

His eyes posed questions, and she nodded.

She'd come completely under his spell like Dora, it seemed.

He took her hand and kissed the inside of her wrist, his breath hot against her cool skin.

She lifted her other hand to his cheek and stroked his cropped beard. It felt surprisingly soft.

'*Posso baciarti*?' Can I kiss you?

She wanted to run.

She wanted to stay.

'Yes.' Her voice trembled.

He opened his arms and she went into them.

But the kitchen door crashed open and they sprang apart.

Lucrezia erupted into the passageway. She stopped dead and burst into laughter.

'I knew it,' she chuckled. '*L'inglese ha una cotta per te, sorella*.' The Englishman has the hots for you, sister.

Rosa's cheeks flamed.

'I don't know what you're talking about,' she said.

* * *

Later, in the bed she shared with Lucrezia, Rosa curled herself into a ball. Tom had stoked a fire in her and she couldn't stop thinking about him.

'What's it like when a man puts his *uccello* inside you?' Lucrezia asked out of the blue.

'What a question!'

'No one will tell me, even though I'll be seventeen soon. Mamma refuses to discuss the subject. At least you have a child to prove it happened to you.'

'I'm sure it would depend on the man.' Rosa heaved a sad sigh. 'Francesco made me feel wonderful, but I don't know if that's always the case.'

Lucrezia snuggled up for warmth.

'Tom *vuole scoparti*.' Tom wants to fuck you.

Rosa gave her sister a soft slap.

'Watch your language, *cara*. The *bambine* might hear.'

'I'm only stating the obvious. He can't take his eyes off you. I tried to get him to notice me, but he ignores me. I just don't get it. I'm younger and prettier than you...'

'That's just it, little sister. You're far too young for him.'

Lucrezia gave a moan. 'I wish there was someone for me,' she said in a wistful tone.

Rosa turned to face her sister. 'There will be one day, you'll see.'

'If there's anyone left when this cursed war is over.'

'We can only pray for the fighting to end soon.'

They lapsed into silence and soon Lucrezia's soft snores bore witness to the fact that she'd fallen asleep.

But Rosa couldn't drift off. Thoughts of Tom flittered through her mind. He'd wanted to kiss her and she'd wanted to kiss him back. Was Lucrezia right about his intentions? If so, Rosa didn't know how she'd react. She wasn't the type of woman to have sex outside of marriage. She and Francesco had waited until they were wed.

She gave a wry smile. Lucrezia was imagining things; she'd always been fanciful. Tom had shown himself to be a true gentleman by asking her permission. He certainly wouldn't want anything more than a kiss.

She hugged herself. If the situation arose again, she'd let him kiss her.

But only because she'd like to find out if he was a good kisser.

What could be the harm in that?

9

Emma hugged herself for warmth as she gazed out at the valley from her bedroom window. The snow had melted a week ago, but the weather was still extremely cold. Punctuated by inky-green cypress trees standing tall like upright pencils, the desolate, barren earth would become verdant with young wheat soon. Spring was her second favourite time of the year after Christmas and she couldn't wait to enjoy the pink cherry blossom and purple wisteria edging the garden. Perhaps the Allies would break through before the new season arrived.

A sigh escaped her. The British and Americans were still being held up by the Germans and bitter fighting was occurring at Cassino, halfway from Naples to Rome.

Movement caught her eye. Luigi, the gardener, was raking up leaves from the pathway between the hedges below. On Boxing Day, he'd waited for the fascist militiamen to come and arrest him after he'd refused to let his boy, Sandro, turn himself in as a draft dodger. In preparation for imprisonment, Luigi had even changed into his best shirt. But no one came and a few hours later, to everyone's relief, they heard that the order to detain parents in place of their sons had been revoked.

For the time being.

Emma stepped away from the window and went to meet her father in the courtyard. Unease tickled in her chest. Hofmann was due to arrive and inspect the fortress. Papà had said they needed to be civil to him, for making an enemy of a Nazi would only cause trouble. For moral support, Emma had offered to accompany her father on the inspection. Much as she disliked the captain – the man who'd requisitioned their horses – she'd decided to follow Papà's advice. She wouldn't go as far as to turn Hofmann into a friend, but maybe if she pretended she liked him he would be less severe in his attitude towards her father. And he might even return Bella and Zorro.

The roar of the Moto Guzzi's engine echoed in her ears.

'Good morning,' Papà greeted the captain.

'Lead the way!' Hofmann commanded, his feet planted either side of the bike.

'*Jawohl*, Herr Kapitän!'

Emma climbed onto the lorry next to her father. Before too long, they'd made their way up the unmetalled road and had arrived at the fortress.

A fresh breeze blew the loose hair back from her face and she shivered, not just from the cold but also from apprehension. There were Germans billeted in Chianciano, paratroopers who'd come from Cassino to recuperate and train new recruits before returning to the front. Their rations weren't arriving regularly because of Allied bombing, and they saw no reason why sheep, pigs and geese from the local farms should not replace them. At night, when they were drunk, they would bang on the doors of the Chiancianesi houses, shouting, 'Out with the women!'

It would be too awful if that happened on the Bivio estate.

Emma walked through the wide entrance to the fortress behind Papà and the captain. After he'd been shown around, Hofmann exclaimed that the facilities were rather primitive.

'Well, it's hardly the Grand Hotel,' Papà chuckled wryly. 'We housed prisoners here, as you know.'

'Hmm. It will be all right for about one hundred of our enlisted men, I suppose, but I think your villa would be more suitable for the officers.' Hofmann looked her father up and down. 'You should prepare to leave as soon as possible.'

Emma's spirits sank. How could she possibly be nice to this man? He was vile and he made her feel nauseous. But she assumed a sympathetic expression and forced a sweet smile.

'We'll do so willingly,' she said in what she hoped wasn't a sarcastic tone. 'Anything to help the Reich.'

The captain's cold eyes fell on her and he smirked.

'I'm pleased you see it that way, *vermissen*.'

'My daughter has echoed my sentiments,' Papà added. 'When can we expect your men?'

'I'll return with our billeting officer in a day or so.' Hofmann remounted his motorcycle. 'Just be ready at short notice.' With a surprisingly soulful look at Emma, he turned the bike and roared back down the road.

Emma removed the fake mask from her face, letting her consternation show.

'Oh, Papà. Where will we go?'

'To our only empty property.'

'Le Faggete? It's not empty. Marco and the partisans are there...'

'There'll be enough space for us, I'm sure.'

She wrinkled her brow. Her father was used to being waited on hand and foot. How would he cope camping with a band of rough men? More to the point, how would *she* cope?

'Maybe we should start packing,' she said, her heart heavy.

Papà ran a hand through his thinning hair.

'We'd better get on with it...'

* * *

After helping Papà bury his papers and Mama's jewellery in the rose garden, Emma was on constant tenterhooks, waiting for Hofmann to return. Several anxious days went by. They moved their best furniture and precious books to outlying farms and tried to keep occupied to ease the uncertainty of not knowing what would happen. Emma spent her time helping in the school or making clothes. She thought about Marco, whom she hadn't seen since Christmas. The partisans were building up their supply of arms, from what her father had told her, ambushing German trucks and stealing what they found. She worried about Marco and longed to see him. If she and her father moved to Le Faggete, at least she would see him soon.

Then news came through that the Allies had landed at Anzio, near the town of Nettuno about thirty miles south of Rome. Almost immediately, long columns of German troops started to head south and the paratroopers destined for the fortress went to join them. Hofmann phoned Papà to tell him.

It was a reprieve, of sorts.

'They'll be back, mark my words,' her father said as he lowered himself into his armchair by the fire. 'The Allies will push them northwards and we'll be ordered to make way for them again.'

Emma looked up from where she was sitting, knitting a scarf. She allowed the momentary relief to sink in, but couldn't help a prickling of her scalp that the stay of execution was only tempo-rary. She felt a sudden longing to see Marco.

'Do you still want to go and find out if we can live at Le Faggete?' she asked her father.

'Perhaps it would be safer for you to stay in Montepulciano.'

Their close friends, the Brandinis, had issued an open invita-tion just yesterday. Edoardo was the mayor of the town and Agata, his wife, often helped him in the town hall. Their comfortable palazzo would make a good bolthole, perhaps.

'Not only me. You too, Papà.' Emma wished he wouldn't still treat her like a child. She'd turned nineteen in the new year; she was a grown woman.

'I can't leave the estate, *mia cara*.'

'Then neither will I.'

Papà opened his mouth, clearly about to argue, but he was interrupted by the appearance of Vittorio, their butler.

'The Maresciallo of the Montepulciano Carabinieri is here, marchese. He says that he needs to speak with you immediately.'

A sinking feeling spread through Emma. The visit was unprecedented. Something must be wrong.

Papà rose to his feet.

'Please, ask him to come in.'

'Shall I go to my room?' Emma asked for the sake of politeness.

'No, darling. If he's here on urgent business it will probably concern you as much as me.'

She went to stand by her father. He'd known the Marshal for years. She knew him to be an honourable man of the old school. Rumour had it he'd yet to take the oath of obedience to the Republican government and that, if ordered to do so, he would hand in his notice. Throughout occupied Italy, many gendarmes were taking a similar stand and, apparently, 70 per cent of the officers and 90 per cent of the NCOs would prefer to resign from the service rather than swear loyalty to the new regime.

Vittorio took the Maresciallo's dark blue overcoat as he ushered him into the living room.

The Marshal shook hands with Emma and her father, accepted the glass of wine offered, then went to warm himself by the fire.

'It's freezing out there,' he said. 'I wouldn't be surprised if we had more snow.'

'Indeed. Please, take a seat.' Papà indicated towards the nearest armchair. 'To what do we owe the pleasure of your visit?'

'I would have phoned, marchese, but the lines are tapped.' The Marshal paused to sip his wine. 'I've come to warn you. The Prefect of Siena, Giorgio Chiurco, has asked me to keep you and your daughter under special surveillance as "suspect persons".'

'Whatever for? We've done nothing wrong.' Emma's father frowned.

'They believe you are giving money to the partisans and inciting your sharecroppers not to report for military service. Word is you are paying each man fifty lire if he fails to register.'

'How ridiculous!' Emma laughed.

'Absolute rubbish,' her father added.

'Just be careful,' the Marshal said. 'I'll turn a blind eye to Chiurco's request. But watch your backs and be vigilant.'

'We'll do that,' Papà said.

'Oh, and another thing.' The Maresciallo lowered his voice. 'I've heard Chiurco will soon be in this area to search for any escaped POWs and draft dodgers.' He gave a wink. 'A warning might be opportune...'

Emma's hand flew to her mouth.

Her pulse raced.

She needed to go and tell Marco as soon as possible.

* * *

The next morning, heavy cloud hugged the tops of the hills as Emma set off at first light. Once more, she'd had to insist with her father that it be her who went to deliver a message to the partisans.

'No one would ever suspect a woman going for a walk,' she'd said. 'And the woods are ours, which makes it even more unsuspicious.'

'I wish you weren't so headstrong, daughter,' he'd said. 'But as you keep saying, you're grown up now...'

'Exactly. I'll be fine. Please don't worry.'

'Easier said than done.' He kissed the top of her head while she hugged him.

A sparrowhawk gave a loud *kekekeke* cry from a nearby tree, startling her. When it flew off to hunt for prey, she laughed at her own jumpiness. She was alone in the forest, apart from the wildlife, and there was nothing to be concerned about. If Chiurco and the fascist militiamen were in the vicinity, they'd be making so much noise she'd have heard them.

She carried on walking and, after about an hour, she'd reached the last bend in the track before Le Faggete.

A clearing opened up with a terracotta-coloured house in the centre. A couple of partisans were guarding the path and hurriedly she gave them the password.

'I need to speak to Leandro.' This was Marco's battle name. 'Urgently.'

'He's out on patrol,' the taller of the two men said. 'Come through to the kitchen and warm yourself by the fire.'

Fulvio, the cook, offered her a cup of acorn coffee which she accepted gladly. Although she'd exerted herself hiking, she'd fought through bitterly cold wind and her face was freezing.

She took off her coat and went through to the long, narrow living room. She didn't have to wait long. Marco's cheerful voice preceded him.

'It's snowing,' he said.

She leapt to her feet.

'Ciao, Leandro.'

'Daria!' He called her by her battle name, went to her, and kissed her on both cheeks.

'I have a message for you,' she whispered.

'Come.' He took her hand, and led her back into the kitchen, where he helped himself to a coffee while she pulled out a chair at the big oak table.

She explained about the Maresciallo's visit. 'I came to warn you.'

'The *fascisti* aren't likely to come up here in the snow,' Marco said. 'But we'll watch out for a visit after it thaws. *Grazie.* You did well to come and tell me.'

She basked in his praise. 'I'd better head back down before the weather gets worse.'

'It's already bad, *cara.* Best you stay here.'

'But Papà will worry about me.'

'He knows where you are. Knows I'll look after you.'

'*Va bene.*' Okay. A warm feeling spread through her. She felt unaccountably safe with him. 'I'll help Fulvio with lunch, make myself useful around the place.'

'Perfect.' A smile creased his face.

* * *

It snowed all day, the snow settling and forming a slushy carpet. Whenever Emma glanced out of the window, the flakes were swirling so fast she couldn't make out the trees. She and the others were completely cut off; there'd be no danger of an unwelcome visit from the fascists. She hoped her father wasn't too worried, hoped he'd realise she was in safe hands.

That night, after a meal of bean stew washed down with copious amounts of red wine, she found a place on a floor cushion to sit next to Marco. A huge log fire crackled in the old-fashioned stone fireplace. It threw out enough heat to warm the entire room. The twenty or so men who were with them passed around a bottle of grappa.

Emma took a sip and the strong alcohol burnt her throat.

Sandro Salvadori, Luigi's son, began to strum his guitar and sing 'Camicia Rossa'.

Everyone joined in, some more melodiously than others. The spirit of camaraderie in the room was tangible. The partisans' morale was sky high.

The food, drink and warmth had made Emma sleepy, and she yawned.

'I'll take you upstairs,' Marco said.

She felt a little guilty that she'd been assigned a bedroom to herself. But he had insisted, saying she was the only woman among them and he refused to listen to her pleas that she be treated like everyone else.

They stopped at the door to her room.

Their eyes locked.

Marco tilted her chin up.

He kissed her.

Her heart thudded and she arched up on her toes to kiss him back, threading her fingers into his sweater and clinging to him.

He pulled her closer and his lips became more demanding.

She opened her mouth, losing herself in the kiss.

He drew back, stroked a finger down her cheek. 'Buonanotte, *cara*.' Goodnight.

She turned her face into his palm and kissed it. 'Sleep well, Marco.'

The room was like an icebox, so she got into bed fully clothed. It took a while for her to drop off. All she could think about was Marco and that kiss. What did it mean? Had he developed feelings for her like she'd done for him?

She was so tired, though, that when she eventually fell asleep she slept deeply. At dawn's light, she woke and went to the window. The snow of yesterday had turned to rain.

Downstairs, she found everyone packing their rucksacks.

'We've decided to hike across to Castiglioncello,' Marco said, handing her a cup of coffee. 'There's another group of partisans in the Spineta woods, living in a charcoal burner's hut. Mainly British and American escaped POWs. By all accounts, one of them came down by parachute. It's said that they have a radio transmitter, and that supplies are dropped to them from planes.'

'Will you stay there?' She took a sip of coffee, then told him that her father was thinking of moving into Le Faggete.

'Not planning on anything, really. We need to go with the flow.' He met her gaze. 'I doubt the *padrone* will be comfortable in this place. Hopefully, it won't come to that.'

'I agree.' She quickly finished her drink. 'Well, I should get going.'

'I'll come with you. Just in case.'

'In case of what?'

'The fascists might have set off for this area when it stopped snowing.'

The thought had already occurred to her, but she'd kept it to herself.

After Marco had made arrangements to meet his men in Castiglioncello, he walked with her down the track that led to the Bivio.

When they were almost at the bottom, he halted, listened.

He placed a finger to his lips, then pointed at the trees.

Stealthily, they headed into a thicket, then deeper into the woods.

And not before time.

Emma's pulse pounded.

An open-top lorry laden with men in black uniforms was grinding its way up the dirt road.

10

It was early March, and the weather had turned mild. Rosa was in the kitchen at daybreak, readying herself for the task ahead. She would set aside her usual chore of doing the weekly laundry. Today was for big things: bedsheets, quilts, towels, tablecloths, house cloths. Stained and soiled, they'd been piling up in the laundry chest since before Christmas, waiting for the sun to be warm enough to dry them. And now that time had finally come.

Watched by Nonna, who used to do the job before she became too old for it, Rosa lit the fire in the hearth. She got it going with a wax match and tinder twigs, blowing and shielding the precious flame with her hands. Afterwards, she built a nest of wood, adding more fuel until the fire had assumed a life of its own. Then she ran the tap, filled a pail with water and poured it into the huge pot that hung on the fire.

Nonna stretched out her hands.

'You always make a good fire, *cocca*.'

'You taught me well.'

The kitchen had turned busy. Mama was heating fresh sheep's milk on the electric stove. Papà and Tom were packing their tools.

Lucrezia was wrapping cheese and bread and salami into waxed cloth parcels for the two men to eat mid-morning. Dora and Rosa's younger siblings were dressed for school, ready to climb aboard the oxcart that would take them to the Bivio. They huddled over bread and hot milk, enjoying the warmth of their bowls and chatting about the day ahead.

Rosa made quick work of eating. She was soon seeing the little ones off. When she returned to the kitchen, Mama was lifting the waste pail. The fruit peelings, vegetable skins, stale bread, and uneaten food scraped from plates would be taken to the piglet, who was already being fattened up for next year's slaughter.

'Do a good job with the laundry,' Mama said as Rosa and Lucrezia made their way outside.

Rosa didn't reply. Her eyes were on Tom as he and Babbo, having finished their breakfast, were picking up their bags and leaving the room. Rosa's skin tingled as Tom brushed past her. He'd become a part of the family, but was aware he was putting them at risk. If the *nazifascisti* found out about him, who knew what they would do? Tom kept his kit hidden in a barrel at the back of the pig stall, so there'd be no trace of him in the house if it was ever searched. *Repubblichini* had been to farms nearer the main road. Hopefully, the Vaninis' *podere* was too remote for them to bother about.

Rosa went down to the yard. There, she placed a big wooden tub on its three-legged stand. She checked the pipe at its base, made sure it wasn't blocked, then set the scrubbing board on top and the draining tray below.

With an exhale of breath, she went back upstairs and opened the laundry chest. It smelt rancid, despite Mamma's little posies of lavender. Rosa lifted out as much as she could, making a hefty pile. And then another. Even dry, the laundry was a heavy weight. She put the basket on her head and carried it downstairs, then returned to the kitchen to lift the big pot of hot water from the fire.

'*Brava*,' Nonna said. Good girl. 'And remember to scrub hard.'

'Yes. Yes. I know. Again you've taught me well, *cara*.'

Outside once more in the fresh cool air, Rosa scrubbed the filthy linen with the soft olive soap kept specially for the purpose. The smells of olives, stale dirt and faded lavender filled her senses. It was the scent of spring, the passing of the seasons, and the scrubbing brush felt good in her hands. She was mucky up to her elbows. And she was full of thoughts of Tom.

Her feelings for him had grown from early attraction to something much stronger. A couple of months had gone by since he'd asked if he could kiss her. Now, they would kiss whenever they were alone together. Her tummy fluttered at the thought. She adored being kissed by him; she loved it when his fingers trailed down her body; she loved the warmth and press of his mouth. Their tongues would dance in endless circles of swollen embraces. He'd fuelled a fire within her and she found herself wanting him more and more. Was that so terribly wrong? She barely thought of Francesco these days.

She frowned. Although Tom's Italian had improved a lot, he hadn't spoken of his feelings towards her. Not that there'd been any opportunities for in-depth conversation. There'd only been stolen chances for them to kiss. She remembered wondering if he would be a good kisser. Well, he'd turned out to be very satisfying in that department.

Smiling to herself, she refilled the pot on the fire, pail by pail, trying to be quiet as Nonna was now dozing. The spilt drops sizzled. The kitchen steamed. She heaved more boiling water down to the laundry tub and watched it soak in. Filthy liquid oozed from the pipe, thick and coffee coloured.

Over and over again, she boiled water and carried it downstairs. The liquid eventually became cloudy, sudsy. She would leave the washing to stand and soak until the afternoon, when Lucrezia would help her carry the wet load all the way down to the river, where they'd thrash and rinse it before wringing each cloth into a twist between them. Then they would spread the damp linen onto bushes to be dried by the warmth of the sun.

Bolstered by doing a good job, Rosa returned to the kitchen. Mamma and Lucrezia had come back from feeding the farm animals and were rolling out the pasta dough. She went to help them. She could hear Babbo and Tom chopping wood at the edge of the forest. They would be back soon, hungry as wolves, and joy spread through her at the thought of feeding them.

In the late afternoon, when Dora and Rosa's siblings had returned from school and were quietly drawing pictures at the kitchen table, Rosa made her way down to the river to collect the washing. Everything was as she'd left it, the linen as white as snow. She'd gather it momentarily, after she'd rested. Relishing the warm sunshine, she took off her headscarf, sat on a rock by the water's edge, and closed her eyes.

Thoughts of the progress of the Allies – or lack of progress, to be honest – filled her mind. All night, most nights she'd hear German planes flying overhead. A couple of weeks ago, the fascist government – probably under pressure from the Nazis – had ordered every Italian man born between 1922 and 1925 to report for military service once more. Those that did not do so within a fortnight would be executed on the spot, either at the place where they were captured or in their own homes. All landowners who sheltered or allowed their farmers to conceal draft dodgers on their property would be considered directly responsible.

Rosa feared for the *padrone*: there were many such men on the Bivio estate. In the meantime, the fighting on the Anzio beachhead was continuing, with heavy losses on both sides and no breakthrough by the Allies. It was all too terrible, and Rosa felt so helpless. She was like a leaf being tossed in the wind. Who knew what the future would bring? What kind of world would Dora grow up in? She pulled at a loose lock of hair and twisted it between her fingers.

'Ciao.' Tom's voice made her give a little jump.

'What are you doing here?' She was more than glad to see him; he always lifted her spirits.

He lowered himself onto the rock next to her.

'I thought I could give you a hand.'

His smile went straight to her heart.

'But this is women's work.'

'So you keep saying.' His Italian was so much more fluent these days, but his accent was still endearingly evident.

'Only because it's true.' She tilted her head to the side. 'Do men like you help their womenfolk in Scotland?'

'No, it's not common for men to help women with housework.' He chuckled. 'But I come from a family of women. Didn't I tell you that I have three sisters and I'm the only boy? They expected me to lend a hand around the house...'

'What about your father?'

Tom gave a wry laugh.

'He's a coalminer. When he gets home from work, all he wants to do is sit by the fire, read the newspaper and puff on his pipe.'

'Did you ever want to be a coalminer, Tom?'

He'd told her he'd been a gardener, worked for a 'milord' on a big estate. A bit like Luigi at the Bivio, she imagined.

'Never. I'm claustrophobic. It would be my worst nightmare. I prefer the big outdoors, being amongst the beauty of nature.'

The river burbled its way over the rocks, and a fresh breeze ruffled the branches of the chestnut trees. Swifts had returned to the valley from overwintering in Africa, and were singing their high-pitched songs. Tom was a man after her own heart, Rosa thought, and perhaps in more ways than one.

He reached for her hand.

'It's nice to spend time alone with you, Rosa.'

'I think so too.' She squeezed his strong fingers.

Gently, he wrapped his arms around her and pulled her to lie on top of him.

'You have such beautiful hair,' he said, brushing a lock back from her face. 'I wish you didn't cover it with a scarf all the time.'

'It keeps it clean. We all wear scarves for that reason. It's so dusty around here.'

His eyes were like pools of clear, blue water and she was in danger of drowning in them.

He kissed her on the forehead, the cheeks, the corners of her mouth. His lips were smooth and warm; his beard was a soft tickle.

'I'd like to touch you, please, Rosa.'

'I'd like that too.'

He rolled her off him, lay by her side, and gazed into her eyes as he ran a hand up her thigh. Rosa's breath caught as he slowly pulled her underpants down. When he started to stroke between her legs, she gave a little moan.

'Oh, Tom,' she said, opening her legs for more, 'that feels really nice.'

Using his other hand, he tugged up her blouse and her bra, exposing her breasts. Rosa breathed hard as her nipples tightened, then gasped as his fingers slipped inside her.

'You're so lovely, Rosa. I'm in complete awe of you.'

'*Grazie*, Tom,' was all she could think of to say.

He sucked at her breasts, heavy with desire, swirling his tongue and drawing her nipples deep into his mouth.

She arched her back, whimpered and rocked her hips. She was burning up for him.

Moaning, she clenched around his fingers and bucked against his hand. It felt so wonderful: wanton but liberating at the same time.

'Tom, please don't stop.'

'I won't stop,' he said.

He worked his fingers and kissed her and it took all Rosa's strength not to cry out as wave after wave of intense pleasure seemed to lift her from the ground.

He held her against him until her breathing slowed.

'God, how I love you,' he said. '*Quanto ti amo.*'

'*Mi ami?*' You love me?

'I've loved you from the moment I first saw you. But I hardly dared hope...'

'Tom, you mustn't fall in love with me.' She spoke with a voice of reason. 'There's a war on and, afterwards, you'll return to Scotland.'

'The truth is I want to marry you, my darling. Take you and Dora back to my country. Back home, I'll be due promotion to be head gardener. The job comes with a cottage on the estate. I could give you both a good life.' He gazed deep into her eyes. 'Maybe we can have children together. Brothers or sisters for Dora.'

Rosa was almost too shocked to speak.

'How can I leave Italy? It's my home.'

'We'd come back and visit as often as possible. I wouldn't expect you to sever all ties with your family. And I've grown to love them like my own.'

'I don't know, Tom. Please, let's wait until the war is over before making any plans.'

'If that's what you want.'

'It is. If you'd like to help me gather all the laundry from those bushes,' she pointed, 'I wouldn't say no to you.'

'Of course.'

One last kiss and Rosa straightened her clothes before they gathered up the washing.

Soon they were making their way up the steep track to the *podere*.

Rosa stopped dead.

Lucrezia was running towards them.

'*Fascisti* have come,' she said between panting breaths. 'They're looking for escaped prisoners.'

Rosa's pulse quickened. She took the bag of laundry that Tom was carrying and handed it to her sister.

'Go!' she said to him.

The plan was that he'd head for the forest if ever this happened. He gave her a quick kiss on the cheek.

'I'll come for my kit when it's dark.'

Rosa's chest squeezed with disappointment. There would be no question of him staying on at the farm now. She watched him disappear into the treeline, then walked nonchalantly with Lucrezia into the yard.

Her blood turned icy. A *repubblichino* was standing in front of Babbo, with his gun levelled at his chest. A group of five men with pistols in their hands stood behind him.

Lucrezia went to where Rosa's younger siblings were crouched, sobbing with fear.

'Your children have been telling their fellow school pupils that they are learning English,' the fascist commander said. 'You're harbouring an escaped Englishman, aren't you?'

Oh, blessed Maria, Joseph and all the Saints. Rosa took the laundry basket from her head and stepped forward.

'Pure fantasy.' She squared her shoulders. 'They have vivid imaginations. How can we be sheltering an enemy? We would never do that. My husband was killed by the Allies in Africa.'

The *fascista* raked his dark eyes over her.

'And who might you be?'

'She's my eldest daughter,' Babbo said. 'A loyal Italian.'

Dora ran up to Rosa and buried her snotty face in her skirt. She lifted her into her arms.

'Dora, please stop crying and tell these men that there haven't been any Englishmen staying with us.'

Dora hiccoughed on a sob. She'd since learnt that Tom was Scottish and no longer referred to him as *inglese*.

'It's true,' she managed to say. 'We don't have any Englishmen staying here.'

The fascist commander quirked a fake smile. He tucked his pistol into the halter strapped across his broad chest.

'We'll carry out a search. Put the child down and take us inside the house!'

Her entire body quaking, Rosa led him and his men up the stairs.

Nonna was sitting in her chair by the fire, knitting.

'What do these men want?'

'We believe you are hiding an Englishman,' the *fascista* said.

'*Inglese?*' Nonna shook her head. '*Nessun inglese qui.*' No English here.

Mamma looked up from the worktop. She echoed Nonna's statement, confirming there were no Englishmen on the farm.

But the commander insisted on checking for himself.

Rosa took him into her parents' bedroom, the girls' bedroom and finally to the room that Tom had been sharing with her brothers. Thankfully, there was no trace of his belongings.

'Search the storerooms and animal stalls,' the fascist commanded his men.

Rosa made to leave the room, but the vile man barred her way. He leant into her, and groped at her bottom, pinching it forcefully.

She pushed him away.

'I'm a married woman.'

'A widow. You said your husband was killed in Africa. Or was that a lie?'

'Why would I lie about that?'

'I can see lies written all over your face, signora. You think we're stupid? There are escaped prisoners all over this valley, not to mention draft dodgers. If it turns out that you've been economic with the truth, you and your family will suffer the consequences.' He sniggered a cruel laugh.

'Is everything all right?' Babbo's voice came from the corridor.

'That depends on what my men find,' the fascist said with a smirk.

God forbid they look inside that barrel, Rosa thought.

* * *

Supper that evening was a miserable affair. Thankfully, the fascists hadn't found any trace of Tom. But the children kept crying and asking about him. Mamma and Nonna joined in with their sobs, repeating everyone's feelings that they'd come to love him as one of their own. Even Babbo, not one for showing any sentiment, allowed a tear to trickle from his eye.

After she'd put the children to bed, Rosa went out into the cold night air and crossed the yard to the pig stall.

Her heart missed a beat.

Tom was there.

She went into his arms and they kissed passionately.

'I came to get my kit,' he said. 'But now I must go. I feel terrible for putting you and your family in danger.'

'Where will you go?'

'I'll join the partisans in the forest. There's strength in numbers, as they say.'

'I'll miss you, Tom.'

'Not as much as I'll miss you.' He kissed her again.

'When will I see you?'

'The forest isn't far. When it's safe, I'll try and stop by.'

'Don't take any risks, *amore*.' She'd called him 'love' for that's what he was. She loved him, but she wouldn't tell him. Not yet. She would keep that knowledge to herself until she'd made up her mind about the future. *If there was a future.*

A quick hug, an even quicker kiss, and he was gone.

Rosa's chest ached with sorrow and tears ran down her face. She wiped them away with the back of her hands and, with an aching heart, returned to the kitchen.

11

Emma was on the terrace, reading. Cherry blossom floated in the breeze, its beauty belying the miserable state of her world. She sighed. Just last week, three recruits who'd failed to report for military service had been shot by the fascists in Siena, in the presence of their comrades, 'as an example'. At Piancastagnaio, about thirty kilometres south of the Bivio, two partisans, who'd been caught in nearby woods, had been severely beaten and then executed by Nazi soldiers. Their bodies were then hung on trees at the entrance to the small town, no doubt to intimidate the local population. Her heart wept for the families and loved ones of the poor men. She'd been shocked to the core when she'd heard the news and worry for Marco and his group was keeping her awake at night. She hadn't seen him since Chiurco's abortive attempt to reach Le Faggete last month. Relief had flooded through her when her father had revealed that the *repubblichini* had been too scared about a possible ambush to venture far into the forest. Marco's comrades had been able to get away without a hitch. But he and his men still hadn't returned; they were camping in the forest above Castiglioncello and were focusing on stealing weapons from the enemy to build up their arsenal.

Emma's breathing slowed as she thought about Marco. She missed him terribly, missed their long rides around the estate, missed their closeness. Her hand brushed her lips. Was he missing her as much as she was missing him? It was best that he stayed away, though. Last week, Orazio and his wife, Valeria, had been woken in the early hours by militiamen searching for their son. Marco had been reported as a deserter by somebody, and would be shot on sight if ever the fascists found him. To compound the threat, if proof arrived that his parents had been sheltering him, they too would be summarily executed.

It was all too awful. If only this terrible war would end soon.

It appeared that the Germans had given up all hope of throwing the Allies into the sea at Anzio and had started to move some of their best troops away from that front. Papà maintained they would continue their defences around Rome, for the present, but if or when the Allies broke through at Cassino, the Wehrmacht would withdraw to the area north of Florence and form their defence line along the Apennines from Spezia to Rimini. When she'd asked her father how he knew this, he'd placed a finger to his lips and had directed their conversation to matters closer to home.

Emma drew a shaky breath. That morning, Hofmann was due to arrive with his billeting officer to inspect the fortress. More than two months had gone by since he'd threatened to do so, and she and her father had almost dared to hope he'd decided against it. But it was not to be. Yesterday, Papà had received a phone call to confirm the appointment at 11 a.m.

Emma checked her watch: ten o'clock. She felt hollowed out and could barely focus on her book. Her father was still insisting that she stay with the Brandinis in Montepulciano if they were forced out of the villa. And she was adamant she wouldn't leave him to look after the estate on his own. They'd reached an impasse, neither of them giving way to the other.

* * *

'There are partisans out front,' Vittorio announced, coming onto the terrace about half an hour later. 'Your father is dealing with them.'

Emma smiled.

Marco?

Putting down her book, she got to her feet.

'I'll go and see what's happening.'

She hurried through the villa to the *fattoria*.

Her breath hitched with disappointment.

A group of five fierce-looking men, heavily armed with military-issue weapons, shotguns, and hunting rifles, were loitering in the courtyard. Dressed in Italian army jackets, baggy peasant pants, trousers from German uniforms and other nondescript garments, they appeared older than Marco's companions and slightly uncouth. Emma wrinkled her nose at the stench of stale sweat as she pushed her way between them.

A surprisingly good-looking man had positioned himself at the front of the group. He flicked his light brown hair from his indigo-coloured eyes.

'My name is Casimir, from Dubrovnik in Yugoslavia. Me and my guys escaped from the Laterina POW camp after the armistice.' He paused to take a breath. 'We've spent the winter hiding on one of your farms.'

'First I've heard of it,' Papà said sternly.

'There are one hundred and twenty of us scattered throughout the valley. We plan on going up to Monte Amiata now that spring is here.'

'What is the purpose of your visit to us?'

'We'd like you to give us wheat and oil, boots and clothes.'

'I'm sorry.' Emma's father shook his head. 'We need the little we have left to help our farmers.'

'I think you should leave,' Emma chipped in. 'There's a Wehrmacht officer on his way here to find billets for his men.'

Casimir tapped his dimpled chin. 'Maybe I could play a double-game and act as a spy for the Germans if they make it worth my while.'

'Not on my turf, young man.' Papà pointed towards the gateway. 'Be off with you!'

The Yugoslav stood firm.

'I've heard about you, Marchese Ginori. That you provide assistance to escaped prisoners and refugees from all over. I'm insulted you won't help me and my men.'

'I'm sure Kapitän Hofmann will be fascinated to meet you.'

Casimir laughed. He tilted his head back and slapped his thighs.

'On second thoughts, we'll be on our way. There are rich pickings not far from here, apparently.'

Papà growled.

'You leave my farmers alone, or else...'

'Or else what, old man?' The Yugoslav smirked. 'My guys would take you down in a minute.'

Orazio appeared in the yard with his hunting rifle levelled.

Emma's blood froze.

But her father signalled to his *fattore* to lower his weapon.

'They're leaving now,' he muttered.

Casimir and his comrades had turned on their heels and were making their way through the gate.

'Why did you refuse him?' Emma asked.

'His story didn't ring true. And I've received complaints from a couple of our *mezzadri* about a group of *partigiani* demanding money and food. He's a very fishy customer, I think.'

Emma nodded. The so-called partisan's attractive veneer hid something sinister, and she was glad her father had sent him on his way.

The roar of a motorcycle interrupted her thoughts.

Hofmann had arrived and there was a sidecar attached to his vehicle, with a German officer inside.

She straightened her shoulders and went to greet them.

* * *

In the sitting room, two hours or so later, Emma sat sipping vermouth with her father and the two Germans. The billeting officer had turned out to be a parachutist and was covered with medals from both this war and the last. Unfortunately, he'd declared himself delighted with the fortress and had placed a notice on the door, saying it had been requisitioned. The keepers and their families would move out as soon as Papà found them accommodation in Montepulciano.

'We're not planning on turning you and your daughter out of the villa quite yet.' The bemedalled officer crossed and uncrossed his long legs. 'But we'll probably need to do so when the front moves this way.'

Hofmann put his glass down and cleared his throat.

'On a different subject, marchese. Rumours have reached us that you've been helping our enemies.'

'Rumours aren't facts, Herr Kapitän,' Papà responded calmly. 'The Bivio stands at a crossroads. All kinds of people pass this way. If they are hungry, we feed them, that's all.'

'Be that as it may.' Hofmann creased his smooth brow. 'Be careful not to provoke the Reich.'

'Of course.' A smile gleamed in Emma's father's eyes. 'Can I offer you more vermouth?'

'We should be on our way,' the parachutist said, getting to his feet. 'Thank you for your hospitality.'

'We are nothing if not hospitable,' Papà chuckled.

'I'll show you out,' Emma said. She couldn't wait to be rid of them.

She led the two men across the hall and through to the courtyard, where they'd left the motorcycle.

The parachutist clambered into the sidecar, but Hofmann lingered.

He cleared his throat once more.

'Would you have dinner with me tomorrow, Emma?'

The request came so out of the blue, she couldn't have been more shocked if he'd asked her to dance naked in front of him.

'Why?' she stammered.

'You remind me of my fiancée in Berlin.' He met Emma's eye. 'She has red hair like yours and she also wears it in a braid down her back. My intentions are entirely honourable. It's just that I've been feeling a little homesick lately...'

Emma took a step backward. *A hardened Nazi showing a human side.* Perhaps he wasn't as horrible as she'd imagined. It was a long shot, but if Hofmann had even a tiny bit of kindness in him, having dinner with him might come in useful. She would attempt to persuade him not to throw her and Papà out of the villa. And she'd ask him if he knew what had happened to their horses.

'I'd love to have dinner with you,' she said, pasting a smile to her face.

'Good. There's an excellent restaurant in the hotel where I'm billeted in Chianciano. I'll pick you up at seven o'clock.'

Without waiting for her confirmation, he clicked his heels and mounted his bike.

Emma stood watching until the vehicle had roared out of the courtyard.

What have I done, she asked herself. *And, more importantly, how will I explain it to Papà?*

* * *

The following evening, Emma sat gazing at her surroundings in the elegant dining room of the luxurious Excelsior Palace Hotel. Potted palms stood like sentinels in the corners and gilded chandeliers hung from the ceiling. A crooner, accompanied by a pianist, was singing 'Lili Marlene'. Her stomach tensed; she'd needed to argue long and hard with her father before he'd given his blessing to her going out to dinner with Hofmann. She'd put forward her case with clarity. Hadn't Papà himself said they needed to be nice to the Germans?

'Civil, not nice,' he'd retorted. 'And, besides, Hofmann doesn't come across as a particularly nice man.'

She'd gone on to explain her reasons for accepting the invitation. Hofmann had maintained his intentions were honourable, that she reminded him of his fiancée, and that she'd try to convince him to let them stay in the villa. He might even return their horses.

'I don't trust the man and neither should you,' Papà had said. 'We can't rely on anything he might promise.'

'It's worth a try.' Emma touched her hand to her father's arm. 'I don't want to be in the position of regretting I didn't at least attempt to win him over.'

'I'll telephone the maître d'hôtel and ask him to keep an eye on you,' Papà said with a heavy sigh. 'Please, be careful, my darling. Don't let that Nazi take you anywhere out of public view.'

'I won't,' she promised.

But now she was here, she couldn't keep a frisson of worry from tickling her spine. However, after Hofmann had picked her up and brought her to the hotel in his sidecar, his behaviour was completely gentlemanly. He'd placed her hand on his arm as he'd walked her up the steps to the lobby. He'd desisted from paying any compliments about her appearance – which she'd taken particular care over, dressing in one of her mother's Chanel gowns and pinning her hair up in an extravagant twist – and he'd even asked her politely to call him Gerhardt when she'd addressed him as 'Herr Kapitän'.

'Tell me about your fiancée,' she said after their waiter had brought them both a glass of vermouth and had taken their orders for *ribollita* soup followed by fillet steak.

The captain's erstwhile cold eyes assumed a warm glow.

'She's the sister of a schoolfriend. Her name is Freida. We plan to marry as soon as Germany has won the war.'

'You must miss her a lot.' Emma picked up her fork and placed it down again.

'I haven't seen her in over a year.' Hofmann took a sip of his drink. 'She's young, like you. A student at the university.'

Their conversation continued with Emma encouraging him to talk about himself while they ate. He'd been fresh out of university when the war started, a newly graduated architect.

Such a coincidence that he'd been studying for the same degree as Marco.

She kept the observation to herself, of course, and told him about her love of the Tuscan people, her plan to study law so she could help them.

When they were nearing the end of the meal and were sipping

their ersatz coffees, Emma brought up the subject of the villa's requisition and her beloved Bella and Zorro.

It's now or never.

'My father and I need to stay on the estate,' she said. 'We have a duty of care towards our workers and they would be lost without us. And our horses are needed on the farm.'

Hofmann wiped his mouth with a starched linen serviette.

'The matter is out of my hands, I'm afraid. I'll see what I can do, but can't make any promises.'

With that she had to be content, she supposed.

'It's getting late, Gerhardt. I should head back home. Thank you for a lovely meal.'

She wasn't lying. The food had been delicious.

A smile lit his pale blue eyes.

Eyes filled with sadness.

Was his previous heartless demeanour a sham? He could have been putting it on in front of his men.

'I hope you'll agree to have dinner with me again, if the war should permit.'

'I'd like that,' she said.

* * *

The night had turned chilly and, after Hofmann dropped her off, Emma hugged her coat as she made her way across the courtyard.

Inside the villa, she discerned light coming through the open door of the living room. Her father had said he'd wait up for her, and she went to put his mind at ease.

She gave a gasp of surprise.

Marco was sitting in the armchair opposite her father, a brandy balloon in his hand.

He put down his glass, got to his feet and strode towards her, his handsome face creased with concern.

She stood rooted to the spot.

'Emma,' he said. 'What were you playing at going out to dinner with a Nazi?'

'Didn't Papà explain?'

'He did, but I think you've been foolhardy.'

'We've both been worried about you,' her father added.

Emma went to the fire and warmed her hands.

'I'm perfectly all right. Hofmann behaved like a gentleman. When I asked if he'd be able to stop us being turned out of the villa, he said he'd see what he could do.'

'I don't trust him,' Marco said, lowering himself to the sofa.

'Neither do I.' It was her father's turn to stand. 'But I'm off to bed now that I know you're home safe, my darling. Make sure you extinguish the fire before you come up.'

'Yes, Papà.' She pecked him on the cheek. 'Goodnight.'

'Come, sit with me,' Marco said, smoothing the cushion next to him.

She did as he requested.

'How are you?' she asked, lacing her fingers through his.

'Not so bad. Better for seeing you.' He lifted her hand and brushed a kiss to her wrist.

'Are you back in the area?' She nestled into his side.

'There are seventy of us now and we're camping in the forest behind Le Faggete.'

'Oh, good. I'll be able to courier messages to you again.'

He lifted her chin and kissed her on the lips.

'I've missed you, Emma.'

'And I've missed you too.'

'Please, don't go out to dinner with Hofmann again. I fear he could be using you to get to your father and consequently to us.'

Her breath caught.

'Oh, I didn't think...'

'The story about his fiancée comes across as a little too contrived.'

She shook her head.

'He seemed sincere.'

'I'd rather you didn't see him again.'

'I'll try not to, but I still believe he has a human side.'

'He's a Nazi. A Wehrmacht officer. He will always put the Reich first.'

'You're right, I guess...'

'I care about you, Emma. I'd be devastated if anything happened to you.'

'I care about you too, Marco. I've been worrying about you. You're my best friend.'

'I'd like us to be more than friends.' He kissed her again, possessively. He tasted of brandy and smelt of the forest.

'I'd like that too.' Her heartbeat skittered.

Marco tucked a strand of loose hair behind her ear.

'You're so beautiful. But all dressed up for a Nazi?' He groaned. 'I wish it had been me taking you out for dinner.'

'Let's hope this war will be over soon and then we'll be able to do that.'

'Things are about to hot up around here. We're ready to take on the *nazifascisti*.'

Her stomach gave a lurch.

'Please, be careful.'

'I will.' He yawned. 'It's late and I need to get back to my men. Let's smother the fire and say goodnight.'

Emma went to pick up the poker and spread the embers. But Marco got there before her and soon the fire was out and it was time for them to part.

At the garden door, which opened onto the track leading into the woods, he held out his arms and she went into them.

They kissed for a long while, passionate kisses that begged for more.

'Goodnight, Marco.'

'*Buonanotte, amore mio.*'

He'd called her his love.

Did he love her? Did she love him?

She watched him make his way between the box hedges, her fingers caressing her lips.

12

Rosa exhaled a weary breath as she went down to the terrace. She and Lucrezia were carrying a rolled-up mattress on their heads. Mamma mia, it was heavy. It was the last in a long line of the annual spring-cleaning jobs, preparing the house for a visit from the parish priest, who came every year to bestow his Easter blessing. Just yesterday, she, Mamma and Lucrezia had thrown buckets of water over their red-brick floors. With brooms made of millet stalks, they'd swept the water towards the front door and out through a little hole in the stone landing at the top of the steps. The house smelt fresh and clean afterwards, especially after they'd polished all their furniture with beeswax. Nonna's pride and joy – her walnut wedding *credenza* sideboard – had never shone so brightly, it seemed.

Rosa had focused on her work to try to keep her mind off Tom, but that hadn't stopped her from missing him. She thought about him all the time, longing for him so much that she'd even found herself contemplating joining the Resistance so she could be with him. But her duty towards Babbo came first. He needed her help even more now the Scotsman had left. In any case, she shouldn't encourage Tom. He wanted her to go to Scotland with him when the war was over. How could she possibly do that? She couldn't leave her father in the lurch. Not after everything he'd done for her. And the thought of making such a fundamental change to her life filled her with anxiety. Learning the language would be a monumental task. Tom had taught her a few words of English and she'd found it hard to get her tongue around even them. She didn't know if she was up to it. No, the whole notion was impossible. She didn't know why she was even thinking about it.

'Uffa, this mattress weighs a ton,' Lucrezia grunted, interrupting Rosa's thoughts.

'We can lower it to the ground now,' Rosa said. The mattress would be cleaned with a damp brush, and was an important part of the spring-cleaning ritual. 'Spread it out, sister. We'll give it a good scrub and let the sun dry it while we bring down the next one.'

The sisters had tied yellow kerchiefs round their heads and had pinned up their skirts to one side. Rosa relished the feel of the warm sun on her face. Sunshine was a vital element in the mattress-cleaning process: heavy rain was seen as an ill omen for the household as well as a misfortune on the day. She gazed across the yard towards the rolling hills, green with young wheat, such a beautiful sight. How could she bear to leave this place? She wouldn't do it, and that was that.

She gritted her teeth and concentrated on scrubbing. Before too long, she and Lucrezia had finished the task at hand.

'Let's go and fetch the next one,' Rosa said.

The sudden sound of male voices made her turn around. *Dio buono.* Good God. She gave a gasp. Five heavily armed men dressed in Italian army jackets were coming toward them.

Who were they and what did they want?

An arrogant-looking fellow swaggered forward. He was

surprisingly attractive, with high cheek bones and a dimple in the middle of his chin. But his eyes looked shifty and they darted around until they landed on Lucrezia.

'*Che bella signorina*,' Shifty Eyes said. What a beautiful young lady.

Lucrezia visibly preened. She puffed up her chest so that her breasts formed peaks in her blouse.

'*Come ti chiami?*' She asked Shifty Eyes' name.

'I'm Casimir. From Dubrovnik.'

'What is the purpose of your visit?' Rosa placed herself between her sister and the man.

'We are partisans. And we need food.'

'I'm sorry, but we can't spare any.'

Rosa wasn't sorry at all. Something about Casimir and his men had put her back up. She wished Babbo was there, but he'd gone to tend to the lower slopes of the vineyard.

Lucrezia came from behind. She'd removed her headscarf and was running her fingers through her hair.

'We have more than enough flour and olive oil.' She beamed an encouraging smile at Rosa. 'Casimir and his men are partisans, fighting for our freedom. We should help them, sister.'

The so-called partisans were now forming a circle around Rosa and Lucrezia. And they were looking at them with hungry eyes. Rosa's stomach grew heavy with dread. She needed to get rid of these men.

'I'd forgotten about the flour and oil,' she said. 'Of course you can take some.'

'*Grazie*.' Casimir smirked.

Soon he and his cohort had filled their backpacks to the brim.

He turned to Lucrezia. 'Can you show us the best road to Monte Amiata?'

Rosa was about to offer to do so – she didn't like the way Casimir was ogling her sister – but Lucrezia got in before her.

'Follow me!'

'With pleasure,' he said.

Lucrezia made her way across the yard, her hips swinging.

A sinking feeling gripped Rosa's chest. Lucrezia had no idea what she was doing. She'd only just turned seventeen and had never had a sweetheart on account of the war. She was sending all the wrong messages to Casimir. As soon as she returned from escorting him and his men to the forest, Rosa would have words with her. She had to warn her sister that her actions might have unwelcome consequences.

Babbo reacted just like Rosa thought he would when she told him about Casimir's visit.

He bunched his hands into fists.

'I've heard about that group of *banditi*. They aren't partisans but brigands.' He gave a growl. 'I would have sent them packing.'

She kept to herself the fact that Lucrezia had been more than willing to donate to their cause.

Rosa decided to bide her time to talk to her sister, and that time came in the early afternoon while Babbo, Mamma and Nonna were having a post-lunch nap.

'Come, Lucrezia, let's go sit outside in the sunshine,' she said. 'It's such a beautiful day.' She picked up her sewing basket. 'We can chat while we darn some socks.'

'You're better at darning than me,' Lucrezia said with a huff. 'Everyone complains that my stitches are lumpy.'

'Then come and keep me company.'

'*Va bene*.' Okay. 'I'd like that.'

Outside, they sat on a bench facing the river valley.

Birdsong echoed and the scent of the wild cherry blossom filled the air.

'So, what did you want to chat about?' Lucrezia asked, squinting her eyes.

Rosa sighed. 'You need to be careful how you behave around strange men.'

Lucrezia shook her head.

'I don't know what you mean.'

'You were flirting outrageously with that Yugoslav. Babbo said he's a *bandito*, not a proper partisan at all.'

'I wasn't flirting.'

'Puffing out your chest, running your fingers through your hair, swaying your hips as you led him away. Those are all the wrong signals. You could have come to harm.'

'But I didn't, did I?'

'Then you were lucky, this time. He's not the man for you, dearest sister. He would gobble you up like a big bad wolf.'

Lucrezia gave a wry laugh.

'What about you and Tom? Didn't take you long to betray the memory of Francesco with him, did it?'

Rosa gritted her teeth.

'Tom is a gentleman. Not a brigand like that Yugoslav.'

Lucrezia laughed again.

'Tom lusts after you. I've seen it in his eyes. He's not the gentleman you think he is.'

Rosa's cheeks burned.

'Just be careful, dearest. I wouldn't want you to come to any harm.'

Lucrezia touched her hand to Rosa's.

'I'm perfectly capable of looking after myself.'

Rosa exhaled a long, slow breath. She didn't know what else to say, so she kept silent and concentrated on her darning until the rumble of the oxcart heralded the return of Dora and the rest of the children from school.

* * *

The next day was Saturday, and Rosa's daughter and her younger siblings only had classes in the morning. Again, the weather was glorious so Rosa decided to take Dora for a walk along the ridge towards the forest. As she walked, she thought about the news Babbo had been told by the *fattore*, who'd heard it from the *padrone*: the other day, in Rome, at a celebration of the twenty-fifth anniversary of the foundation of the Fascist Party, an explosive device had been detonated and grenades thrown by partisans in Rasella Street, killing thirty-two Wehrmacht officers and men. A swift reprisal had then followed: for every German killed, ten hostages had been shot.

Rosa wiped a tear from her eye.

'Too many innocent people are dying in this war,' she'd said.

'It's the way of things, *figlia mia*.' My daughter. 'But it seems that our poor country is paying a disproportionate price. I fear for our safety when the front moves into Tuscany.'

'Mammina,' Dora's high-pitched voice interrupted Rosa's thoughts. 'There are some men up ahead.'

Rosa gathered her daughter to her.

What if the men are Casimir and his fellow banditi?

A tall man stepped forward and Rosa smiled.

'Tom,' she said, lifting Dora up into her arms and rushing towards him.

He took the child from her and swung her around.

'You've grown since I last saw you.'

Dora squealed with laughter.

'I'm four now. You missed my birthday last week.'

'*Mi dispiace.*' I'm sorry. 'But I made you something.'

He set her down and pulled an intricately carved wooden rabbit from his pocket.

'I crafted it for you.'

'*Grazie.*' Dora's eyes glowed. 'It's beautiful.'

'You're very talented,' Rosa said. 'I didn't know you could do that.'

'Something my dad taught me.'

He bent to Rosa's ear.

'I need to get back to my comrades now. But we're camped nearby. I'll try and visit you this evening. Could you meet me in the stable?'

Rosa's heart thudded. How she longed for him to hold her in his arms.

'It will be after everyone has gone to sleep,' she said.

'Perfect. *A dopo,*' he said with a wide smile. See you later.

Rosa watched him walk back to his comrades, her gaze lingering on his broad shoulders. Was she playing with fire by agreeing to meet him alone in the barn? Her chest fluttered as she thought about the last time they'd been on their own together.

She gave herself a shake and reminded Dora not to talk to anyone about Tom as she led her back home. He was a secret to be kept within the family.

'What about my wooden rabbit?' Dora's eyes met Rosa's.

'That too. Only show it to *la famiglia.*'

Dora nodded solemnly.

Back indoors, Rosa got on with her usual chores while her daughter played with her new toy, generously allowing Teresa and Ines to take turns holding it. Afternoon stretched into evening and, before she knew it, Rosa was tucking the little ones up in bed and listening to their nighttime prayers. She went to the bathroom and washed herself from top to toe. Back in the kitchen, she sat with Lucrezia and listened to a light musical programme on the radio until it was time for bed.

'I'm meeting Tom,' she whispered to her sister at the bedroom door. It would have been pointless to pretend otherwise. Lucrezia would almost certainly notice if she tried to sneak out behind her back.

Lucrezia's laugh tinkled in her ears.

'Don't you dare lecture me about Casimir again or I'll tell Babbo what you're getting up to!'

Rosa's stomach was tying itself up in knots. Should she forgo meeting Tom? She rubbed a hand through her hair. No. Chances were the Yugoslav had other fish to fry than Lucrezia. And didn't he say he was heading for Monte Amiata? He and his men would be long gone.

'I'll be back soon,' she said, before pecking her sister on the cheek.

'Take as long as you like.'

Lucrezia's wry laughter echoed as Rosa made her way down the corridor.

Outside, moonlight lit the courtyard. The night had turned chilly and she hurried towards the warmth of the stable. She pushed open the heavy wooden door and breathed in the steamy scent of musky oxen breath mixed with sweet hay.

'Rosa, you came.' Tom's voice gave her a warm, fuzzy feeling inside.

She went to him and he put his arms around her.

He lifted her up so that her face was level with his, and then he kissed her. His lips pressed down softly and the kiss was so slow and sensual it sent tingles through her. He increased the pressure, demanding more.

She opened her mouth for him and their tongues met.

'Oh, Rosa. *Quanto ti amo.*' I love you so much. His hot breath fanned her cheek.

He slid her down his strong body, and desire flamed between them.

Oh, God, she wanted this man. She wanted his strength. She wanted to feel him inside her. She wanted *him*.

She looped her legs around his waist and he walked them both backwards until her spine rested against the wall.

'Make love to me,' she said.

'Are you sure?'

A moonbeam filtered through the high window, lighting his eyes.

'I am.'

She took his hand and led him towards the ladder up to the hayloft.

There, breathing fast, they tumbled onto the straw.

It had been so long since Rosa had been with a man. Tom wasn't Francesco, and she tried not to make comparisons. The heat coiling in her belly and between her legs was familiar, though. She lay back and let Tom undress her, then watched him take his own clothes off.

Her breath caught as she feasted her eyes on him. He was all muscle. Toned to perfection.

He lowered himself onto the straw next to her.

'You're so beautiful, Rosa.'

'So are you.' She lifted her hand and stroked his bearded cheek.

'Just a minute, my darling. I'll sheath myself first.'

He rummaged in the pocket of his discarded trousers.

He kissed his way down her body, his tongue exploring and sending waves of pleasure through her.

Then he was rocking into her and she lost herself to him.

Afterwards, she snuggled into him as he caressed her.

'*Ti amo tanto*, Rosa.' I love you so much. He kissed her. 'I meant what I said before, my love. After the war ends I want to marry you and take you back to Scotland.'

She sighed.

'Please, Tom. Let's not make any plans yet. We don't know what the world will be like when all of this is over.'

'It's not a "no", then?'

'I'm not sure. If I let myself fall in love with you and then you get killed, I couldn't bear it. And the thought of moving away from Tuscany terrifies me.'

He tilted her chin, kissed her deeply.

'I would give you a good life. And I promise we'd come and visit your family as often as possible.'

'You've got it all planned, haven't you?' She couldn't resist a smile.

'I can't stop thinking about you, Rosa.'

She stroked his bearded cheek again.

'And I can't stop thinking about *you*.' She reached for her clothes. 'But it's getting late, *mio caro*, and I really should go up to bed.'

'I'll try and visit again soon,' he said. 'Remember I told you we're carrying out some actions nearby? It will all depend on how everything turns out. Maybe you could come to the stable and check if I'm here for the next few nights? If we leave the area, I'll try and get a message to you.'

'That sounds like a good plan,' she said, buttoning up her blouse.

Tom dressed quickly and they descended the ladder. Out in the courtyard, they kissed passionately before Tom took his leave.

Rosa crept upstairs and slipped into the bedroom. Lucrezia

was fast asleep, thank God, and soon Rosa had fallen into dreams beside her.

* * *

The following three nights, Rosa went to the stable as arranged. But there was no sign of Tom. Just the echo of the oxen rustling in their stalls and the hayloft empty. Disappointment clenched at her stomach, and she'd made her way back to bed, her shoulders hunched.

On the fourth night, something was different.

Noises came from the hayloft. Moaning and grunting sounds.

Her legs trembling, Rosa climbed the ladder.

At the top, her heart filled with dread.

Lucrezia and Casimir were making love in the same place where she'd slept with Tom.

Her sister lay sprawled on her back, and the Yugoslav's pale buttocks shone in the moonlight as he pumped into her.

Rosa made her way back down the ladder.

She felt sick. Quivering with excitement at the thought of possibly meeting Tom, she hadn't even noticed her sister wasn't in their bed.

Had Lucrezia been meeting the Yugoslav in secret?

How Rosa feared for her.

13

Stones scattered beneath Emma's feet as she made her way up the forest track to Le Faggete. Day was breaking and birdsong echoed through the trees. Her chest tingled with anticipation: she had an important message for Marco. Casimir and his comrades had turned up at the Bivio again yesterday, demanding money. The Yugoslav had said he'd seen an English general 'in these parts', but when Papà had pressed him for details, he'd wriggled out of it by saying he couldn't remember exactly where. Casimir had almost certainly been lying, but Emma's father thought Marco should know, 'just in case'.

It was all very strange, but there was a war on and strangeness seemed to have become the name of the game. Emma's thoughts turned to Gerhardt Hofmann. It had been a fortnight since she'd had dinner with him, and he'd phoned twice in the interim to repeat the invitation. Each time, she'd made the excuse that she was busy. She'd kept it vague. Just said she was caught up in a project making warm-weather clothes for the estate's children, as their families had been unable to find any in the shops. The work had been time consuming; she'd been cutting up old curtains and turning them into dresses, trousers and shirts. To be honest, she'd been glad of the pretence. Although he'd been a complete gentleman, she didn't want to spend too much time with the captain. People might think she was a collaborator, like some of the Chianciano women who went with Germans in return for food, clothes and cosmetics. Tarcisia had told her about them, pursing her lips in disdain.

'The *tedeschi* are the enemy,' Tarcisia had said. 'I hope I'm not speaking out of turn, but you should stay well away from that man.'

The dawn chorus of birdsong reduced in volume and the clearing with the terracotta-coloured farmhouse opened up in front of her. Emma stopped dead in her tracks. Men were milling around in the open space.

'Daria!' A familiar voice came from up ahead.

'Leandro!' She used his battle name and ran to him, hugged him and told him the reason for her visit.

'That Casimir,' Marco snarled. 'He's a thorn in our sides.'

'Oh?' She tilted her head.

'They're giving partisans a bad name.'

'You think he was lying about the general?'

'Of course.' Marco gave a derisive snort. 'He'd say anything to ingratiate himself with friend and foe alike.'

'I hope he leaves the valley and goes to Monte Amiata like he said he would.'

'Hmmm.' Marco tapped his chin. 'The partisans up there would soon deal with him. They're a fierce bunch.'

Emma took in the activity taking place around her. Men shouldering haversacks and weapons as if they were about to leave for somewhere.

'What's going on?' she asked.

'We're heading for an inn on the outskirts of Chianciano, to rescue a comrade being held by fascist militia.'

She took an eager step forward.

'Can I come?' She'd been longing to take part in a partisan action.

'Emma, how can you even ask?' Marco shook his head. 'It would be far too dangerous.'

'I could help if anyone is wounded.' She looked him in the eye.

'You don't even know how to fire a weapon. You're a *partigiana non combattente*. A *stafetta*, courier, and an amazingly good one. We need you to stay safe so you can continue helping us.'

'Then can I at least wait here until you get back? I'd worry about you and the others if I went home.'

His smile warmed her heart.

'Alright. *Va bene*. If all goes to plan, we'll be back by lunchtime, then you and I can spend some time together.' He took her hand and kissed her wrist.

'Please, take care,' she said.

'I will.'

'Is that a promise?'

'Maybe.' He chuckled.

With that, she had to be content. After a quick kiss, and an even quicker hug, he shouldered his rifle and was gone.

Emma went into the farmhouse. She'd offer to help in the kitchen to while away the time.

There, she found Sandro rolling out the dough to make *pici*.

'Ciao,' she said.

'Ciao. *Tutto bene*?' Is everything all right?

She caught a hint of homesickness in the young man's eyes.

'Your parents are fine,' she said with a smile. 'Thankfully, the *fascisti* seem to have forgotten all about arresting your *babbo* for your failure to report for the draft.'

'Yes. I heard. I wanted to hand myself in, you know.'

'I know.' She picked up a rolling pin and joined him at the table. Tarcisia had taught her how to make the dish a while ago.

Sandro was more or less her age, but appeared younger. He was gawky, with a prominent Adam's apple. As a little boy, he'd followed his father around while Luigi worked in the villa's gardens, but Sandro's obvious shyness had made him keep his distance. But now he appeared to have come out of his shell. Living cheek by jowl with a band of seventy men clearly left no room for reticence.

Emma fell into easy conversation with him as she told him about recent goings-on in the valley. There'd been a constant parade of escaped POWs passing through. She and her father had fed them, then provided directions for them to try to reach Allied lines. They were also giving assistance to groups of partisans they felt they could trust. But not Casimir, whom Sandro mentioned before Emma could bring up the subject.

'We all wish he'd just disappear,' he said, grimacing.

'We can only hope.' Emma put down her rolling pin. 'The *pici* are made. All that's left for us to do is make a tomato *sugo*.'

'Fulvio has done that.' Sandro indicated towards Fulvio, the elderly widower who'd volunteered his services after the armistice. He and his late wife once operated a small trattoria, but after she'd passed away he hadn't the heart to run it on his own and had closed it down. Fulvio was an expert at incorporating foraged ingredients into his recipes, by all accounts.

On hearing his name, Fulvio approached. '*Grazie, ragazzi.*' Thanks, guys. He gestured to the window. 'Go, take a break outside in the sunshine. The others will be back soon.'

Emma went with Sandro to the open space in front of the farmhouse, where they sat on a bench. A feather of worry for Marco tickled her insides.

Sandro offered her a cigarette, which she was tempted to accept. It might calm her nerves. But smoking didn't agree with her; the only times she'd tried, she'd coughed so much it had made her retch.

She focused on chatting with Sandro about the progress of the war, about how the Allies were still being held back by the Germans south of Rome.

'I expect the British and American armies will break through eventually,' she said. 'And the highway heading north is so close to us we could be in the frontline.'

'I can't wait.' Sandro's eyes glowed with excitement. 'We've been pussyfooting around the Germans in this area. It's time we took them on properly.'

'Hmmm. They're trained soldiers, better armed. I hope the Allies send you backup before that happens.'

Sandro took a deep draw of his cigarette and exhaled smoke slowly.

'We're hoping for a weapons drop soon. Your father will send you to us with a message when that happens.'

After Sandro had finished smoking, he got to work cleaning his rifle. Emma watched him remove the magazine, scrub the barrel with a brush, then apply oil to the moving parts. He told her he'd yet to kill anyone and she was about to ask him if the thought of ending someone's life worried him when a scout came up to say their men had been spotted approaching.

Smiling with relief, Emma rose to her feet and went to greet them.

She stopped dead.

Something was wrong.

In the distance, two partisans were half-carrying another man between them.

Oh, God, has Marco been injured?

She ran forward.

Her knees buckled.

It wasn't Marco. He was one of the men holding up the wounded partisan.

'What happened?' Her voice quavered.

'A stray bullet caught Giorgio in the shoulder,' Marco said. 'Passed right through, but it needs dressing.'

'We should take him down to the Bivio's clinic. Our nurse will be able to treat him.'

'He's bleeding too much to be carried any further. We need to get him lying down so we can staunch the flow.'

'I'll go and see if we can borrow the estate's three-wheeler lorry.'

Marco frowned. 'I doubt that has enough horsepower to make it up this hill.'

'How I wish we still had Bella and Zorro. They'd pull the cart up here and we could take Giorgio down in that.'

'There has to be a solution,' Emma said as she walked with Marco and his comrades across the clearing and into the farmhouse.

They laid Giorgio down on the kitchen table. His face had turned ashen and he was groaning with pain.

Fulvio came up.

'I'll get some clean cloths,' he said. 'This needs stitching, though.'

'Come, Emma. I'll go down to the villa with you. There must be a way we can get a vehicle up here. Either your father or mine will know what to do.'

She agreed and they set off forthwith, leaving Giorgio in Fulvio's safe hands. He'd packed the wound and had covered him with a blanket to maintain his body warmth and ease the shock.

Before too long, Emma and Marco arrived at the villa's front garden.

'Wait here,' Emma said. 'I'll go inside and make sure it's okay for you to come in.'

'Come and get me when you've checked the lie of the land.'

'Will do.'

She opened the door and crossed the hall.

Voices came from the living room.

Her blood froze.

Hofmann was sitting on the sofa, a glass of vermouth in front of him. Her father sat opposite, a fake smile plastered on his face.

'Oh, hello, Gerhardt,' she said, feigning nonchalance. 'How nice to see you again.'

'I stopped by on the off chance you'd be free to have lunch with me,' he said.

She caught her lip between her teeth, collected her thoughts.

'I'm so sorry. But I promised to help out at the school today. Perhaps another time?'

She looked the captain in the eye, prayed he'd believe her.

His face took on a thunderous expression. So briefly she could almost have imagined it.

'You keep putting me off, Emma. I'm starting to believe you don't like me.'

She sat on the sofa next to him.

'That's not true at all. I've been terribly busy, that's all.'

'Well, free up some time for me,' he said.

It was an order, not a request.

'Of course.'

'I'll come and pick you up tomorrow at midday.'

'I'll look forward to it.'

'Good.' Hofmann knocked back the rest of his drink, stood and clicked his heels together.

Emma and her father jumped to their feet.

'I'll see you out,' she said.

In the courtyard, he lifted his motorcycle off its stand.

Emma's skin prickled.

Marco had come into the periphery of her vision. He was standing under the archway leading to the garden.

Her heart thudded as she took a step sideways to block him from view.

'*A domani*. See you tomorrow, Emma,' the German captain said.

She waved him off then watched him pass through the gates and up the road.

What had she got herself into with that man? Now was not the time to worry, though. Now was the time to join Marco and find a solution to their problem.

He'd gone back into the garden and was waiting where she'd left him. She went up to him, and he gave a low growl.

'I wish you'd never allowed yourself to pretend friendship with that Nazi.'

'A bit late for regrets,' she said. 'Come, let's go find my papà.'

Inside, Emma's father listened to them explain their dilemma.

'You're right that the lorry won't make it up there.' He drummed his chin. 'But the tractor will manage it easily. We can hitch a trailer to it, put Giorgio on it, and take him to our clinic.'

'We'll need to involve my father.' Marco's face broke into a smile. '*Grazie*, marchese. Thank you.'

'Just take care. And Emma, you stay here with me. Let Marco handle this, he's more than capable.'

'But...'

She wanted to protest, wanted to insist that she go with them. But the look on her father's face brooked no argument. 'Yes, Papà.'

Marco left the room and Emma's heart swelled with pride and love.

14

The next day, nerves trembling in her stomach, Emma waited for Hofmann in the courtyard as arranged. She'd decided not to make any special effort with respect to her appearance; she'd simply put on a plain skirt and blouse and, after remembering the captain had said his fiancée plaited her hair in a long braid, she'd tied hers up in a bun.

She thought about yesterday. Marco's father had gone with him in the tractor to take Giorgio to the clinic. After he'd been treated, his wound cleaned and stitched, he'd been taken to a nearby farm where the arrangement was that he'd hide during the day and return to the surgery after dark for his dressings to be changed. Marco had stopped by briefly to see Emma before heading back to Le Faggete. She'd told him about her plans to have lunch with the captain and he'd urged her to be careful, then added that he hoped it would be the last time. Keeping her fingers crossed, she'd responded that she'd do everything possible for that to be so.

He'd kissed her and she'd wrapped her arms around his waist, breathing in the scent of him before he'd vanished into the night.

Emma caught Papà gazing down at her from the upstairs window. He'd offered to come and greet the captain, but she'd put him off.

'I'll tell him you're visiting a sharecropper,' she'd said. 'This is my mess and it's up to me to deal with it.'

The roar of the Moto Guzzi alerted her to the captain's arrival. He swept into the yard, sending gravel flying, then came to an abrupt halt.

'*Buongiorno*, Emma,' he said in his guttural accent as he pushed his goggles up his forehead. He leapt off the bike and helped her into the sidecar, then handed her a pair of goggles.

She was glad the noise of the engine prevented any conversation en route to Chianciano; she was saving up her small talk for lunch. Hofmann was taking her to the same restaurant where they'd eaten last time. She prayed no one would recognise her and mistake her for a collaborator.

They sat at a round table in the centre of the dining room, in full view. There were few diners, thankfully. All German officers, some of whom were entertaining local ladies. Emma didn't blame the women. How could she? They must have valid reasons for collaborating. Everyone was short of food and perhaps they had children at home who needed feeding. As for her, she'd got herself into this situation by acting rashly. How to get out of it? She had no idea.

'You look different today,' Hofmann said, breaking into her thoughts.

'Oh? How?' She met his eye.

'It's your hair. I prefer it when you wear it in a braid, like Freida.'

'Have you heard from her recently?' Emma took a sip of water.

Get him talking about his fiancée. That way he'll continue to be a gentleman.

'She wrote to me just last week.' He gave a sigh. 'The Allies have been bombing Berlin practically every night for months, it seems. Thousands of people have been left homeless. I fear for her safety.'

'I hate this war. I wish it would end.'

Hofmann's mouth twisted. 'I blame Churchill for the whole debacle. He's an ardent imperialist and won't let Britain be thrust aside by us.'

It was on the tip of Emma's tongue to say she thought it was all because of Hitler's ideological beliefs and overconfidence. She didn't want to get into a discussion with the captain on the topic, though; she needed to keep things light between them.

'Tell me about your family, Gerhardt,' she said. 'Do you have any brothers and sisters?'

'No, I'm an only child,' came his abrupt reply.

She sighed inwardly; she'd have to think of another topic.

'Shall we order?' She picked up a menu and, with a curt nod, the captain did the same.

It always amazed her that the hotel could offer such a wide choice of dishes in these times of so many acute shortages. She supposed billeting the enemy had its advantages as far as supplies were concerned.

Their waiter approached and they both ordered *pappa al pomodoro*, a Tuscan soup made with tomatoes, bread, garlic and olive oil. Emma chose grilled chicken breast for her main course and Hofmann opted for steak.

Emma tucked in when their soup arrived. It was a dish she'd enjoyed regularly in the past, but Tarcisia hadn't prepared it in a while given that their reserves of olive oil were running low. Likewise, they hadn't eaten chicken in a long time. All their birds were kept for egg production nowadays.

Thankfully, Hofmann talked at length about his fiancée. Freida was a talented musician and had ambitions to become a concert pianist.

'How about you, Emma?' he asked while they sipped ersatz coffee at the end of the meal. 'Is there anyone special in your life?'

She couldn't tell him about Marco, so she lied, saying there was no one. She hoped her flaming cheeks wouldn't give her away.

The captain put down his coffee cup and lit a cigar, his pale eyes piercing hers. He sucked on the cigar and let out two little puffs of smoke before licking his lips.

She knew what was coming before he said it.

'I have the rest of the afternoon free, dear Emma. Why don't you come up to my room and keep me company? I'm a little lonely...'

Her head spun and so did her stomach. Nausea gripped her, her skin turning cold and clammy.

'I'm sorry, Gerhardt. I'm not feeling very well. In fact, I'm going to be sick.' She clapped a hand to her mouth.

Her belly heaved and vomit rose in her throat. She scraped her chair back and ran for the bathroom, where she vomited up every morsel of her lunch.

Tears stung her eyes, and she wiped them away with the back of her hands.

You've been a fool, she told herself. Of course the captain wanted more from her.

On wobbly legs, she made her way back to the table.

Hofmann stared up at her.

'You've gone very pale, Emma. Was it something that I said?'

'No. No. I'm so sorry.' She thought quickly. 'I think it was the cigar smoke that made me sick.'

He stared at her for a moment, distrust in his eyes.

'Please,' Emma said, holding her stomach, 'I really should go home and lie down.'

It was his turn to scrape his chair as he shot to his feet and swiped up his gloves, smacking them on his hand as he did so. 'Very well. I'll take you home.'

She released a shaky breath and walked behind the captain as he made haste for the exit.

What a nightmare. She only hoped she made it home safely.

* * *

Two days later, in the late afternoon, Emma was sewing in the sitting room when her father came through the door.

'The Maresciallo of the Montepulciano Carabinieri phoned to say he's on his way over, my dear. He wants to talk to both of us.'

Emma put down the child's dress she was making.

'I wonder what he has to say.'

Papà shrugged. 'It's something he can't talk about over the phone.'

'I'll go and tell Vittorio we're expecting company,' she said, getting to her feet.

She relayed the message to their butler, then went to wait in the courtyard. She was glad it was the Marshal who was visiting and not Hofmann. Hopefully, her reaction to his suggestion that she keep him company in his room had put him off. It was a slim hope, but she clung to it, encouraged by the fact that he hadn't been in touch since.

Other 'visitors' had turned up yesterday. While she was out in the garden, she'd heard some rustling in the bushes and had come across a party of fifteen men, armed with Tommy guns and muskets. Three of them were wearing the Communist red star. They said they were lying in wait for 'anyone who comes to make trouble'. Emma had suggested it was better to avoid unnecessary bloodshed, that there was a bigger group of partisans nearby who were watching out for them, and they should head south instead. She'd left them there and they seemed to have followed her advice as afterwards no one had reported seeing them.

The purr of a car engine alerted her to the Maresciallo's arrival. She greeted him and took him to her father. After Vittorio had brought a decanter of Vino Nobile red wine and had poured three half glasses, Papà asked the Marshal about the purpose of his visit.

'I'll get straight to the point,' he said before taking a sip from his glass. 'I've been informed that a wounded partisan has been treated in your clinic.'

Emma's stomach tensed.

'Who told you that?'

'Your nurse's little niece has been telling people that he comes every night to get his wound dressed. I'm afraid I'm going to have to arrest the woman.'

'He's accompanied by armed men,' Emma's father said. 'She has no choice but to treat him. But I've heard the man in question has left the district. You'll no longer find him there.'

The Marshal took another sip of wine.

'Are you also threatened by these *partigiani*? If so, there's nothing I can do to protect you.'

'Indeed.' Papà refilled the Maresciallo's glass. 'We shall probably receive further demands for wheat and oil and will be obliged to grant them.'

'I suppose that's inevitable.' The Marshal sighed. 'The partisans are guarding all the roads leading to the Bivio. In fact, my men are on excellent terms with them and the *partigiani* only fire on fascist militiamen.' He gave another sigh. 'We've heard that the government is about to order us to wear the same uniform as the *repubblichini*. If that happens, I fear that many of my men will desert and join the Resistance.'

'What would you do then?' Emma asked.

'God only knows.' The Maresciallo drained his glass for the second time.

'If the Allies get here first, that might not happen,' she said.

'From what I've deduced, I doubt we'll see the British and Americans anytime soon.' Papà drank down his wine, refilled both his and the Marshal's glasses.

Emma decided to leave them to it. She'd barely touched her own glass, she wasn't in the mood for wine. She made her excuses and went up to her room. There, she gazed across the green valley towards Monte Amiata. She was missing Marco and hoped her father would have a message for him shortly.

* * *

After breakfast the next morning, Emma decided to take the bull by the horns. She didn't have anything to relay to Marco, but that shouldn't prevent her from going up to Le Faggete to see him. The farm was on the estate, and she had every right to go for a walk in the forest.

She slipped out without telling anyone where she was going. It was wrong of her and she knew it. If her father discovered she was missing, he'd worry. But he would no doubt advise her not to go and she didn't want to get into an argument with him. Chances were, she'd be back soon enough anyway.

Before too long, she'd reached the clearing in front of the farmhouse and had given the password to Marco's sentry, who happened to be Sandro that day.

'I'll take you to him,' he said, smiling. 'He's gone for a forage farther up the hill.'

'Emma, you came.' Marco opened his arms to her in the forest glade where he was gathering young dandelion leaves for salad.

She ran to him and they kissed while Sandro surreptitiously slipped away.

'Let's sit here,' Marco said, spreading his jacket on the grass. 'Tell me about your lunch with Hofmann.'

She'd never kept secrets from Marco and she wasn't about to do so now. She told him everything and he growled with anger.

'First chance I get, I'll kill that filthy Nazi,' he muttered.

'Please, Marco. I don't want you to put yourself in danger.'

'You think I can't do it?' His gaze snapped to hers.

She placed her hands on the sides of his face, looked him in the eye.

'I don't doubt you, *caro*. You fill me with awe.'

He crushed her to him, kissed her deeply.

She wanted this so much. Wanted his kisses, his touch, his caresses.

She relaxed into his embrace, let his hands explore her body.

'Darling Emma, I'd like to make love to you.' He kissed her again. 'But not here, where we could be seen. I'd like our first time to be perfect.'

'I'd like that too.' Happiness bubbled in her chest. 'Even if we have to wait until the end of the war.'

'I hope it won't be that long.' A smile glimmered in his eyes. 'I love you too much.'

'I love you too, Marco. I've loved you my whole life.'

'We were children together, but now we are adults. I want us to have a future together, *amore mio*.' He stroked her cheek.

She was too caught up with emotion to speak. All she could do was kiss him, let her lips do the talking.

And she prayed, oh, how she prayed.

A future with Marco was everything she'd ever wanted she realised now.

15

It was a week before Easter and the parish priest, Don Franco, had arrived to bless Rosa's family's house. He took a bottle from his bag and walked from room to room, sprinkling holy water in every corner and saying prayers. Rosa was pleased everything looked *tutto pulito* – spick and span. The children were dressed in their Sunday best: clean clothes, the girls with ribbons in their hair and the boys' cheeks scrubbed spotless. Late-afternoon sunshine came through the newly washed windowpanes, lighting the rooms in a golden glow.

'*La tua benedizione sia sempre sopra di noi. Per Cristo nostro Signore. Amen*,' the priest said as he lifted his crucifix. '*Ho finito.*' I have finished.

They all sat around the table while Don Franco enjoyed a glass of wine before heading off on his mule back to the fortress. Rosa had heard the building had been requisitioned for German troops. But they'd yet to arrive, and the priest had refused to leave his comfortable apartment, where a housekeeper attended to his every need.

'I'll stay in my home until the *tedeschi* come,' he'd said. 'Hopefully, they'll decide to go elsewhere.'

Everything was up in the air, Rosa mused as she and Lucrezia began making supper after the priest had left. No one knew when the Allies would break through. No one knew what the Germans would do. No one could predict if the front would pass through Tuscany and, if so, how long the fighting would last.

After they'd eaten, Lucrezia offered to tuck the little ones up in bed and hear their prayers. Rosa was tired, so she accepted gladly. She sat and listened to the radio until she started to yawn.

Strangely, her sister hadn't reappeared, but she was probably tired too and had gone to sleep early.

Rosa wished her parents and Nonna good night, then went to her room.

No Lucrezia. How odd. Was she meeting that Yugoslav again?

Gritting her teeth, Rosa returned to the kitchen.

'I've left Dora's pinafore drying on the line outside,' she said. 'I'd better bring it in in case it rains.'

Her muscles quivering, she made her way downstairs and out into the yard.

The night was dark with only a sliver of moonlight. But she knew the courtyard *come il palmo della sua mano*, like the back of her hand, and could see the shadow of her sister standing by the well up ahead.

Rosa went to her. 'What are you doing?'

'Nothing.' Lucrezia was clasping a bag to her chest.

'Doesn't look like "nothing" to me. Are you going somewhere?'

The fact that her sister had packed a bag was a dead giveaway.

Lucrezia released a loud breath.

'If you must know, I'm leaving. Casimir has rented an apartment in Montepulciano. He's coming to get me any minute now and we'll live together until we can be married.'

Rosa's jaw dropped.

'How can you betray the good name of the family like that? That man is an outlaw. He and his men have been looting nearby farms.' Her voice rose. 'You think he'll marry you? He'll do no such thing, my dear. He'll use you then discard you. Mark my words!'

'You're a fine one to talk. I know what you've been up to with Tom. Fornicating with him like a bitch in heat,' Lucrezia spat.

'Have you been spying on us?' Rosa took a step back.

Lucrezia laughed.

'I know you saw me and Casimir the other night. You can't accuse me of anything you haven't done yourself, Rosa.'

'What's going on?' Babbo's voice came from the top of the stairs.

'Nothing.' Lucrezia dropped her bag into the shadows behind her, then lowered her tone. 'If you tell Babbo about me and Casimir, I'll tell him what I saw you doing with Tom.'

'I want you both to come inside. This minute.' Babbo sounded angry. 'It's bedtime and you're keeping everyone up.'

Rosa and her sister did as requested. They went to bed and soon Lucrezia was snoring softly as if she hadn't a care in the world. How odd that she should drop off to sleep so quickly. Surely she'd be worried about Casimir not finding her waiting. Perhaps she was pretending to be asleep so she could slink out again as soon as Rosa had dropped off?

She tossed and turned, wondering whether the Yugoslav had come to fetch her sister. If so, and finding her not there, would he wait for her, or would he return another night?

How Rosa cursed the war. It brought more than bombs and senseless deaths; it brought people together, like her and Tom, as well as others, who were not as good a match.

Filled with worry for her sister, Rosa stayed awake and kept half an eye on her sibling. She wouldn't be getting much sleep tonight.

* * *

Tom visited the next day. He arrived at midday with Marco and Sandro to ask Rosa's father if he could spare any olive oil.

Babbo invited them into the kitchen, and they all sat around the table to eat lunch together.

'I've missed your cooking so much, Rosa,' Tom whispered as she passed him a bowl of minestrone soup.

She couldn't resist a smile, tempted to ask him quietly if that was all he'd missed. Her face became hot at the thought and she glanced away.

'What have you been up to lately?' she asked instead.

Tom's eyes crinkled with mirth.

'We commandeered a government lorry. You'll never guess what it was transporting.'

'Wine?' Babbo chipped in.

'No!' Tom chuckled. 'It was full of cognac. We took it to Marchese Ginori, who hid it in his cellar. We found out the alcohol was intended for the Germans. They'll be missing it, for sure.'

'We were hoping they were transporting flour to their stores. But we've heard from an informer there's due to be a transport tomorrow.' Marco took over the conversation. 'So we'll attack and then distribute the grain to the people of Montale. We've learnt they're in dire need.'

The large medieval village was about eight kilometres away. Rosa remembered thirty-one men had given their lives during the last war, a disproportionately high number given the population of only 750, which included women and children.

'A bit like Robin Hood robbing the rich to give to the poor,' she said, catching her sister's eye. She and Francesco had enjoyed the film with Errol Flynn before the war. She hoped Lucrezia realised how different Tom, Marco and Sandro were from Casimir and his men.

* * *

Tom and his comrades set off with a cannister of oil as soon as they'd finished eating, but not before he'd whispered to Rosa that he'd try to come down to the stable that night.

But, when she went to meet him, he wasn't there. Her heart sank as she made out the sound of Lucrezia and Casimir canoodling above her. At least she'd managed to persuade her sister that it wouldn't be a good idea to move in with the Yugoslav in Montepulciano. She'd used the argument that people would call her a 'fallen woman', that her reputation would be soiled forever and, if Casimir should lose his life in the war, she'd have no entitlement to a widow's pension.

Rosa went back to bed and pretended to be asleep when Lucrezia drew back the covers and slipped in beside her. She squirmed away from her sister's cold feet.

'Are you awake?' Lucrezia asked.

'I am now.' She sighed. 'You've been with that renegade, haven't you?'

'Yes.' Lucrezia huffed. 'He seemed relieved when I said I'd decided not to go and live with him. Apparently, the apartment isn't available any more.'

Rosa turned to face her sister. 'I know you're upset, my darling. But this will pass and eventually you'll realise it's for the best.'

'Is falling in love always so painful?' Lucrezia asked in a plaintive tone.

'It depends, I think.' She kept to herself the thought it would depend on the person you'd fallen in love with. 'Let's try to get some sleep, Lucrezia. *Buonanotte.*'

* * *

The following morning, after the little ones had left for school, Rosa got on with her chores while Babbo set off in the oxcart to collect supplies from the communal stores in the *fattoria* home farm.

He returned in time for lunch, and Rosa sat down with him, Nonna, Mamma and Lucrezia for their midday meal.

'The *fattore* just told me that the villainous Yugoslav has been spying for the *fascisti*,' Babbo said, as he mopped up tomato sugo with a piece of bread. 'The marchese found out from a contact in the Liberation Committee. If Casimir ever dares to come back here, I'll send him packing.'

'*Madre di Dio.*' Mother of God. Nonna shook her head. 'What a terrible fellow he is.'

'Indeed,' Mamma agreed. 'A vile character.'

Rosa met Lucrezia's gaze. Her sister looked mortified, her cheeks burning with shame. She dropped her head, stirred her pasta. Rosa hoped this would be the end of her sister's reckless dalliances.

Later, after she and Lucrezia had done the washing-up and her parents and grandmother had gone for an afternoon rest, Rosa suggested to her sister that they sit on the bench overlooking the river valley.

'It's another beautiful day,' she said. 'We can enjoy the sunshine.'

Lucrezia wiped her hands on her apron.

'You want to gloat about how Tom is so perfect in comparison with Casimir, don't you?'

'Nothing of the sort. I won't even mention him.'

'*Va bene.*' Okay. 'I'll go outside with you.' Lucrezia sighed.

They sat in silence, each lost in their own thoughts. Rosa thought about Tom, about how he and his fellow partisans were heading for Montale. She hoped their mission would be successful.

'Rosa.' Lucrezia drew her eyebrows together. 'I might have said something to Casimir last night.'

'What?' Dread spread through Rosa.

'I told him that Tom and the others were going to rob grain from the fascists and then distribute it to the people of Montale.'

Rosa covered her mouth with a hand.

'Why did you do that?'

'Because... because I wanted him to be like them. Wanted him to help people.'

Rosa's stomach convulsed with horror. What her sister had done would lead to terrible repercussions, of that she had no doubt.

'He's a spy, Lucrezia. He'll have sold the information to the enemy. You've put the lives of so many people in danger. How could you?'

'But I didn't know.' Lucrezia gave a sob. 'I would never have told him otherwise.' She wrung her hands together. 'I'm so sorry.'

'It's too late for that.' Rosa sprang to her feet. 'Come with me.'

Her heartbeat pounding, she raced upstairs with Lucrezia in her wake. She had to tell her father. Had to tell him about Lucrezia and the Yugoslav. If her sister retaliated by spilling the beans about her and Tom, then so be it.

Babbo growled with anger after she'd told him.

'I must go and warn them.'

'I'll go with you.'

'No. Far too dangerous.' He was already reaching for his hunting rifle.

'Please,' Mamma said, coming up to them. 'Take Rosa with you. She has a good head on her shoulders and will keep you from harm.'

Rosa hugged her mother.

'I'll try my best.'

'In the meantime, I'll deal with Lucrezia,' her mother said. 'I wish you'd told us what she was up to before now.'

'It's my fault,' Lucrezia said through her tears. 'I didn't want Rosa to tell you so I threatened her.'

'There's no time to get into this right now,' Babbo interjected. 'We have more pressing matters to attend to. As soon as I'm back from Montale, I'll sit you both down and you must explain everything.'

Lucrezia nodded and Rosa kissed her cheek.

'You did well to confess to your slip-up, sister. If you hadn't, things might be a whole lot worse.'

'I just hope we're not too late.' Babbo was already heading out of the door. 'Come on, Rosa. We'll make our way across country.'

She took off her apron and ran after him, beads of sweat breaking out on her forehead. Fear spread through her. They had to reach Tom and his comrades. Nothing else mattered. She would not contemplate failure. The alternative didn't bear thinking about.

16

The unmetalled road to Montale, lined with cypress trees, wound through rolling conical hills, but Rosa and her father took a direct path over the clay knoll known as *Lucciola Bella*, 'beautiful firefly', before cutting across fields, and eventually the castle tower dominating the village came into view. Perched on top of a high mound, the tiny medieval town boasted a fortified entrance gate and was encircled by crenelated walls dating back around 800 years.

Rosa followed Babbo up the steep track and soon they found themselves in the middle of a throng of residents. Partisans were distributing flour from the back of a government lorry, passing the bags to the locals, who'd formed a long line.

Rosa spotted Tom and she and Babbo ran up to him and told him the reason for them being there.

'Leandro,' he called out, using Marco's battle name. 'Listen to what Rosa and her father have to say.'

Marco joined them and they recounted their story again.

'I bet Chiurco in Siena won't let this rest. We can expect a visit from his men any minute now,' Marco muttered.

He swept his gaze over the women and children of Montale.

'I'll need your help, Rosa, to inform the local population and suggest that they leave before we're attacked.'

Rosa did as Marco requested. She and her father went from house to house, knocking on door after door, explaining the situation. Although Montale was small, there must have been over sixty dwellings lining the narrow streets. It was exhausting work in the warmth of the spring afternoon, but it had to be done.

'If you leave now, you'll be safe,' they said, but practically everyone they spoke to affirmed that they wanted to stay. They would keep their children secure in their cellars until the danger had passed.

Finally, Rosa and Babbo had done their rounds.

'Should we go home?' she asked as they stopped to catch their breath. The sun was dipping lower in the sky and soon it would be evening.

'No.' Babbo shook his head vehemently. 'I told your mother we might not be back today as I thought we'd be needed here.'

'Let's go and find Tom and the others, then.' She longed to see him, longed for a hug and a kiss. She'd been so busy rushing around she hadn't felt afraid. But now her stomach churned with anxiety. Would she find herself in the middle of a battle? And, if so, how would she cope?

The partisans were setting up camp in the church hall. As was the norm at that time of the year, the late afternoon had brought a chill to the air. They'd unpacked blankets from their haversacks and were sitting on the floor, smoking and chatting.

Rosa stood at the edge of the group; she felt a little out of place. Her father had slotted right in, but he'd been a soldier in the first war and clearly felt at home. He'd gone to sit with the sons of their neighbours and was laughing at something one of them had said.

Someone tugged at her sleeve. A dark-haired young woman who was roughly her age.

'My name's Claudia, what's yours?'

Rosa introduced herself.

'Would you like to help me and some of the other women prepare food for everyone?'

Rosa accepted the invitation gladly. She went to tell Babbo and Tom where she was going.

Tom pecked her on the forehead.

'*Grazie*. You've put yourself in danger coming here, my darling. But we're all immensely grateful.'

Rosa sighed. 'I wish Lucrezia hadn't blabbed.'

'Chiurco would have found out anyway, I suspect.'

'You could leave now, get away before his men arrive.'

'Marco gave us all the chance, but no one wanted to go. Luckily, we brought our Breda heavy machine-gun in the lorry we commandeered. We hold the high ground and we're all spoiling for a fight.'

'Let's hope that doesn't happen.' Rosa hugged Tom and then went with Claudia to the village inn, where she helped make a big cauldron of bean stew in the kitchen. She was given the task of chopping carrots and soon the familiar aroma of simmering garlic and tomatoes filled her nostrils. The known of an everyday recipe mixing with the unknown of what was to come. She was so afraid she could barely hold her knife.

Back at the church hall, she helped ladle out more than seventy plates for the partisans and the women who'd come to serve them. She sat next to Tom while they ate, taking comfort from his reassuring presence.

'Don't be scared, my love,' he said. It was as if he'd read her mind. 'I won't let any harm come to you.'

'It's all so different from what I'm used to, Tom. I never imagined I'd find myself doing something like this.'

'You're managing brilliantly. I'm so proud of you.' He held her close, kissed her in front of everyone.

'Babbo told me earlier he's looking forward to camping here with you and the other men. But my new friend, Claudia, has invited me to stay the night at her place.' Rosa looked him in the eye. 'Would you mind if I did that?'

'I think it's a good idea. Try and get some rest, my dearest. I have a feeling tomorrow will be a long day.'

He kissed her again.

'*Buonanotte, amore mio*,' she said. Good night, my love.

* * *

Claudia's family home was crowded as she lived with her parents and younger sisters, and Rosa was truly grateful to them for putting her up. She was given the sofa in their downstairs room, where she found herself restlessly shifting position as she tried to get some sleep. Her head was so full of the day's events that it was difficult to drift off.

Claudia had told her that her husband, Silvio, was missing in Russia and, in turn, Rosa told her about her brother, Maurizio, and how they all hoped he'd managed to survive. She also mentioned that she was a widow, that Francesco had died in Africa.

It had been strange to talk about Francesco with her new friend. She would never forget him and, each day, she could see more and more of him in Dora.

Francesco had been such a good man, kind and caring. A wonderful husband. Tom was like him in so many ways.

Oh, blessed Virgin Mary, please don't let Tom get killed.

Rosa stayed awake for hours, it seemed, but she must have dropped off for she woke to dawn light and the sound of heavy machine-gun fire. Her pulse raced and she leapt off the sofa.

Claudia and her sisters ran into the room.

'The *repubblichini* have arrived and the partisans have taken up positions on top of the walls,' Claudia said. 'We're going to help them by loading their guns.'

'I'll come too.' Rosa grabbed her shawl and put on her shoes.

They hurried up the steep stone steps to the battlements and Rosa went to stand between Tom and Babbo.

'I've come to give you a hand,' she said when they expressed surprise. 'I can pass you fresh magazines of ammunition when needed.'

'Only if you keep your head down,' Babbo said.

'Of course. Goes without saying.'

With nervous perspiration prickling her brow, Rosa took a peek over the parapet. A column of armoured cars had made their way up the road below, but had now ground to a halt. Fascist militiamen were shooting from the woodland underneath the village, but the partisans' Breda, placed in the medieval tower, appeared to be keeping them at bay. Shells curved through the air and landed in the middle of the *repubblichini* position.

A bullet whistled past Rosa's ear, and she ducked back down.

The gunfire was continuous from both sides and Rosa's heart hammered against her ribs. After crouching nervously for some minutes, she took her courage into both hands and got to work, passing ammunition to Tom and her father whenever needed.

The sun rose higher in the sky and the day wore on. The older village women came with refreshments: boiled eggs and flasks of water.

Rosa's ears rang from the hellish noise and her hands turned clammy as she handed Tom and her father magazine after magazine until, eventually, an apparent stalemate had been reached.

'The *fascisti* are retreating,' Marco shouted. 'Let's go get them!'

Before Rosa had time to realise what was happening, Tom and Babbo were rushing down the steps with the rest of the men.

She peered over the battlements. The other women were doing the same, and she joined them in shouting, '*Forza, ragazzi!*' Come on, guys!

Turmoil raged below. Men running. Yelling. Shooting.

Every nerve in Rosa's body screamed with fear for Tom and her father.

The fighting seemed interminable. Groups sallying to and fro. Gunfire echoing everywhere.

She gave a gasp.

A group of *repubblichini* were running to their armoured cars, climbing into them and setting off without an apparent thought for their comrades left behind.

But where were Tom and Babbo?

A magnificent sunset pinked the sky and it was difficult to see anyone in the muted light of dusk.

Rosa rushed down the steps, out through the gates of the village and into the road.

Hordes of villagers milled around.

'Rosa!' Tom came up, breathless.

She hugged him and he kissed her on the lips.

'Where's Babbo?'

'I'm here.' Her father appeared, his arm around Marco, whose hand was bleeding and who'd gone terribly pale.

'*Mamma mia!* What happened?' Rosa's voice trembled.

'Grenade exploded right by him. He's caught some shrapnel, I think.'

'What shall we do?' Rosa glanced from her father to Tom and back to her father again.

'Drive me in the lorry to the Bivio. I can be treated there,'

Marco managed to say. 'But wait until darkness falls.' His expression turned grave. 'Bring Sandro too.'

'Sandro? Where is he?'

Tom grasped her gently by the shoulders, looked her in the eye.

She took in his devastated expression, and her heart sank.

'I'm so sorry, my darling. Sandro has been killed.' Tom's voice broke.

'He volunteered to run back to the village to get more ammunition.' Babbo took over the tale. 'So brave of him. He almost made it...'

Rosa burst into tears.

Tom wrapped his arms around her. And Rosa was so very glad of them.

She sobbed against his chest.

* * *

Later, after a tourniquet had been applied to Marco's wrist and Sandro's body had been carefully wrapped in a sheet and loaded onto the lorry, Rosa said goodbye to Claudia then climbed into the back. Tom was already waiting there with Marco. Babbo got behind the wheel and they rumbled down the road with the headlights off.

'What a bloody awful day this has been.' Tom put his arms around Rosa on one side and Marco on the other.

'I agree,' Marco said softly. 'But it's a day that will never be forgotten. Just like Sandro. Henceforth, we shall be known as the Salvadori formation of partisans in his honour. His sacrifice will go down in the annals of history.'

'Such a waste of a young life.' Rosa sighed, glancing at Sandro's body, the senselessness of war weighing heavily on her. 'What will happen now?'

'Our men will interrogate those *repubblichini* who didn't flee and get them to bury their dead.' Tom's mouth twisted grimly. 'At least they left a massive number of weapons behind in their haste to run off. Those arms will be very useful to us in the weeks and months to come.'

Rosa gave another sigh. *More fighting. Would it ever end?*

She kept her thoughts to herself for the rest of the drive back to the Bivio estate. Babbo knew the way, but driving in the dark wasn't easy and it took more than an hour for them to reach the villa.

At the gates, Babbo brought the lorry to a stop. Rosa expected everyone to be asleep, but that was not the case. As soon as she and her companions climbed down from the lorry, they were greeted by Emma, the marchese, and Marco's father.

'We heard the sounds of the battle coming from Montale,' Emma said by way of explanation. 'We've been so worried.'

Emma visibly blanched at the sight of Marco staggering from the lorry, and she rushed towards him.

Marco's father had already wrapped his arms around his son.

'We have bad news, I'm afraid,' Tom said. 'We've brought Sandro with us.'

'Why is that bad news?' Marchese Ginori asked.

'He didn't make it,' Babbo announced without preamble.

'Oh, my God!' Emma's eyes welled with tears. 'Poor dear Sandro. How will we ever tell his family?'

'I'll handle that.' The marchese exhaled a deep breath. 'In the meantime, come inside, Marco. Your father can go and fetch the nurse.'

'I'll take my daughter home now, if we're no longer needed

here.' Babbo shouldered his rifle. 'My wife will be worrying about us.'

'Yes, of course. Please take the lorry and hide it somewhere safe.' Marco waved his good hand. 'Thank you for helping us today. I don't know what we'd have done without you.'

Tom hugged Rosa. His embrace was tight, pulling her to him. He kissed her nose before letting her go. It seemed their love was out in the open now, and no one appeared the least bit surprised. She caught Babbo smiling at her.

'Come, daughter,' he said. 'We must get a move on.'

Tom brushed a kiss to her cheek.

'I'll see you soon, no doubt, my love.'

'Take care, Tom.'

'I will.'

After another quick hug and a kiss on the lips, she climbed onto the lorry next to her father. He was a man of few words, and after he'd praised her for her actions in Montale, they lapsed into silence.

Rosa stared out of the window as they headed towards the *podere*. There wasn't much to be seen in the darkness and the going was slow. Tiredness seeped through her and she closed her eyes. She tried to stay awake, but it was impossible.

Her last thoughts before she fell asleep were of Tom. Of his warm embrace. Of how brave he'd been. How decisive. How loving. Could there be a future for her and Dora with him?

Don't think about it, she told herself. *Life is too uncertain in these terrible times.*

17

Sandro was buried late in the afternoon of Easter Monday, four days after the battle of Montale. Perched on a southern slope beneath the villa, the cemetery overlooked the wide valley below. Rain sheeted across the sky as Emma stood next to her father by the open grave, both of them holding black umbrellas. Luigi and his wife had positioned themselves opposite and were sobbing loudly at the loss of their only son.

Emma's gaze was drawn by movement under the dripping branches of the cypress trees to her left. A group of about twenty partisans, guns slung over their shoulders and pistols in their belts, had come to pay their respects to their fallen comrade. Not openly, but in the shadows.

She'd wept brokenheartedly for the gardener's son. His death so senseless, so tragic. It occurred to her that it could have been Marco lying in that wooden coffin. She gave a shiver of fear for him. He'd decided to rejoin his comrades, heading up to Monte Amiata with them tomorrow, even though there were still a couple of sutures in his right hand. The Bivio's nurse had removed a small piece of shrapnel from the flesh below his thumb, and now he'd declared himself to be well on the mend. He would return in about a week for the stitches to be taken out and had promised to keep it bandaged to avoid infection.

'Luckily I'm left-handed and can still shoot,' he'd said.

Emma glanced towards the window of the room where he was staying on the top floor of the villa. He'd be watching the funeral from up there, filled with regret that he couldn't attend in person.

Don Franco's cassock swayed as he committed Sandro's body to the grave. Everyone bowed their heads in prayer. Emma's father put his arm around her, and she gave in to her emotions, crying hot tears of grief for the shy boy who'd only recently come out of his shell.

Such terrible sadness for all who had known and loved him.

Papà squeezed her shoulder.

'Come, Emma. We should go back indoors. There's nothing more to be done here.'

She nodded, her throat so tight she couldn't speak.

Later, after dinner, Emma went to visit Marco. He was sitting in an armchair in the corner of the room, the supper tray and carafe of wine his mother had brought him earlier on the table opposite.

Emma glanced at the empty plates and glass.

'Your mamma has enjoyed cooking for you these past few days. She told me she wished you'd stay longer.'

It was what Emma, herself, wished. But she knew her pleas would fall on deaf ears. Marco's prime objective was to lead his men in their search for Casimir and make him pay for what he'd done. The Yugoslav would receive a summary trial and, if found guilty, would almost certainly forfeit his life.

'I'll be back before you know it, Emma. Remember I'll need to get my stitches taken out.' Marco gave her an encouraging smile. 'Come, sit on my lap. I want to hold you.'

She did as he requested, snuggling into his chest.

'I feel really sad about Sandro,' she said.

'Me too. He truly was a hero.' Marco held her tight.

He kissed her deeply and he tasted wonderful – of red wine and Marco.

With a groan, he drew back and gazed at her.

'You're incredibly beautiful, *amore*.'

She wound her arms round his neck.

'So are you.' She slid her fingers into his wavy dark brown hair.

He kissed her again, and his tongue found hers.

'I'd like to make love to you, my darling.'

'I'd like that too.' And she would. Her best friend, the boy she'd grown up with, had become a man. A man who'd woken the woman in her. It wasn't wrong. There was a war on and they must seize the moment.

He rose to his feet and lifted her before carrying her across the room to the bed. There, he laid her on the soft white blanket.

Her eyes locking with his, she unzipped her slacks, lifted her bottom, and slid them down her legs, followed by her underpants. Then she unbuttoned her blouse and unclipped her bra.

He stared in evident wonder at her body, his forest-green eyes glowing with love.

'Touch me, please, Marco,' she begged. 'I need you.'

He cupped her breasts in the palm of his uninjured hand, tugging at her nipples and sending ripples of desire through her.

'You're absolutely perfect, my love.'

'Let me undress you,' she replied, brushing his hair back from his face and caressing his lips.

'Little Miss Bossy.' He chuckled.

He was still laughing while she shrugged off his shirt and removed his trousers, taking his shoes and socks with them.

Licking her lips, she feasted her eyes on him.

'I think you're perfect too,' she said.

He came down on top of her and kissed her passionately.

She pushed at his hard, lean body, trying to manoeuvre him between her legs.

'Ah, ah, ah. Not so fast.' He chuckled again before mouthing her breasts and drawing them into his mouth.

Tingles coursed through her and her body hummed with need.

'Please,' she whimpered.

'I'll try not to hurt you, Emma. I know this is your first time.'

And then he was rocking into her with such gentleness, she barely felt a twinge.

'That feels amazing,' she said, urging him on.

Marco picked up the pace and it felt even more amazing. The pleasure built and built until it was truly intense and her release made her call out his name.

He brought his mouth to hers, kissing her with such passion that tears of emotion welled in her eyes.

'You were incredible,' she said.

He rolled off her and onto his side, then took her in his arms.

'I love you so much, Emma. Marry me. As soon as possible. I want us to be husband and wife.'

Her heart beat so fast she almost stopped breathing.

'Yes. Oh, yes. I love you too. But maybe we should wait until the war is over?'

'What if I've made you pregnant?' He stroked a finger down her cheek, gazed into her eyes.

'Let's wait and see.' She smiled. 'I doubt it could happen so quickly.'

'If that's what you want, my love.'

'It is. There's a lot we need to organise first. You want to go back to university, don't you?'

She was putting obstacles in their way, she knew she was. It was all too sudden. She loved him so much, though. There would never be anyone else for her, so maybe she should simply say 'yes'?

'I was going to suggest you study law in Florence instead of Siena,' Marco said.

'I suppose I could.' She cuddled into him and yawned with tiredness. 'I wonder if they have accommodation for married students...' Her eyelids felt heavy; she was on the cusp of sleep.

He lifted her hand and kissed it.

'You'd better go to your own bed now, *amore*. I'm not sure how your father would react if you were discovered asleep here.'

She giggled, kissed him on his stubbled cheek, untangled herself and reached for her clothes.

'Don't leave tomorrow without saying goodbye, promise?' she asked as she dressed.

'I promise. Wait for me at the breakfast table. I'll join you for a cup of barley coffee before I set off.'

He was still stretched out on the bed, his beautiful body exposed. She gazed at him, committed him to memory. He was everything to her; she couldn't imagine her life without Marco.

'*Buonanotte, amore mio*,' she said. Goodnight, my love.

'*Buonanotte*, Emma. *A domani*.' I'll see you tomorrow.

She gave him one last loving look, then turned with a heavy sigh and made her way from the room.

* * *

The next morning, Emma was still sitting in the dining room after Marco had left, when her father burst through the door. His tanned face had lost all its colour. He twisted his gold wristwatch and muttered under his breath.

'I've just received a coded message from the Liberation Committee.' His voice sounded disbelieving. 'An informer has revealed that a group of Germans and Italian fascists will head for Montale tomorrow to execute the entire local population for helping the partisans.'

Emma's veins turned to ice.

'Oh, dear God. I can't believe they'd be so barbaric.'

'It's hard to believe, but it's true, I'm afraid.' Papà paused, as if he was struggling to find the right words. 'Reprisals of this kind are happening throughout occupied Italy. The enemy seems to believe such actions discourage further aid to the Resistance.'

'There must be something we can do. We can't let those poor, generous people suffer such a horrible fate.'

'What can we do?' Papà spread his hands wide. 'We don't have the resources.'

Emma bit at her lip. Her thoughts chased each other like the chaff of the fields before the wind. Somehow, the Germans needed to be convinced that the villagers had been forced into helping, that they hadn't done so voluntarily. But how?

An idea came to her. She could go and ask Rosa. The share-cropper's daughter had been there during the battle. She'd met the locals, had experienced the village first-hand.

Emma shared her idea with her father.

'I'll drive you to the *podere* in our three-wheeler lorry,' he said. 'We could be clutching at straws, but it's worth a try.'

'*Grazie*, Papà.' Emma was already heading out of the room.

Her father was right behind her. They climbed onto the truck and, before too long, had arrived in front of the Vanini farmhouse.

Rosa was hanging washing out to dry on a line stretched between two olive trees. She wiped her hands on her apron.

'*Buongiorno.*' She swept her gaze from Emma to her father and back to Emma again. 'Is anything wrong?'

Emma explained and Rosa clapped a hand to her mouth.

'We can't let this happen.'

'My thoughts exactly,' Emma said.

'My daughter thinks we can try and convince the Germans that the locals were forced to help the partisans. You've met the villagers and have been in their homes. Do you think there's any way the *tedeschi* would believe such a story?'

Rosa made a *hmmm* noise in her throat.

'You know about the Yugoslav and how he and his band of *banditi* have been going around looting farms? There are other groups of outlaws in the area, from what I've heard. The Germans probably know about them.' She furrowed her brow. 'I'll go to Montale and warn the villagers. Those who want to leave can do so. Anybody who prefers to stay should trash their home to make it look as if they've been looted. That might convince the enemy they were coerced into assisting the *partigiani.*'

'Why would anyone want to remain in Montale once you've warned them?' Emma asked.

'The Germans would realise there's a spy in their midst if all the villagers suddenly left. From what I've learnt about the Montaliani... remember they preferred to stay and fight rather than flee last week... I expect most will remain. They hid their children in their cellars during the battle and are a brave bunch. I wouldn't be surprised if the majority of them agreed to the ruse.'

'We can only pray that will be the case,' Emma's father said. 'Thank you, Rosa. You are an excellent *partigiana.*'

'I'll try my best.' Rosa blushed. 'Claudia, the friend I made, will help me convince people, I hope.'

Rosa's father appeared in the periphery of Emma's vision. He approached.

'What's going on?' he asked.

Emma's father told him everything.

'I'll go to Montale with my daughter,' the sharecropper said. 'Then I'll bring her back home. It would be too dangerous for us to stay in the village.'

'*Grazie*.' Emma touched her hand to his arm.

'Now we must leave,' her father said. 'We have to inform the enemy about how the villagers were coerced.'

'Good luck with that.' Rosa's father smiled. 'I will pray you are successful.'

'So will I.' Rosa squeezed Emma's hand.

She climbed into the small lorry next to her father and they took the unmetalled road back to the villa.

'I'll phone Hofmann as soon as we get home.' Papà drove around a pothole filled with rainwater from the day before.

Emma breathed in and then slowly exhaled.

'No, Papà. I'll do it. Remember I told you that I reminded him of his fiancée? He likes me. If anyone can convince him, it will be me.'

'I can't let you do it, Emma. He's a Nazi. He has but one agenda and that is to rid Italy of any opposition to German occupation. You could be putting yourself in danger if he doesn't believe you.'

'And you wouldn't be putting *yourself* in danger?' she retorted.

'I'm older than you and have lived my life.'

'It will be fine. I'll meet him in Chianciano at his hotel. Make sure we are in a public room while I talk to him. You know the maître d'hôtel. He can keep an eye on me like he did the first time I had dinner with Gerhardt.'

Her father shook his head and huffed.

'You're incorrigible, my dear. When you get the bit between your teeth, there's no stopping you.'

She laughed ruefully. Laughed to cover her nervousness. She hadn't told Papà about what had happened the last time she'd met the captain. She hadn't told anyone. But she had to try to save the villagers. There was no other option.

18

Emma experienced a sense of déjà vu as she waited for Hofmann in the courtyard behind the villa. Just like the last time, nerves fluttered in her chest, but unlike before, she'd taken special care with her appearance and had put on a blue cotton dress she'd sewn herself. It incorporated padded shoulders, a nipped-in waist, and a hem to just below the knee, and she'd been pleased with her reflection in the mirror. She'd also plaited her hair in a long braid because the captain had said he preferred it that way – the way his fiancée always wore it. With a sigh, she smoothed down her skirt. She would have to tread a fine line between being pleasant to him and pleasing him too much.

The roar of the Moto Guzzi alerted her to Hofmann's arrival, making her heart race and her stomach churn.

Oh, dear Lord. Please let my mission be successful.

The captain skidded to a halt, sending gravel flying. He jumped off the motorcycle and handed Emma a pair of goggles.

'Get into the sidecar,' he said without preamble. 'I've reserved us a table for lunch.'

She did as he ordered. He'd been curt on the phone when

she'd rung him. Was he still annoyed with her for being sick last time?

Soon they'd arrived at the Excelsior, where they were shown to a table in the corner.

'I must admit I was surprised to hear from you.' Hofmann took a sip from his glass of wine after they'd ordered from the menu and their waiter had brought them a bottle of Vino Nobile. 'The last time we met was a complete disaster, and I have no wish to repeat the debacle.'

'I'm sorry, Gerhardt. It was your cigar smoke, I think.' She gave him what she hoped was a sincere smile.

He huffed, then swept his gaze over her. 'You're looking very beautiful today, my dear.'

She felt the heat of a blush.

'Thank you.'

How to introduce the plight of the villagers? It wouldn't be easy as she wouldn't have known about it unless intelligence had been leaked by a spy. She would have to lead the captain into revealing the information himself.

Their waiter brought them their starters of chicken liver pâté on *crostini* toast. Emma forced herself to eat; apprehension had stolen her appetite. Although she tried, she couldn't find an opening in their conversation to bring up the real reason for her contacting the captain. So she listened to him rant and rage about the Allied bombing of Berlin.

'We are developing a secret weapon,' he let slip. 'It is so deadly that Churchill will be forced to capitulate.'

'Is it gas?' Dread washed through her.

'Worse than that.' Hofmann smirked. 'Goebbels wanted to use it before now, but the Fuhrer hesitated. Now, after so many bombs had been dropped on our capital, he has given the go-ahead to retaliate without mercy. London will soon be obliterated.'

Emma gave a gasp.

'So much death and destruction.'

'It will bring an end to the war, we expect.' The captain smiled, sipped more wine, then polished off the rest of the food on his plate.

Emma forced herself to finish her *crostini*. She'd ordered baked sea bream for her main course, which she was looking forward to, despite her lack of appetite. Tarcisia hadn't been able to buy any fish in the Montepulciano markets for months.

But the bream tasted like soggy paper. It had been overcooked and under seasoned.

Emma put down her knife and fork.

'I can't eat another mouthful,' she said.

'Would you like a glass of cognac to finish?' The captain wiped his mouth with a serviette, then clicked his fingers to summon their waiter.

'I'm sorry, but we are out of cognac, sir.' The middle-aged man shook his head. 'Would you like a glass of grappa?'

'No. Can't stand the vile stuff.' Hofmann grimaced. 'I presume your stock was stolen by those outlaws?'

'I'm afraid so.' The waiter took their plates. 'I'll bring your coffees,' he said.

The captain took his cigarette case from his pocket.

'I won't risk smoking a cigar, Emma. I don't want you to be sick again.'

'Thank you, Gerhardt.' She paused to collect her thoughts. 'I'm intrigued to hear about the cognac theft. What happened?'

At last, an opening to ask him about the villagers.

'Those bastards stole the brandy intended for us,' he said. 'The next day, they apprehended a lorry taking grain to the government stores and gave it to the people of Montale. The villagers helped them retaliate when Chiurco, the Prefect of Siena, sent his men to punish them.'

'Oh, my goodness.' Emma feigned shock. 'But I think you have the story wrong.'

'Wrong?' The captain shook his head. 'What do you mean?'

He lit his cigarette, his eyes on Emma's chest.

She cleared her throat, took a sip of wine. 'One of my father's maids comes from Montale and she told us that the villagers were forced to help the partisans. They looted their houses and threatened even worse if they didn't comply.'

Hofmann exhaled a cloud of cigarette smoke. 'Seems a little unlikely. I mean, from what I've learned, the whole valley is helping the Resistance. We can't allow it to continue and we must make an example of the village.'

'What kind of example?'

Emma looked the captain in the eye. He had to believe she knew nothing about his intentions.

He poured himself a glass of wine, staring at her warily, and took a long drink before answering.

'The entire population will face a firing squad at dawn.' He placed his glass on the table with a sneer.

'But they are not guilty. I promise you, Gerhardt.' She widened her eyes, feigning innocence. 'It would be a terrible miscarriage of justice.'

'How do I know you're telling the truth?' He took another drag of his cigarette.

'You could send someone to the village to check. Their houses have been trashed. All their food stores emptied, their money stolen.'

Hofmann leant back in his chair.

'I could do that, I suppose, if I knew you were sincere.' His gaze dropped to her chest once more and he licked his thin lips. 'Last time we met, I invited you to my room. Show your sincerity by accepting the invitation now, Emma, and I might believe you.'

She gripped her hands together in her lap. Oh, God, could she really do this? But of course she had to, for the sake of the villagers. So many blameless lives at stake.

'I would like nothing better,' she said, a little relieved when the waiter returned with their coffees.

But the captain waved the waiter away and rose to his feet. He held out a hand.

'Come, dear Emma.'

Her stomach twisting, she placed her hand in his cold fingers, feeling the eyes of everyone else in the room upon her. Thank God, the maître d'hôtel was nowhere to be seen. She didn't want this getting back to her father.

In a blur, she allowed Hofmann to lead her to the lift, and she kept her gaze down as they rode up to the third floor in silence. She walked with him along the carpeted corridor to a room at the end. He took his key from his pocket and opened the door.

She stepped inside, but she barely had time to take in her surroundings. In a flash, he'd grabbed her and pushed her against the brocaded wall, turning her so she was facing away from him.

'You will be Freida for me,' he said, his hands squeezing her breasts. 'Then I will believe you.'

Bitter bile filled Emma's mouth and she wanted to flee. But she couldn't. The fate of the villagers rested in her hands.

The captain was kissing the nape of her neck, slobbery kisses that made her want to vomit. Maybe he would stop there, she thought? It was a slim hope.

She yelped when he dragged her away from the wall and pushed her across the floor to the big double bed.

'Get on your hands and knees,' he barked.

'I don't understand.' Her voice trembled.

'Face away from me.' He picked her up and threw her onto the bed, face first, before grabbing her hips and tugging her into position. Her dress was lifted over her back and her underpants roughly pulled down.

Emma dropped her face into the mattress and closed her eyes. If she pretended this wasn't happening, perhaps it wouldn't be so bad.

But it was bad. It was horrific. Within seconds, it seemed, he was slamming into her. And it hurt. It hurt terribly. Pain shot through her private parts as he thrust like a madman, grunting and moaning Freida's name.

Emma gritted her teeth to stop herself from screaming.

When will it be over? He was taking a long time to finish.

Finally, he emitted a long groan of release. He withdrew and slapped her on the backside.

'You did well,' he said, rolling her over. 'Make yourself presentable and I'll take you home.'

'And the villagers?' she managed to ask, her throat scratching with unshed tears.

'I will send my men to verify what you've told me. Then, I might reconsider, depending on the outcome.'

She inhaled a shaky breath. If she'd saved the Montaliani, this would have been worth it. If not, she might just die of shame.

19

The morning after she and her father had gone to Montale to warn the villagers, Rosa arrived at the Bivio villa to find out about the outcome of the ruse. She was shown onto the terrace by the marchese's butler, where Emma and her father were sitting sipping barley coffee in the shade of a potted palm tree.

'*Buongiorno*, Rosa.' Emma's hand shook as she placed her cup down on the saucer, and Rosa's heart sank as she returned the greeting.

But the marchese's daughter gave her a smile.

'It worked,' Emma said. 'We received a phone call from a representative of the Liberation Committee a short time ago. A lorry-load of Germans and fascists went to Montale at dawn. The villagers showed them the so-called damage caused by the partisans and the *nazifascisti* decided to accept their story and have spared them from the firing squad.'

Rosa's knees buckled with relief.

'Thank God.' She lowered herself to the chair Emma pulled out for her.

'We are immensely grateful to you,' Marchese Ginori said. 'If you and your father hadn't convinced the Montaliani, the horrific outcome doesn't bear thinking about.'

'It's a good thing the German captain was willing to listen to Emma.' Rosa glanced at the padrone's daughter. Emma's cheeks had turned pale.

'Yes, well. It's done, now,' Emma said curtly. 'Let's hope this is the end of it.'

Emma had echoed Rosa's own sentiments. The partisans' ongoing actions could well lead to further reprisals. Local people would continue to help the Resistance, without question. And, even if they didn't, they might be used as scapegoats and pay the ultimate price.

'Can we offer you a coffee, Rosa?' Marchese Ginori asked, breaking into her thoughts.

'*Grazie*, but I really should head back home. My little girl was feeling a bit unwell this morning. I must go and tend to her.'

'I'll walk with you to the road,' Emma offered. 'I need to stretch my legs.'

Rosa shook Emma's hand at the entrance to the courtyard, but the marchese's daughter kissed her on both cheeks.

'Thank you again for what you did,' she said.

'I doubt it was as difficult as your mission.' Rosa looked Emma in the eye, giving her the chance to clarify. Emma remained silent, though, so Rosa took her leave, and set off down the winding track through the valley.

While she walked, she thought about the day before, how she and her father had rushed to the village, how Claudia had helped them go from house to house, knocking on the doors and explaining the situation. Half the inhabitants had left straight away, to hide in the woods with about thirty of the children. The others decided to stay and brave it out. They said they would do as Rosa and her *babbo* suggested, ransack their homes and pretend they'd been robbed. Rosa and her father had left before they'd found out if the ruse had worked. Last night, she'd barely slept for the worry.

A sudden droning sound echoed around her. Rosa shaded her eyes with a hand and glanced up. She squinted. Was it a German or an Allied plane? The aircraft circled low. It was British – there were concentric circles under its wings.

What's it doing here?

Without warning, black egg-shaped pellets spilled from its belly. Bombs!

Massive explosions resounded around the hills. Smoke rose from the clay crests and an acrid smell stung Rosa's eyes.

Why were they bombing the valley? Were they heading back to base and dropping explosives to lighten their load?

Engines screaming, the plane suddenly dived.

Machine-gun bullets burst from between its propellers.

Mamma mia, it was firing on the road!

Stones ricocheted and the ground beneath Rosa's feet shook.

Her stomach lurched and she ran for the ditch.

Trumpets of mud spewed into the air, showering her with debris.

She crouched low and covered her head with her hands.

As suddenly as it had started, it was over. The plane tipped its wings and turned towards the coast.

Every bone in her body shaking, Rosa clambered out of the ditch.

Coils of black smoke snaked upwards from a burning cypress tree. More smoke spiralled from the surrounding hills.

Rosa sucked in a sharp breath, wiped her hands on her skirt, and set off at a run for home, fearful that the plane may come back.

Her heart thumped a painful beat against her chest. Her

breaths became choking gasps. But she didn't stop running until she'd reached the courtyard in front of the *podere*.

Mamma was just getting a loaf out of the bread oven. She gasped at the sight of her.

'What happened to you? Your cheek is bleeding.'

Rosa hadn't realised. She touched a hand to her face, saw blood on it.

'I must have been hit by a flying stone.' Her voice quaked.

'We heard the bombing. Thank God you are safe.'

Rosa nodded. It had been the most frightening experience of her life.

'I'll go and put some iodine on the cut.'

She turned to go, but her mother went on to say, 'Dora has a fever and has been asking for you.'

Distraught, Rosa set off at a run up the stairs.

She found Nonna sitting by the fire with Dora on her lap.

'I'll take her,' Rosa said. 'I'll need to cool her down.'

She lifted her daughter into her arms and took her to the bedroom, where she laid her on the bed.

The child half opened her feverish eyes.

'Where were you, Mammina?'

'I was at the villa, darling. But I'm home now and I'm going to look after you.' She pecked her on her heated forehead.

Rosa went to the bathroom, where she applied the iodine, making her cheek sting, before soaking a washcloth in cold water. She returned to the bedroom, stripped Dora down to her underpants, and then wiped her face and chest.

Guilt caught at the back of her throat. She shouldn't have left Dora, shouldn't have gone gallivanting about the countryside. She wasn't a partisan; she was a mother. And her duty lay with her child.

* * *

Rosa stayed by Dora's side the entire night. She kept her in her own bed, Lucrezia bunking down with their small siblings. Rosa's skin had turned clammy with worry. Dora's fever was taking a long time to break.

Throughout the night, Rosa carried on sponging her down; she even opened the window so the cool night air would reach her.

What a day it had been! Rosa touched her hand to the cut on her cheek. She'd never imagined being struck by machine-gunned bullets from a plane. Her skin prickled with fear at the thought of it.

At dawn, Dora's fever broke and she fell into a peaceful sleep. Rosa was so tired that she, too, dropped off and it wasn't until mid-morning that she woke to find Lucrezia standing by the bed, staring down at her.

'Tom and Marco are here. They want to talk to you and Babbo. I'll stay with Dora, if you like.'

'*Grazie.*' Rosa thanked her sister.

She found Tom and Marco sitting at the kitchen table with her father, cups of coffee in front of them.

Tom got to his feet.

'Oh, my goodness. What happened to your cheek, Rosa?'

She explained and his nostrils flared with evident anger.

'How can they have done that to you? It's outrageous.'

'I agree,' Marco added. 'There are far too many trigger-happy gunners on both sides in this conflict, I fear.'

Rosa kept to herself the notion that it wasn't only gunners on aircraft who were trigger-happy. From all accounts, when the partisans were carrying out their actions, they would let rip with their weapons without a thought for the consequences. Perhaps it was the way of war? If that was so, more innocent civilians were bound to suffer.

'It's good to see you both safe and sound,' she said, her eyes on Tom.

'We can't stay long.' Tom met her gaze. 'We're on our way to inform the marchese that Casimir has been executed.'

She couldn't help gasping. Much as she detested the man, it was the severest punishment possible.

'We found him up on Monte Amiata. Gave him a fair trial,' Marco said. 'In the end, he confessed to everything. He'd been passing information to the enemy for months, spying on the *padrone* and picking up intelligence wherever he could.'

'I see.' Rosa swallowed hard. It would fall to her to tell her sister. Lucrezia would surely be devastated. Even though the plan to run away with Casimir had come to nothing, she still talked about him and was clearly still infatuated.

Tom and Marco finished their coffees, scraped back their chairs and shouldered their rifles.

'We'll return to our formation on the mountain,' Tom said. 'Rumour has it that the Germans are about to start a mopping-up operation of partisans in the valley and we'll avoid it up there.'

Marco shook hands with Rosa's father. He thanked her mother and grandmother for the coffees, then said to Rosa, 'We know about your involvement to help save the Montale villagers. It was very brave of you.'

'Emma was the true heroine. She braved the lion's den and managed to persuade the German captain of their innocence.'

'Hmmm.' Marco's expression darkened. 'I wish she hadn't felt the need to do that, despite the successful outcome.'

Rosa didn't know how to respond, so she kept silent and led the men down the outside stairs.

In the courtyard, Tom hugged her and she lifted her face to receive his kiss.

'I hope we'll be back in Le Faggete soon, my love. I don't like being so far away from you.'

He kissed her and she wrapped her arms around his waist. How she wished he didn't have to leave. When she was with him, the war receded into the background and she felt secure.

'Stay safe, my darling Tom. Come back to me. Promise!'

'I promise.' He spoke the words with certainty and kissed her again. '*Arrivederci, amore mio.*'

She watched Tom and Marco make their way down the dusty road until they were but two specks in the distance.

With heavy steps, she headed for the stairs. How would she tell Lucrezia about Casimir? It wouldn't be easy, but it had to be done.

20

On a mild afternoon, three weeks or so after the battle of Montale, Emma was helping Luigi weed the garden. He'd come down with the 'flu after his son had died and had only just come back to work. The world seemed to have gone increasingly crazy since that tragic event, she mused.

Sadness washed over her as she remembered Papà receiving a letter from a cousin in Rome not long ago, saying that the authorities had yet to publish a list of the 320 hostages shot in reprisal for the death of the thirty-two Germans who'd been killed by the Resistance. People didn't know if friends or relatives who were political prisoners had been executed or not. It had made her realise that allowing Hofmann to have his way with her must surely have been worth it. The villagers would have been murdered without a doubt.

Even so, she couldn't help wishing her sacrifice hadn't been necessary. She'd felt sullied afterwards, had scrubbed herself from head to toe, and now she tried to avoid thinking about it.

When Marco had unexpectedly arrived with Tom the next day, she could barely look him in the eye. She'd been relieved when

Marco and Tom had rushed off to get Marco's stitches removed and had then gone back to Monte Amiata. She hadn't seen him since and she missed him terribly. Under no circumstances must he find out what she'd done with Hofmann. She'd never kept secrets from Marco in the past. If only she didn't have to do so now. But the truth was too raw, too painful to share. And what if it put him off her? She wouldn't be able to bear that.

Emma carried on weeding. From time to time, she glanced up at the sky and listened out for the drone of aircraft engines. Recently, the Allies had stepped up their bombing of Tuscany. Last week, she'd gone to Siena in the small lorry with her father to do some shopping for essentials. They'd left home at 6 a.m. to avoid the Allied planes, and had driven past umpteen burnt-up trucks and cars by the sides of the roads. They arrived in Siena about twenty minutes before the first air raid. The sirens had wailed throughout the day, and during the attacks they'd had to go down to the shelters with the rest of the locals. She'd cowered with her father, her heart pounding while the air around them throbbed from explosion after explosion.

Then, only yesterday, the Allies dropped their bombs on the estate, shaking the villa and scaring everyone. The British were aiming for the bridge over the River Orcia, Emma's father had said. The bomber formation had flown over their heads, going on to bomb Chiusi and the railway line. Papà went on to explain their intention was clearly to stop all German traffic by air, road and rail.

Emma gave a shudder. War had come to the valley, and it was absolutely terrifying.

Movement at the garden gate caught her eye. Her father was approaching.

'Orazio just came to say that Marco is at our usual meeting place in the woods. He'd like to talk to us.'

A smile spread over Emma's face. She put down her weeding fork and fell into step beside Papà.

But when she saw Marco, she averted her gaze. He knew her so well he might notice she was different somehow.

'I've come to warn you about a German mopping-up operation,' he said. 'It started early this morning on the lower slopes of Monte Amiata.'

'Good God,' Papà exclaimed. 'What happened?'

'About 400 Germans surrounded the villages of Vivo d'Orcia and Campiglia. We scattered into the forest, but they arrested around one hundred villagers.' Marco's gaze fell on Emma, but she still kept her eyes down.

'Were any of you captured?' her father asked.

'No. The *tedeschi* subsequently released the villagers but went on to raid several farms, helping themselves to pigs, flour, bedding, etcetera.'

'The *bastardi*,' Papà muttered.

'Did you hear the rumour that the German line at Cassino has been broken?' Marco said, changing the subject. 'Apparently the *tedeschi* have started their retreat.'

'I'm sorry, but we listened to the BBC news earlier, and there was no mention of that.' Emma's father shook his head. 'The latest report from Rome to the Liberation Committee predicts that the Allies aren't expected to break through until mid-May at least.'

'It's all taking so long,' Emma said. She shot Marco a quick look. 'Half of me dreads what will happen when the German army retreats through here, the other half can't wait for it.'

Marco reached across the space between them and gathered her in for a hug.

'Stay strong, Emma. You're so brave...' He kissed the top of her head.

Her father cleared his throat.

'Is there something you two haven't told me?' he asked with a chuckle.

Emma took a step back, her cheeks aflame.

'What do you mean, Papà?'

With twinkling eyes, he glanced from her to Marco, then back to her again.

'You have my blessing,' he said.

'Thank you, sir.' Marco shook his proffered hand. 'I was a little worried you'd think the son of your *fattore* not good enough for your daughter.'

'Not the case at all, dear boy.' A smile spread across Emma's father's face. 'I'm extremely proud of you.'

'So am I,' she echoed. 'Don't get yourself killed, Marco. Be careful, please.'

He hugged her again, kissed her on the cheek.

'I'll bring my men back to the valley as soon as possible. In the meantime, stay away from that Nazi captain. Promise me, Emma!'

'I promise,' she said.

* * *

The days went by and the weather turned warmer. Marco and his men had returned to Le Faggete and were carrying out raids on German supply lines. An entire year had passed since the British POWs had arrived in the valley, Emma reflected as she gazed out of her bedroom window. The wheat was ripening in the fields. How would they harvest it without help?

She plaited her hair and put on a pair of cotton slacks and a blouse. Papà would be waiting for her to have breakfast with him.

He was listening to the radio while drinking a cup of coffee.

Emma breathed in the aroma. It was a smell she'd always

found pleasant, but for some reason it suddenly made her feel sick.

'Are you all right?' Papà asked. 'You've gone very pale.'

'I'll be fine.' She poured herself a glass of water and took a sip. 'Just not very hungry this morning.'

The radio crackled and her father put a finger to his lips, indicating she should remain silent.

Her heart gave a leap. An announcement was being broadcast that brought a smile to her face. The Allied attack on the Cassino front had begun at last.

Emma and her father hardly left the radio for the next twenty-four hours. A day later, it was announced that Cassino had fallen and the Allies were set to break the German Gustav line.

'They'll advance on Rome next,' Papà said, his tone jubilant.

Next day, Emma and her father learnt that partisan activity in the district had hotted up. Marco and his men had broken into the barracks at San Casciano, disarming the Carabinieri. They'd also disarmed two German soldiers at Contignano, only ten kilometres away.

The following morning, Emma woke early. Nausea swelled in her stomach and she hurried to the bathroom to be sick.

What's wrong with me? she asked herself.

She dressed and went downstairs. A cup of tea might settle her tummy.

But, before she could make her way to the kitchen, the rumble of lorry engines echoed from the courtyard and Vittorio rushed into the hallway.

'The German captain is here and he says he needs to see your father immediately,' he said.

Emma tensed. What had brought Hofmann to the villa?

She hurried back upstairs and knocked at her father's bedroom door.

'Good God, it's only 7 a.m. and I haven't shaved yet,' Papà muttered. 'It's probably some routine matter. The Kapitän will just have to wait.'

'I'll stay with you,' Emma said. The thought of spending time with the captain sent shivers of dread through her. She sat on the chaise longue in her father's bedroom while, in his en suite bathroom, he shaved and dressed.

A knock sounded at the door.

'I'm sorry, marchese, but the captain wants you to come downstairs straight away,' Vittorio said. 'He threatened to come up and fetch you himself if you don't appear at once.'

Emma's father released a heavy sigh.

'Come, daughter. Let's go and find out what the man wants.'

'I don't like to be kept waiting,' Hofmann spat as they approached.

Papà ignored the captain's rebuke. 'Good morning to you, Herr Kapitän. To what do we owe the pleasure of your company?'

'We've been to Contignano and have taken nine men as hostages in reprisal for the partisans' action yesterday.' Hofmann indicated towards the lorries. 'One of the prisoners has told us your staff have been helping the rebels. So, we've come to examine their quarters.'

Emma stepped forward.

'Whoever told you this is mistaken.'

'Why should I believe you?' Hofmann lowered his cold blue eyes and raked them over her body.

Papà placed himself between them.

'You're welcome to carry out a search, but you won't find anything.'

'That remains to be seen.'

The captain requested that Emma show him and his men to the kitchen.

She stood by, aghast, while they ransacked the place, helping themselves to bags of flour and cannisters of oil in the process.

Tarcisia had burst into tears, the two helpers with her, whimpering.

Emma went to them, and put her arms around them.

'It will be all right. The Germans will leave as soon as they realise there's nothing to be found.'

But Hofmann insisted on continuing his quest in the staff quarters, which were housed in a wing behind the kitchen.

'Send someone to tell your employees to wait in the courtyard,' he barked.

She did as he ordered, running to Vittorio, who was still with her father in the hallway.

'The man is deranged.' Papà shook his head. 'Vittorio, gather our people together. I'll go with Emma.'

Emma stood as far from Hofmann as she could while his men went from room to room, pulling open drawers and upending mattresses. From the corner of her eye, she discerned her father remonstrating with the captain.

Finally, the search was over.

'Tell your employees we will examine their papers,' Hofmann barked again at Emma.

She conveyed the message to Tarcisia and her helpers, the laundress, carpenter, blacksmith and stable hands.

Thank God, it was market day in Montepulciano. Marco's parents went there every week and their house was far enough away from the villa not to have attracted the captain's attention.

After Hofmann's men had checked the Bivio workers' documents, he puffed himself up to his full height.

'I'm warning you all that any further help to the partisans will be given at the risk of your lives.' He clapped his hands together.

'Go! Get on with your work! I need to speak to the marchese and his daughter in private.'

The nausea in Emma's stomach threatened to overwhelm her. She inhaled a deep breath.

'I include you and Emma in my caution, marchese.' The captain sneered. 'And I require you to reveal to me where the rebels are hiding. I know you have your finger on the pulse of the valley. I'm not stupid enough to believe your lies.'

'We aren't lying, Gerhardt.' Emma steeled herself, looked him firmly in the eye. 'You know I always tell you the truth.'

He leered at her, bent and whispered in her ear. 'I'm rather busy at the moment, but as soon as the war allows me some free time, you could prove your sincerity to me again.'

She stepped away, appalled.

Her father positioned himself between her and the captain like before.

'You asked me about the partisans, Herr Kapitän. Well, they are to be found everywhere on the chain of hills running from Cetona to Montale – about eighty kilometres – and are seldom more than twenty-four hours in any one place.'

'We'll see what our hostages have to say about that,' the captain retorted, stamping his boots in obvious anger.

Emma felt the blood drain from her face.

Oh, God, please, not again.

She'd given herself to Hofmann once. And it was one time too many. Her head began to spin and dizziness overcame her.

Don't faint, she told herself as she crumpled to the ground.

21

Emma blinked open her eyes to find herself lying on her bed with her father sitting in the armchair by the window.

'W... w... what happened?' she stuttered.

'You fainted, my darling, and no wonder. You went without breakfast and aren't eating properly overall.' Papà frowned. 'Vittorio carried you up here and I called for the nurse, but she's come down with the 'flu. There's a lot of it about, unfortunately.'

Emma raised herself on her elbows. The fuzziness in her head had cleared and her stomach rumbled with hunger.

'I'm feeling fine now. Whatever it was has passed. I'm starving and would love a plate of pasta.'

'Good to hear.' A smile creased her father's face.

Emma's breath caught as she remembered Hofmann's visit, his threats and insinuations.

'Has the captain gone?' Her voice quivered.

'Yes. He didn't even wait to find out if you were all right.' Papà sighed.

'I hate that man. I hope he dies. If I knew how to fire a weapon, I'd kill him myself.'

'Well, I'm glad you're a *partigiana non combattente*, Emma. It's not as dangerous.'

'Hmmm. Any news on the Allies?'

'Only that they're advancing on the Adolf Hitler line. From what I've heard, it will be a tough one to break.'

'I thought they'd be in Rome by now,' Emma said, disappointment making her shoulders drop.

'Might take another week or so, my dear.' He glanced at her. 'Are you feeling up to coming downstairs, or should I ask Tarcisia to prepare a tray for you?'

'I'm feeling a lot better, Papà. Just give me a minute or two to use the bathroom and I'll meet you on the terrace.'

She did as she'd suggested, then strolled through the glass doors leading to the patio. She breathed in the sweet scent of the wisteria lining the walkway in the garden below and went to pull out a chair at the table where her father was sitting.

'Tarcisia will bring you a big dish of *pici* momentarily,' he said. 'I shall enjoy watching you eat it all up.'

The food arrived and she thanked the cook, who told her she'd managed to keep a store of flour hidden from the Germans. Emma relished every mouthful. When her plate was empty, she put down her fork.

The drone of aircraft engines rumbled above.

'Oh, no!' She scraped back her seat, ready to head for the cellar.

But pieces of paper were fluttering down, not bombs.

She gasped. 'They're dropping leaflets.'

Papà picked one up and started to read aloud.

'*Whoever knows the place where a band of rebels is in hiding, and does not immediately inform the German army, will be shot. Whoever gives food or shelter to a band or to individual rebels will be shot. Every house in which rebels are found, or in which a rebel has stayed, will be blown up. So will every house from which anyone has fired on the German forces. In all such cases, all stores of food, wheat, and straw will be burned, the cattle will be taken away, and the inhabitants will be shot. The German army will proceed with justice, but with inflexible hardness.'*

'Oh, dear Lord.' Emma pulled at a loose strand of hair. 'Whatever next?'

Her rhetorical question was soon answered. The rumble of aircraft engines resounded again, and more leaflets fell from the sky.

'*At all costs refrain from reporting yourselves to the army,*' she read. '*Commit acts of sabotage on the communication lines. Enter into contact with the foreigners in the German army. Go on organising groups. The moment for decisive action is near at hand.*'

Emma's father took the leaflet from her.

'The Allies have their own propaganda machine,' he said. 'All of this is bound to upset our farmers. They won't know what to do for the best.'

'All they want is peace. To get back to the land. And to save their sons.'

'Indeed.' Her father crumpled the leaflet in his fist. Then he stared up at the sky. 'I fear for them all. None of our young men have reported for military service. Instead they are hiding in the woods, trusting luck and the Allied advance to protect their families from reprisals.'

Emma's heart wept.

* * *

Emma was sitting at her sewing machine making children's clothes from unused curtains. The afternoon sun came through the open window, slanting across the spare room and lighting the walls with a tangerine glow. She listened out for the drone of planes, but it was the chattering sound of female voices that filled her ears. Curious, she rose to her feet and went downstairs.

Her father was standing in the hallway, surrounded by a group of around ten women, all talking at once. Dressed in what was obviously their Sunday best – clean blouses, tailored skirts, narrow-brimmed straw hats – they varied in age from around forty to fifty years old.

'We've walked all the way from Chianciano,' one of the women, a stout lady with a big bosom, said, managing to be heard above the others. 'Our husbands and brothers were taken as hostages by the Germans in Contignano and we went to take food to them.'

The babble of voices drowned out whatever the woman went on to say next.

Emma positioned herself next to Papà.

'Please, don't all talk at once,' he said, lifting his hands. 'How can I help you?'

The buxom woman stepped forward.

'We've learnt that you know the German captain. We're begging you to intercede with him on our behalf. Our menfolk are too old for the draft. They've done nothing wrong. We all work hard and keep our noses clean.'

'I'll do what I can.' He smiled reassuringly. 'But I truly believe the *tedeschi* are detaining your husbands and brothers simply as a warning to the rest of the population that they shouldn't be helping the Resistance.'

The stout woman huffed.

'Those partisans have a lot to answer for. They go around causing trouble for the rest of us. I can assure you we've had nothing to do with them.'

'Can I offer you some refreshments?' Emma chipped in.

It might smooth the women's ruffled feathers if they had something to eat and drink, she thought. They must be terribly worried, though. She would be devastated if she were in their shoes.

'A glass of water would be nice,' a younger woman responded. 'We have miles to walk before we get home.'

'I can organise an oxcart to take you back to Contignano.' Papà glanced at his watch. 'It's getting late and would save you walking in the dark.'

The women thanked him and, after they'd drunk the water and nibbled on *biscotti*, Emma and her father led them through to the courtyard where Vittorio had organised one of their stable hands to lead the oxen that would pull the big cart.

'Do you really believe their men are being held only as a warning?' Emma asked as she and her father waved the contingent off.

'I do.' He nodded.

Papà's optimism was usually contagious. But now, doubt overcame Emma. A bad feeling assailed her senses and, for the rest of the day, she kept the women and their menfolk in her thoughts.

* * *

Next morning, she woke up nausea free. She must have had some kind of tummy bug and she was glad to be rid of it.

She was enjoying a cup of coffee with her father when Vittorio appeared.

'The German captain has arrived. Shall I show him in?'

Emma's stomach tensed.

'Dear God,' Papà said. 'Will that man ever leave us in peace?' He wiped his mouth with a serviette. 'I suppose you'd better bring him through.'

Emma wanted nothing more than to excuse herself and go up

to her room. But she couldn't. What if Hofmann had come to relay
something important?

Vittorio had arrived with the captain before she knew it. She
stiffened her posture and bit down on her lip, trying not to show
how much she was trembling.

'Herr Kapitän, how nice to see you again.' Her father held out
his hand.

But the captain ignored it. He swept his cold gaze from Papà to
her and back to Papà again.

'I've come to inform you that the hostages from Contignano
will be shot, if, after forty-eight hours' reprieve, the arms the partisans took from my men are not returned.'

Emma couldn't help a gasp.

'Yes, dear Emma,' Hofmann sneered. 'I've made up my mind
about this and *nothing* will change it.'

Her stomach squeezed at his words. Again she felt sullied,
violated. He was looking at her as if she was nothing but a worth-
less *puttana*.

'What makes you think we have a means of communication
with the partisans?' Her father risked the question.

'We need to rid this area of the rebel filth who are draining
your resources, stealing food from you and your farmers and
attracting the anger of the Reich to your *peaceful* community.'
Hofmann smirked. 'I'm sure you will find a means of communication in order to help us, marchese.'

But it was Emma he was looking at, piercing her with his ice-
blue eyes.

She squared her shoulders and stared right back at him.

Her father gave the captain a curt nod.

'If that is all, would you mind if my daughter and I got on with
our day, Herr Kapitän? We have matters to attend to on the estate.'

'Busy bees, the two of you, eh?' The captain tapped his nose. 'I can guess what's been going on. Don't take me for a fool. My warning stands. Either our weapons are returned or the hostages will be shot. And remember what I said.' He glanced at Emma, his lip twitching into a sneer. '*Nothing* will make me change my mind.'

He looked as if he wanted to spit on the floor at Emma's feet.

'Enjoy your day,' he said and left the room with a door slam.

* * *

Emma argued with her father. She needed to go to Marco and tell them about the German threat.

'The *partigiani* are hardly likely to want to return the arms.' Papà shook his head.

'If it means saving people, I think they will.' She knew Marco, knew he wouldn't want innocent civilians to suffer.

'You've only just recovered from being ill, Emma.' Her father furrowed his brow. 'I could ask Orazio to go.'

'It has to be me, don't you see? I take regular walks in the forest. Orazio never has the time as he's always occupied helping you run the estate.' She smiled. 'A hike will do me good. No one will think anything of it.'

'If you say so, dear girl. I know better than to try and stop you. But be careful. Keep to the treeline, promise?'

'I will.' She was already heading out of the room. 'Don't worry!'

She changed into a pair of shorts and a cotton blouse, and set off as soon as she'd filled her water bottle. The day had turned warm and she was sweating as she made her way up the steep track under the conifer trees. Her step lightened at the thought of seeing Marco. She swallowed her fear that he'd notice something different about her. What she'd done with Hofmann was now firmly buried in the past. She wouldn't think about it. His stance towards her that morning, his coldness, surely meant he no longer expected her to give herself to him to prove her sincerity. She could put what had happened behind her, and look forward to being with Marco.

'Emma!' He held out his arms after his sentry had taken her to him, and when they were alone.

She hugged him and lifted her face to be kissed.

His mouth claimed hers and she sighed with happiness. This was where she should be. In Marco's arms. Her heart beat only for him.

But the matter at hand needed to be dealt with, much as she wished it didn't.

'I have bad news, I'm afraid,' she said before going on to explain the reason for her visit.

Marco took her to the stable at the back of the farmhouse, and sat her on a bale of straw. He perched next to her.

'I will need to devise a strategy. It won't be easy, but of course we must save the hostages.'

She snuggled into his side, breathed in his comforting scent. Woodsmoke, resin and musk. The essence of Marco.

'I wish Hofmann hadn't arrested those men,' she said.

'And *I* wish that vile Nazi would leave you alone. It worries me that he keeps on finding reasons to visit you.'

'The Allies will be here soon, won't they? The captain will retreat with the rest of the Germans and I'll never see him again.'

Marco drew her into his arms and kissed her. She relaxed into the kiss. Her lips were Marco's. The captain had never kissed her, thank God.

But when Marco smoothed his hands down her body, she stiffened. She still felt violated. Dirty. *Oh, dear Lord.* She thought she'd put what had happened behind her.

'We can't do this,' she said by way of excuse. 'Someone might see us.'

'You're right, *amore*.' He lifted her hand and kissed it. 'You should go back home, darling. It's dangerous for you to be here. Dangerous for us all to be in any one place for too long.'

'You're leaving?' Her vision blurred with sudden tears.

He kissed a tear from her cheek.

'Only for a short time. We'll be back once we've saved the hostages.'

'You have a plan?'

'I think so.' He helped her to her feet. 'I'll stop by the villa once it has all been sorted.'

'You won't tell me?' Her voice choked with more tears.

'Best not. I haven't worked it out yet.' He wrapped his arms around her. 'Don't cry, *amore*. Be brave and I'll see you again soon.'

'I can't bear it,' she sobbed.

'You're strong, Emma. You're the most beautiful, courageous girl in Italy.'

He rocked her until her sobbing ceased.

She touched her hand to the side of his face, gazed deep into his forest-green eyes.

'You're everything to me, Marco. I wouldn't be able to live without you.'

'You won't have to. The fighting will end and we'll have our future together.'

'I hope so.' She hugged him hard, not wanting to let him go.

She cried hot tears all the way down to the valley. It was unlike her to be so emotional, she thought, as she stepped into the villa's garden. It was because she was worried about Marco. She feared for him all the time and today even more so than usual.

22

Rosa paused on the top step of the outside staircase and lifted the tray of freshly baked breakfast loaves from her head. The enticing aroma made her mouth water, and she licked her lips in hungry anticipation.

The distant rumble of aeroplane engines echoed in the air. She stared across the valley in the direction of Siena. It was a cloudless, limpid morning; she could easily make out a big formation of Allied bombers, attacking what she presumed were German troops on the highway.

'*Mamma mia!*' Lucrezia exclaimed from the open doorway.

The *tedeschi* were counterattacking, the flak from their anti-aircraft gunners bright flashes on the skyline.

The boom of explosions resounded. Lucrezia grabbed hold of Rosa's arm, almost making her drop the tray of bread.

One by one, the enemy were shooting down Allied planes. Rosa counted four of them. What looked like small silver balloons opened and drifted down through the melee. Parachutes. The airmen in the stricken craft were attempting to save their lives, although God only knew what horrors awaited them. Her stomach knotted as another plane exploded on hitting the ground. A huge column of black smoke coiled upwards and, even from this distance, her eyes stung.

'I wish we could hurry to the downed men and take them first aid,' Rosa lamented.

'The *bastardi tedeschi* would get there before us, sister.' Lucrezia tugged at her sleeve. 'There's nothing we can do. Come inside, everyone is waiting to eat.'

Rosa got to work slicing the bread. She passed a basketful around the table. Eager hands grabbed a piece each and spread it with the cherry jam she'd made a couple of weeks ago. Dora and Rosa's younger siblings dipped theirs in milk. Rosa, Lucrezia, their parents and grandmother dunked *theirs* in cups of barley coffee. As if by unspoken agreement, no one mentioned the explosions they must have heard, and Rosa and her sister kept quiet about what they'd just witnessed; they didn't want to upset the little ones.

A knock sounded at the door.

'I'll get it.' Babbo rose to his feet. 'Who is it?'

'It's Marco,' came a voice barely above a whisper. 'Will it be safe for me to come in?'

'Absolutely.' Babbo opened the door. 'Is anything wrong?'

Rosa took in Marco's stricken expression, and her blood froze.

Mamma quickly ushered the younger children from the table.

'Hurry up or you'll miss the oxcart for school.'

Marco pulled out a chair and sat himself down.

'Prepare yourself for what I have to say, Rosa.' He creased his brow, obviously searching for the right words.

Rosa's heart skittered a beat.

'What's happened? Is Tom all right?'

Marco shook his head.

'I'm sorry, but he's been captured.'

'*Oh, Dio!*' She clapped a shaky hand to her mouth.

'I went with him and a couple of others to the village of Castglioncello yesterday to move the stash of arms we took from the Germans in Contignano. Our plan was to take the weapons to Chianciano and exchange them for the hostages.' Marco exhaled a deep breath. 'Someone must have ratted on us. We were outnumbered by a squad of Germans.' He looked Rosa in the eye. 'We decided to retreat, but Tom fell as he jumped down from a wall. Before we could get to him, he was arrested.'

'Do you know where he's being held?' Rosa's father asked.

'I'm about to head for Chianciano.' Marco was already rising from his chair. 'When I know for certain he's there, my men and I will try to spring him from the prison.'

Rosa's eyes brimmed with tears.

'Please, don't let him die.'

'He's a POW,' her father said. 'They won't execute him.'

Rosa glanced at Marco, but he'd looked away. He knew full well what the Germans were capable of. It wouldn't matter to them that Tom would be covered by the Geneva Conventions. They'd caught him with the Resistance and might make him pay the ultimate price.

* * *

Her heart heavy with worry, Rosa took a pail of peas outside and sat in the shade of an olive tree to shell them. She lifted her gaze as Lucrezia approached.

'Tom will be fine, you'll see.' Her sister gave her an encouraging smile.

'I hope you're right.' Rosa's throat constricted. 'I don't know what I'd do if... if they execute him.'

Lucrezia gazed into the distance, and Rosa remembered the

despair her sister had clearly felt when she'd told her about Casimir. She'd sat with her in the privacy of their bedroom and tried to break the news to her as gently as she could. Lucrezia had been distraught and hadn't stopped crying for days.

A droning sound suddenly reverberated. Rosa grabbed her sister's hand.

'We should go inside. The Allies are at it again.'

All day long, planes flew over – big formations of up to thirty-six planes – on their way to bomb trains and other military objectives. It was better than the small, swift-flying groups of six or seven fighters that would swoop down in an instant, machine-gunning any vehicle on the road. She remembered the attack she'd experienced over a month ago – she worried every time the children were on their way to and from school. Thank God the summer break would start next week.

Today, the bombing was going on far from the valley. But, even so, relief flooded through her when the 'school bus' rumbled into the courtyard later that afternoon. She'd been immersing herself in her daily routine to keep occupied. Washing, peeling and chopping vegetables, cleaning. Tom was never far from her thoughts, though. Had Marco found out if he was being held in Chianciano? And how would the partisans break him out of prison?

Rosa helped make supper, then got the little ones ready for bed. After hearing their prayers and tucking their sheets around them, she returned to the kitchen to listen to the radio with her family. But there was no news on the Allied approach to Rome. Why was it taking them so long? The American Fifth Army had already joined up with the British Eighth on the Anzio beachhead, she'd learnt. Rosa wished they would hurry up. If Marco and his men failed in their quest to liberate Tom, then the Allies would do so, for certain.

Back in the bedroom, she glanced out of the window as she put on her nightdress. There was a full moon. She shivered; she knew from what had happened last full moon that the Allies would continue bombing all night long.

She got into bed and prayed. *Dear Jesus, please keep Tom safe.* She would go with him to Scotland if he survived, she decided. He was a good man. She wished she'd told him that she loved him. What if he died without knowing? Tears spilled down her cheeks, wetting the pillow, and her body shook with sobs.

'I'm here for you, sister.' Lucrezia pulled her in for a hug. 'Like you were for me when I lost Casimir.'

'*Grazie, cara.*' Rosa breathed out a long sigh. Lucrezia had grown up of late, maybe because she'd suffered losing the man she'd loved. All over the world at war, women were experiencing similar sorrow. How Rosa wished it didn't have to be so.

She fell asleep at last to dream of happier times with Tom. Their kisses. Their lovemaking. Their deep connection.

Shrill screams and the thrumming of engines jolted her awake.

Her heart pounded painfully.

Dora, Ines and Teresa were sitting up in bed, their cries competing with the grumble of low-flying planes.

Rosa and Lucrezia leapt up and hurried to comfort the little girls.

A loud whistling shrilled, growing ever louder and louder.

Rosa stared out of the window. *Oh, blessed Mary!* A shiny egg-shaped object was dropping from the moonlit sky.

'Get under the bed, everyone!' Rosa managed to say before she was drowned out by a deafening explosion.

Should she try to lead them downstairs to a storeroom? But there wasn't time. Another boom, followed by another and another.

'Cover your ears with your hands,' she said, praying that the bedframe would protect them from any falling masonry.

The bridge over the River Orcia was only a couple of hundred metres or so down the road. The Allied pilots must be targeting it, but their aim was poor, Rosa thought.

During a lull, Babbo came to see if they were all right. He agreed that the safest place for them was under the bed. Nonna had managed to scramble beneath hers, as had the boys. He went back to Mamma before the next load of bombs fell. Rosa could only hug Dora close and tell her not to be afraid.

'*Tutto andrà' bene.*' All will be well.

Finally, after what seemed like hours, there was silence. Only the ticking of Rosa's beside clock remained. Five a.m. It would soon be daybreak.

Babbo returned to check on them and suggested they try to get some sleep. They did as he advised and climbed into their beds.

Sometime later, Dora's pleading voice came from right by Rosa's ear.

'Mammina, I'm hungry.'

Rosa flickered her eyes open, surprised that she'd even slept.

There wasn't time to bake any bread, so they dunked *biscotti* in their milk and coffee. Everyone except for Nonna, who'd declared she was too exhausted to get up.

'Four huge bombs have exploded within fifty metres of the *podere*,' Babbo said as he came into the kitchen. He ran a trembling hand through his hair.

Rosa's skin tingled. *We might all have been killed.*

'What will we do if they come back again?' Mamma asked, passing Babbo a cup of coffee.

'I really don't know.' Babbo stared down at the table with vacant eyes.

* * *

The children stayed home from school as their transport never showed up. Mid-morning, Rosa was out in the courtyard sweeping up debris.

The grinding sound of gears changing heralded the arrival of the marchese's three-wheeler lorry, followed by the *fattore* in the estate's tractor, pulling an enormous trailer.

Rosa wiped her hands down her apron and went to greet them.

'We've come to take you and your family back to the villa,' Marchese Ginori said. 'Emma is organising accommodation in our staff quarters. This is the closest farm to the bridge. It's highly likely the planes will come back. I hope you're all all right?'

Rosa forced a smile. 'We're fine.'

'Thank God! You've been extremely lucky but we shouldn't tempt fate a second time.'

When Babbo appeared, he listened to the *padrone*'s proposal, then scratched at his ear.

'What about our animals?' He frowned. 'We can't leave them to fend for themselves...'

'There's room for them in the home farm. You can tend to them there.'

The children helped to pack everything up and, eventually, they'd loaded their wheat, Nonna's precious furniture, their clothes, personal items as well as their chickens, rabbits, pheasants and guinea fowl onto their oxcart and the padrone's trailer.

Every now and then, the dreaded droning drummed overhead.

'Here they are again!' the little ones cried out.

They all took cover under the olive trees until the bomber formations had passed.

Rosa went to stand next to her father, to help lead their oxen and Nino, the donkey – tied to the back of the trailer – down the dusty track. She glanced at her family, who were sitting on benches down the sides of the big cart. Nonna, her lined face pale with tiredness. Mamma, her arms around Dora and Ines. Lucrezia, Teresa and the boys.

With a heavy feeling in her chest, Rosa gave the farmhouse one last look. When would she see it again? And, when she did, would it still be standing?

Focus on what's important, she reminded herself. *We've escaped with our lives.*

Oh, how she prayed that Tom would escape with his life too. And, keeping him in her thoughts, she grasped hold of the leading rope and took the first step of the many that would lead to the Villa Bivio.

23

Emma was in the garden with the Vanini children, keeping an eye on them while Rosa and her sister were helping Tarcisia in the kitchen. She wiped the perspiration from her brow. Although it was early in the day, it was already hot. She gazed across the valley. Their wheat was almost ready for harvesting, but they needed many more hands than were available for the job.

She bit down on her lip, remembering how shortly after Rosa and her family had moved into the staff quarters two days ago, she and her father learnt that the Allies were within ten miles of Rome. They'd hoped that the German retreat would be cut off, thereby saving Tuscany from becoming a battleground. But yesterday, they'd listened to the BBC and found out that the American Fifth Army had entered the city from the south. Papà had been horrified, saying that the American commander, General Clark, had obviously disobeyed orders. The German 10th Army had been allowed to escape capture. The Wehrmacht was heading north and would use all its considerable resources to stop the Allies from following.

Emma leant forward in the garden chair. Events had started to move too quickly for her to fully process. She touched a hand to her belly. Her breasts were feeling sore and enlarged and she needed to pee more often than usual. She hadn't had her monthlies since the end of March and it had dawned on her that she could be pregnant. Her first missed period was probably due to anxiety, she'd thought. Except now she'd missed a second one and could no longer ignore the situation. Her mind couldn't stop racing. If she were pregnant, who was the baby's father?

Yesterday, she'd gone to see the nurse, who'd felt her tummy to judge the size of her womb.

'Baby will arrive soon after Christmas, all going according to plan,' she'd said, glancing at Emma.

Emma had been stunned, although she'd expected to receive confirmation of her pregnancy. She'd sucked in a quick breath and had asked about pre-natal care.

The nurse gave her an information leaflet, advised her to try to eat as much spinach as possible in order not to become anaemic, and to come back and see her in a month.

Emma had only been grateful the woman hadn't questioned her. She knew from experience, though, that the nurse would be discreet. She'd kept the partisans' secrets and would keep Emma's.

My baby will be a secret until I've worked out what to do.

She'd repeated the words to herself like a mantra all the way home. That night, she'd fallen into a deep sleep. She was much more tired than usual, it seemed. She should be rejoicing that she was bringing a new life into the world. Except the world was in a terrible state. An image of Marco came to her. His beautiful forest-green eyes.

Would her baby have eyes like his? She shuddered. Or would they be ice blue like Hofmann's?

The Vanini children were making enough noise to wake the dead as they got ready to run in the egg and spoon race she'd organised. Emma breathed in the heady scent of roses from the flower bed. Footsteps sounded. Rosa was approaching.

'There are three German officers in the courtyard,' she said. 'Your father is dealing with them.'

Emma's spirits fell.

'I'll go and see what they want…'

* * *

Emma was quaking as she hurried out the back door. Would she come face to face with Hofmann? He was the last person she wanted to see.

But the sight of three ordinary-looking men greeted her. They'd arrived in an obviously commandeered Fiat saloon and were getting back into it.

'Who were they?' she asked her father.

'Doctors, from a hospital relocating here from Monterotondo on the outskirts of Rome,' he explained.

'What did they want?'

'They said they required our fortress, but not for the wounded. They'll quarter their injured men in Chianciano hotels. The hospital staff will arrive here this evening, and they'll also need room in the home farm for provisions, etcetera.'

'Oh, dear Lord. We knew the fort would be occupied sooner or later.' Emma grabbed hold of Papà's arm. 'I suppose it's better having medical personnel rather than troops.'

'For the time being.' Her father huffed. 'Come, let's go and see what those children are up to…'

The egg and spoon race had been won by Giulio and the little girls were complaining that it wasn't fair as he was thirteen years old and could run much faster than them.

'I tell you what,' Emma said. 'You can re-run the race and we'll give the little ones a head start.'

'You're so good with them.' Papà's smile went straight to Emma's heart.

How would she tell him about the baby? And, more to the point, that she didn't know who the father was? *He'll be ashamed of me*, she thought. And Marco? How would she break it to him?

He'll be furious and won't want to marry me any more.

She spent the rest of the morning with the children, playing games like hide-and-seek and getting them to perform a makeshift theatrical performance of *Sleeping Beauty*, with Teresa playing the role of the princess.

At around midday, Rosa came outside and pulled up a chair next to Emma's.

'The *fattore* told us about the German hospital staff.' Rosa gave a shudder. 'My family and I will keep well out of their way.'

'As will we.' Emma glanced at Rosa, catching the sad expression on her face.

'I heard what happened to Tom,' she said.

'Marco promised he would try and break him out of prison.' Rosa lowered her voice to a whisper. 'But won't that be terribly dangerous?'

'It most certainly will be. Maybe they should wait until the Allies get here. They'll free him, I'm sure.'

'If he isn't executed beforehand.' Rosa's hands visibly shook. 'That German captain is vengeful. He won't rest until he's made an example of Tom. He must have confessed to taking the arms. Otherwise the *tedeschi* wouldn't have let the prisoners go free.'

'Mammina!' Rosa's daughter, Dora, ran up. 'We did a play of *Sleeping Beauty* and I was one of the fairies.'

'How lovely.' Rosa picked Dora up and kissed her loudly on the cheek. 'I'm very proud of you, darling.'

Emma touched a hand to her belly. Was she carrying a girl or a boy? She'd always longed to be a mother one day. Fate had dealt her such a cruel blow.

* * *

At around 7 p.m., Emma looked out the window. The Germans had arrived, and were filling the courtyard with their Red Cross lorries, leaving them in full view of the Allied planes which continued to fly low overhead.

'I suggested they put their vehicles under cover,' her father told her at supper. 'But their officers are still in Chianciano, and the enlisted men seem incapable of doing anything without their orders.'

'Indeed.' Emma spooned soup into her mouth.

Her appetite had increased of late, part of being pregnant, she supposed. Vittorio served them *panzanella* for their second course. Emma had always loved the cold stew. Made with dampened bread, raw tomatoes, red onions, crunchy cucumbers and bright green basil, its fresh lightness was ideal for hot weather.

Her stomach was still as flat as a board, thankfully.

No one will notice.

24

Rosa pushed open the door to the laundry. Her jaw dropped. Five fair-haired men were standing soaping themselves in the concrete tubs. *Naked as the day they were born.* She took a step back, averted her gaze. Then she turned on her heel, the basket of washing almost falling from her head, and rushed to the kitchen.

Tarcisia looked up from stirring a pot of soup on the stove.

'What's wrong, *cocca*?'

Rosa placed her basket on the floor.

'There... there... are naked young men in the laundry,' she stuttered out the words.

'A company of German sappers arrived last night.' Tarcisia put down her spoon. 'Their captain is staying in one of the guest rooms. But the men will sleep in their vehicles, parked under the trees behind the *fattoria*. The *padrone* agreed they could use the laundry to wash in.'

'*Mamma mia*, someone might have told me,' Rosa said. 'I was so embarrassed I didn't know where to look.'

Tarcisia snorted out a laugh.

'A feast for the eyes, eh? I took a peek earlier. It's been a long time since I saw such fine male flesh.'

Rosa felt her cheeks grow hot. She slapped Tarcisia playfully on the arm.

'I can't believe you said what you just said.' She giggled despite herself.

'I've been a widow these past ten years. Haven't caught a glimpse of you know what since my dear Piero died.' Tarcisia's eyes twinkled. 'He was hung like a horse, I can tell you.'

Rosa's burning cheeks threatened to self-combust.

'Can I do our washing in here?' she asked, quickly changing the topic.

'Of course. Use the spare sink.' Tarcisia winked. 'We can't have you dying of embarrassment, can we?'

'*Grazie.*' Rosa lifted her basket. 'I'm not a prude,' she added. 'It was just a shock.'

'Whatever you say, sweetie.' Tarcisia chuckled. 'I'll leave you to it while I take a short break. *Buon lavoro.* Enjoy your work!'

Rosa filled the sink with warm water, took a bar of soap from the pocket of her apron, and began to scrub at the family's under-clothes. Her thoughts drifted while she worked. It was nearly the middle of June now and there'd been no news of Tom since Marco had told her about his capture. The partisans were keeping well away from the Bivio, it seemed.

She gave a sigh. Just the other day, the Allied commander, General Alexander, had broadcast to the Italian patriots, saying the hour of their uprising had come. They were to risk all and attempt to cut off the German army by destroying roads, bridges, railways and telegraph wires. No mention they might suffer reprisals afterwards. Ordinary workmen with no military experience had been urged to commit acts of sabotage as well. Soldiers and police had been encouraged to desert. Rosa had been amazed when she'd learnt the entire force of Carabinieri in Montepulciano had run off to join the rebels. *What a turn of events!*

The main road heading north that was being used by German convoys had been strewn with propaganda leaflets promising the retreating *tedeschi* 'safe conduct' if they surrendered. They would receive food, medical attention if needed, and be removed from the combat zone.

All the while, Allied planes continued to drone overhead and to swoop down on the valley roads. Thank God for the cellars at the villa, where Rosa and her family took refuge during the air raids. She was only grateful the children gave the impression they'd lost their nervousness and she hoped they would stay that way. The fighting was getting ever closer, though. She hadn't had a proper night's sleep for a long time, she was so nervous. And Tom. Dear, darling Tom. When would she see him again? She sighed once more and stared down at her hands.

25

Emma was in the library with Papà, waiting for the BBC news to start. The German hospital unit had left a week ago, saying a company of paratroopers would soon arrive to occupy the fortress.

Thankfully, the captain of the sappers had turned out to be an entirely different kettle of fish to Hofmann. Unlike Emma's nemesis, he kept his own counsel, availing himself of the guest bedroom assigned to him and spending most of his time out and about with his men. She couldn't help a shudder, though, as she thought about the mines they were laying. It was obvious the Germans expected the Allies to arrive in Tuscany soon.

Emma touched her hand to her belly, praying that her baby would stay safe.

Yesterday, she learnt that the Allies had been held up in the area around the lake of Bolsena about seventy kilometres away, where they'd met with tough German resistance. From all accounts, they were fighting a panzer division, sent to reinforce the Wehrmacht troops already there. The Allies would defeat them, Papà had reassured Emma, but it might delay their advance. In the meantime, they continued to rain down havoc from the skies. That afternoon, they'd bombed the bridge over the Miglia river north of the villa and fighter planes had machine-gunned the road to the fortress, hitting two German lorries.

The radio crackled and the broadcaster announced that the Americans were proceeding towards Grosseto, on the coast, and had taken Pitigliano, on the other side of Monte Amiata.

'They are getting closer.' Emma could hear the excitement in her voice. 'It shouldn't be long now.'

But, when the newscaster went on to say that South African troops, reinforced by the 1st Battalion of the Scots Guards, were still fighting the Germans at Bolsena, her head pounded with despair.

'I really thought we were about to be liberated.'

'Have faith, my darling.' Her father patted her hand. 'Brighter days are on the way.'

'I hope so, Papà.' She got to her feet and went to kiss him good-night. 'I'm off to bed now.' She yawned. '*Buonanotte.*'

She fell asleep immediately, but woke in the early hours to use the bathroom, and then couldn't get back to sleep again. What would the future hold for her and her baby? She'd talked with Rosa yesterday afternoon, and had asked her as diplomatically as she could what it was like to bring up a child on her own.

'I couldn't do it without the help of my family,' Rosa had said.

And therein lay the conundrum. Emma wouldn't be able to raise her baby as a single mother. How would she support them both? Society would shun her and she couldn't shame her father. She had no idea how Marco would react, once she'd told him she was pregnant and didn't know if he was the father. He'd said that he loved her, but did he love her enough to live with the doubt that he could have taken on another man's child? If the worst came to the worst, she would have to go to Rome and live there incognito until she could give the baby up for adoption.

Her eyes grew wet, and her vision blurred. She wiped away the tears with the back of her hand. *Get a hold of yourself, Emma. Stay strong.* Crying wouldn't solve anything.

* * *

'More Germans arrived during the night,' Emma's father said at breakfast the next morning. 'The woodland around us is full of stray units, straggling north.'

'Oh, God, I hope they won't be here for long. I thought we were being sent a detachment of paratroopers...'

'I expect they'll arrive any day now. One of the Red Cross doctors warned me about them, by the way. He said the paratroopers had been at Anzio and had been attacked by an Italian division who'd been fraternising with them only the previous day. The Germans suffered many casualties and now evidently hate all Italians, no matter if they are civilians or military.'

Emma couldn't help a quiver of fear.

She spent the rest of the morning indoors while her father drove to Montepulciano in the three-wheeler lorry to meet with his friends, the Brandinis.

While she was having lunch, the door to the dining room swung open, and Vittorio appeared. Nothing unusual about that, except he wasn't carrying a tray.

'A sharecropper has come to see the marchese,' the butler said. 'He's extremely agitated about something. I told him the *padrone* was away and he asked to see you instead.'

'Bring him through, please.' Emma wiped her mouth with a serviette and got to her feet.

Vittorio reappeared with the *mezzadro* in tow. It was Giovanni, who farmed the *podere* nearest to the villa.

'How can I help you?' Emma asked.

'Three *tedeschi* are at my place, stealing things. They've taken a ham, some cheese, a thousand lire, my wife's wristwatch and some hens.' Giovanni growled out the words. 'I think they're still rooting around in my barn.'

'Oh, no! How terrible!' She made for the door. 'I'll go straight to the *tedesco* sapper captain who is staying here. Hopefully, he can put a stop to this outrage.'

She left Giovanni with Vittorio while she went to the German's room. She rapped at the door.

'Those men certainly don't belong to *my* unit,' the captain muttered after she'd explained. 'It's not my problem, I'm not my brother's keeper...'

'My father is temporarily away. I need help and would be grateful if you'd give it to me.' She stood firm. 'Your countrymen are involved, after all.'

'All right. I'll let you have one of my sergeants. Take him with you to the farmhouse and he'll deal with the troublemakers.'

Soon, Emma found herself climbing into the front seat of a Fiat saloon while Giovanni sat in the back. The sapper sergeant got behind the wheel, turned the key, revved the engine and they tore off down the unmetalled road, leaving a cloud of dust behind.

The sergeant brought the car to a halt in front of a two-storey farmhouse with the ubiquitous outside staircase. A middle-aged woman was sitting on the bottom step, dishevelled and weeping.

Giovanni's wife, Mafalda.

'They've gone.' She hiccoughed a sob. 'They... they... raped me.' She clutched at her hands. 'And then they took what they wanted.'

Emma stared at the woman, aghast. She was in her fifties but looked a lot older. She ran to her and held her in her arms.

'I'll kill them.' Giovanni bunched his fists.

'No need for that,' the sergeant said. 'We punish any of our soldiers who are caught raping civilians. Leave it with us.'

After she'd tried to console Giovanni and his wife as best she could, Emma climbed back into the lorry. Her father was going to be furious about this.

He returned from Montepulciano shortly before supper, and reacted as she'd expected he would. His lips curled with anger and he telephoned the general of the Hermann Goering Division, which had just arrived in Chianciano, to lodge a complaint.

'There's nothing he can do,' Papà said afterwards. 'His *feldpolizei* have their hands full preventing rape and looting in the towns. He can't spare any more men to police the countryside.'

'I never imagined the war would bring such terrible events to our valley,' Emma lamented, her heart aching.

'I'm sorry that I wasn't here to deal with things. You did well, though, my darling. I'm extremely proud of you.'

He held out his arms, and she went into them for a hug.

Later, while their meal was served, she asked her father about his day in Montepulciano. He recounted that he'd had to jump down in the roadside ditch twice on the way there while Allied fighter planes had swooped down over his head.

'What about on the way back?' she asked, relieved he'd made it home in one piece.

'I had a lovely drive in the sunset – the red clover in flower, the green cornfields waving in the breeze, the hedges full of briar roses. Met a few German cars, heavily camouflaged with branches, the troops sitting on the bonnet or roof so they could keep an eye on the sky. But there were no air raids.' Papà paused to collect his thoughts. 'I wonder if the Allies have diverted some of their planes to France?'

Emma exhaled slowly. The British and Americans had landed in Normandy a couple of weeks ago. Both she and her father feared their resources in Italy would be depleted as a result.

'I hope not,' she said. 'How were things in Montepulciano?'

'Everyone is jumpy. The Germans have installed an anti-aircraft battery at the gates of the town.'

'Oh, dear God! Will they evacuate the population?'

'It was rumoured, but hasn't happened.'

Emma shook her head in despair. She could find no words. No words at all.

* * *

The next day, Emma woke to the sound of cannon-fire. She dressed quickly and ran down to the terrace.

Her father had got there before her.

'The Allies are firing at the southern side of the Radicofani hill and Piancastagnaio,' he said. 'The front is very near.'

She didn't know whether to feel happy or afraid, and said as much to Papà.

'All we can do is sit tight, my dear. And hope for the best.'

'I'm scared for Marco and his men, up in the woods.' She pulled at her braided hair. 'At least we can go down to our cellars...'

'I suspect they'll have built themselves a bunker.' Emma's father met her eye. 'Try not to worry, darling girl.'

After breakfast, the sapper captain came to say goodbye. His unit was being moved northwards and he thanked Emma and her father for their hospitality, also expressing his conviction that Germany would not be beaten. The Fuhrer had promised as much and had never failed to keep his promises to his own people.

Emma fervently hoped he was wrong.

She spent the morning helping Rosa with the children,

marvelling at their resilience and ability to laugh and play while the world around them was falling into chaos.

That afternoon, the cannon-fire grew louder. Emma was reading in the library with her father. Without warning, a massive explosion reverberated.

'We're being shelled by the Allies!' Papà sounded incredulous.

Sure enough, Vittorio rushed in to announce that a shell had fallen beside Giovanni's *podere*.

'The poor man,' Emma gasped.

As if what happened to his wife yesterday wasn't bad enough.

At dusk, Emma went to switch on a light. Nothing.

'There's no electricity,' she said.

Her father picked up the telephone.

'The line is dead.'

Their wireless accumulator needed recharging, so they couldn't listen to the radio.

They ate supper by candlelight and, all the while, shelling of the valley continued. The cannon-fire was relentless.

'I hope our farmers are safe. And Marco and his men.' Emma put down her soup spoon. She'd lost her appetite.

'We'll find out in the morning, my dear. In the meantime, we'll just have to have an early night.'

* * *

For hours, Emma's ears rang with the thunder of explosions. She tossed and turned, the sheets wrapping themselves around her body; she barely slept a wink.

After breakfast, she helped with the children out in the garden, organising a new theatrical production, this time of *Snow White*. Rosa and Lucrezia participated as well, playing the principal roles while the kiddies took on the parts of the seven dwarves. They had to improvise, though, and reduce the number to five.

'That was fun,' Rosa said when the play was over. 'You're a natural with them, Signorina Emma.'

'Please. Call me Emma. I enjoyed it too,' she said, glad she'd managed to cheer Rosa up.

'I'll take the children back to our quarters now. You look a little tired, Emma.'

When she explained that she'd found it hard to sleep last night, Rosa said it had been the same for her.

'I fear for our farm and for Tom,' she added. 'Babbo has gone to check on the *podere*. He should be back soon.'

'I hope all is well. I'm trying not to worry about Marco, and you should try not to worry about Tom. Easier said than done, I know.'

Emma left the garden and went to find her father. She discovered him in the living room, drinking vermouth with Hofmann and a heavy-set German colonel, whom the captain introduced as having arrived fresh from the front.

'The Allies have broken through at Orvieto and are halfway to Chiusi,' the colonel was saying. He went on to express how bitter he felt about Hitler's order to spare Rome and not use any of the bridges.

'My men had to swim across the Tiber,' he added. 'There were many casualties.'

Emma felt she had to say something in response. 'How terrible!' Though she left it at that.

Hofmann smirked.

'Did you listen to the news today?' He swept his cold gaze from Emma to her father and back to Emma again.

'We still have no electricity.' Papà shook his head.

'We've started our *vergeltung* retribution against England.' The colonel rubbed his pudgy hands together.

Emma's chest tingled with apprehension.

'What are you talking about?' her father asked with a frown.

'Rocket planes. Without a crew. Carrying the deadliest explosive. We're firing them at London and the south coast.'

'Oh, my God!' Emma gasped.

'When the rockets explode, they bring utter devastation to a radius of over a kilometre,' Hofmann said, taking up the story. 'There are nearly two hundred thousand fatalities in London alone.'

'Apparently, the Lord Mayor has stated there are only five shelters deep enough to be of any use,' the colonel added. 'So they are evacuating the city.'

Emma stared down at her hands. She couldn't bear the look of glee in Hofmann's eyes nor the lecherous glances he was giving her.

* * *

After the Germans had left, Emma tried to get on with the rest of the day. But she felt haunted by what Hofmann and the colonel had recounted. Had they told the truth or was some of it fabricated? There was no way of finding out. If true, it made what was happening in Tuscany seem child's play in comparison.

In the late afternoon, a German billeting officer turned up. Emma's father went to deal with him, and then came up to Emma's bedroom, where she was resting.

'What did that *tedesco* want?' she asked, her courage shrinking at the sight of Papà's grim expression.

'He requires quarters in the villa for the general of his division and a major. And he will take the school buildings for his officers.'

'Oh, dear Lord. Are they those paratroopers we were warned about?'

'I'm afraid so. They will arrive tonight, my darling. All I can suggest is that you and our female staff keep well away from them.'

Fear unfurled in Emma's stomach. Fear not just for herself and her unborn baby, but also fear for everyone she loved. She still hadn't found out how Marco and his men were faring in the shelling. And now that the villa and its surrounding buildings would be inundated with the worst kind of *tedeschi*, it would be far too dangerous for him to stop by.

She mustered a smile for her father so as not to worry him.

'I'll give the Germans a wide berth,' she said.

26

Rosa stepped into the kitchen and lifted the basket of washing from her head.

'There are naked men in the laundry again,' she said to Tarcisia. 'But these ones look like the most ruthless set of ruffians I've ever set eyes upon.'

'A group of paratroopers arrived last night, *cocca*.' Tarcisia creased her brow. 'Their officers have taken possession of the villa, set up a field telephone in the dining room and a bed for their colonel in the marchese's study.'

'The men I saw didn't seem like officers.' Rosa turned on a tap at the spare sink. 'They were too uncouth.'

'Vittorio told me the enlisted men are sleeping rough. They've been lounging about the place since the early hours, complaining about the heat and wearing emerald-green or scarlet bandanas and loin cloths.' Tarcisia huffed. 'The *padrone* has given orders that we should avoid them as much as possible.'

Rosa muttered under her breath. The Germans in the laundry had talked among themselves when she'd gone into the room, and it was clear they were making lewd comments from the way they were eyeing her. She wouldn't go anywhere near them, not even for a bar of gold.

She swished soap flakes into the water and started to scrub.

'Signorina Emma!' Tarcisia's voice made her glance up. 'You look as if you've seen a ghost.'

The marchese's daughter had come into the room.

'The paratroopers have broken into our clinic and have stolen the last of our antiseptics,' she said. 'They've also taken food from the home farm's larder. They're everywhere, wandering about, sleeping under bushes and trees in the garden.' She swept her arm wide. 'I saw two donkeys in the courtyard, obviously robbed, laden with stuff they've taken from our farms. It's clear all discipline has come to an end. Please keep your doors locked.'

'We will,' Tarcisia said, and Rosa echoed her words.

With a sinking feeling in her stomach, Rosa rushed off to warn her family. She found Babbo and Mamma sitting in a miserable heap. They'd been like that since Babbo had returned from their *podere* yesterday – with the news that the roof had been destroyed by shelling and all the belongings they hadn't brought with them to the villa had been looted. How would she tell him about the paratroopers? But tell him she must.

'*Cazzo*,' he swore. 'I want to kill all of them.'

Rosa widened her eyes in shock. She'd never heard her father use such language before.

Mamma put her arms around him, soothingly.

'It will be over soon,' she said. 'We have to be resilient.'

All day long, terrified sharecroppers arrived for help, which the *padrone* was unable to give. All had had their food stores stolen. Some had been turned out of their houses altogether. One had been shot because he'd made a fuss about handing over his pig. Three of their daughters had been raped.

It was all too terrible to imagine.

Rosa spent the morning in the small apartment assigned to her family, playing games with the children to keep them occupied, and fending off requests for them to play outside. Lucrezia helped her as best she could and Rosa couldn't help marvelling at the change in her sister since Casimir had been executed.

Towards midday, Tarcisia came to their door. Rosa opened up and took a step backwards in surprise. The cook had brought a young girl with her.

'This is Silvia,' she said. 'The marchese has asked if you can take her in.' She lowered her voice. 'The girl was left here by her father, who saved her at the last minute from being raped by a couple of *tedeschi* soldiers. He's afraid they'll return to his farm and will try again.'

'Oh, blessed Jesus,' Rosa gasped. 'Of course she can stay with us.' It was on the tip of her tongue to ask how the farmer had managed to prise his daughter away from the rapists, but she decided to save her questions for later.

Lucrezia took charge of the traumatised girl. Silvia was only twelve years old and had been milking a cow when the Germans had grabbed her, Rosa subsequently discovered. They'd only let Silvia go when her father had come into the cowshed and had bribed them by saying he'd take them to where he'd hidden his prized hams and cheeses.

The heat of anger flushed through Rosa. War had brought such tragedies with it. What was the point? As far as she could see, it was innocent civilians who bore the brunt of the suffering.

In the afternoon, the weather broke and it began to rain. That made it easier to keep the children indoors, and more so when the air throbbed ever louder with deafening explosions.

'The *bastardi* Germans must have moved their big guns closer,' Babbo growled. 'The Allies are sure to respond.'

* * *

In the morning, after a sleepless night listening to gunfire and worrying about Tom – who was still in prison, as far as she knew – Rosa learnt from her father that the paratroopers had placed their batteries all around the villa, machine-guns behind the parapet of the lower garden, and they'd even mined the road to Chianciano.

Soon, the *tedeschi* began to fire on the Allied positions across the valley and it wasn't long before the Allies responded in kind.

Heavy artillery boomed nearby and explosives whooshed overhead.

Icy sweat beaded Rosa's forehead and she held Dora close.

A loud knocking came at the door.

'Everyone must come underground!' Orazio, the *fattore*, shouted. 'Shells are landing on the fortress hillside. It's too dangerous to stay here.'

Rosa picked Dora up and ran. She ran as if the hounds of hell were at her heels, her family and Silvia following behind.

In the cellars, they found the *padrone*, Emma and the house-hold staff blocking up the windowpanes with sandbags. The villa had been built into the side of the hill, and the cellar had high windows on the side facing the valley.

'The children can help,' Emma said. 'It will keep them from boredom.'

How could they be bored with everything that was happening? Rosa asked herself.

But her father had suggested they keep the severity of the situation from them so they wouldn't be scared.

Of course they would be bored, she thought.

They turned it into a competitive game, with the children reporting if they could see any daylight around the edges of the bags. Those that discovered a chink were given a piggyback ride around the cellar by Babbo as a reward.

* * *

The day dragged on with sporadic shelling on both sides. A lull came in both the shelling and the rain, so Rosa took the children outside to play by the door down to the cellar.

She shaded her eyes with a hand.

In the distance, five tanks were making their way along the winding valley road.

'They're Allied Sherman tanks.' It was the marchese, who had come to stand next to her.

Rosa inhaled a hopeful breath.

'Surely they will get to us before too long?'

'The Germans have placed batteries all around, my dear, and the roads are mined. I had a word with the paratroopers' colonel a short while ago. Allied troops did, indeed, break through about a mile away, but were soon driven back. Now they're circling, trying to come down the hill track from Sarteano, apparently, but there are German batteries there too.'

As if on cue, the shelling started up again and the explosions rang in her ears.

Crestfallen, Rosa gathered the children to her and hurried them back underground.

That night, the cacophony of explosions echoed without let-up.

At one point Dora grabbed Rosa's trembling hand.

'If the bangs get louder still, they won't hurt us, will they, Mammina?' The child trembled.

Rosa tried to reassure her. 'We're safe here, sweetheart.'

A sudden scream came from Nonna.

'We're being bombed!'

Rosa leapt up and rushed across the flagstone floor.

A sack of bread, which had been placed between two vats of wine, had fallen on top of her grandmother's head.

Mamma had got there before Rosa, and was rocking her sobbing mother-in-law in her arms, telling her they weren't being bombed at all, while Babbo stood helplessly by.

'We should try and get some sleep,' he said after his mother had calmed down. 'Tomorrow will probably be a long day.'

* * *

The following morning, during the first lull in the shelling, a tragic procession of sharecroppers began to arrive. People who'd been sheltering in the woods. Men too old for the draft. Women and children. About sixty more mouths for the *padrone* to feed and shelter. Rosa's heart went out to them all.

An old grandmother from a neighbouring farm, a friend of Nonna's, collapsed with exhaustion.

Babies whimpered from hunger.

The older children whispered tales to Rosa's daughter and her young siblings, frightening them with gory stories of rape and pillage.

'Are the Germans really going to come and gobble us up?' Dora asked Rosa, plaintively.

'Of course not, *cocca*,' Rosa said.

Tarcisia and her helpers came down from the kitchen with hot barley coffee, bread and milk.

Emma and the *padrone* then brought a gramophone player downstairs and they all sang along to 'Tulipan' and 'Rosamunda'.

But the happy interlude didn't last long. A massive explosion boomed too close for comfort, the walls of the cellar vibrated and the glass in one of the windows crashed outward, causing the children to scream and cry. Rosa and the others comforted them as best they could.

When another lull came, a German sergeant rushed in.

'You need to make room for our troops,' he said.

Rosa glanced around. The vaulted underground chambers were already filled to overflowing.

Before the *padrone* could remonstrate with the sergeant, an officer appeared.

'You must get out, marchese,' he barked. 'We require your cellars. If you go now, you might be able to get out of range before shelling starts again.'

Rosa couldn't believe what she was hearing. How could they leave? Where would they go?

'There's nothing else to be done,' Emma said to her as a crowd of terrified people besieged her father. 'Papà and I discussed this eventuality earlier. Everyone must go either to Chianciano or Montepulciano. Wherever they have friends who will take them in. They should only take what they're able to carry with them. The clothes on their backs and some food.'

'Isn't the road mined?' Fear twisted Rosa's stomach.

'Only the sides. If we stick to the middle we should be fine.'

Emma hadn't met Rosa's eye.

Was she deliberately trying to sound more positive than she felt?

Whatever the case, they were caught *tra l'incudine ed il martello* – between the anvil and the hammer.

'*Va bene,*' Rosa said. All right.

27

Rosa's stomach jittered as Babbo lifted Dora onto his shoulders. Everyone grabbed what they could – sacks of bread, bottles of water. The marchese stood by the cellar steps, making sure people made an orderly exit.

'You must spread out when you get to the road,' he said, 'so as not to attract the attention of Allied aeroplanes.'

Outside, Rosa felt exposed. The cellars had been a safe haven in comparison to the harsh reality of acrid smoke stinging her eyes, distant gunfire ringing in her ears, and the smell of sulphur from exploded shells. It was mid-morning, and the sun beat down mercilessly. There would be no shade at all in the middle of the road.

She and the others scurried out through the villa's back gates.

'Mammina, where are we going?' Dora chirped from Babbo's shoulders.

The Vaninis had no friends or family they could stay with, neither in Chianciano nor Montepulciano. Rosa chewed at her lip.

'We're going on a big adventure, darling. And I need you to be very brave.'

'Yes, Mammina. I'll try.'

Rosa offered Nonna her arm.

'*Forza, coraggio*, Nonna.' Have strength and be of good courage.

'I'm composed of stronger stuff than you think, my dear. I'll manage.'

'*Brava*, Nonna.' Rosa squeezed her hand.

The long, straggling line of people made slow progress. Babies were being carried. Older children clutched at their mothers' skirts. Elderly men and women stumbled.

They passed German sappers laying yet more mines, who looked up at them in evident astonishment.

Without warning, a foul stench hit the back of Rosa's throat. It was much worse than the smell from the annual pig slaughter – it filled the air, lodging in her mouth, clinging to her tastebuds. Unburied German corpses had been left to rot in the hot sun.

She gagged and saw that up ahead, Emma was retching.

Mamma mia. Why haven't they collected their dead?

She supposed there hadn't been time.

All around her, people were placing themselves between the horrific bodies and their children, shielding them from the grisly sight.

Babbo lifted Dora down from his shoulders.

'What's that stink?' she asked.

'Just some meat that's gone off,' Babbo said. 'It's not very nice, so don't look.'

They walked on, and the echo of shellfire pounded in their ears.

From time to time, a child would cry out they couldn't walk so fast, and the adults would pick that *piccolino* up and carry them for the next hundred yards or so.

Every stumbling, weary step was taking them farther away from the shelling and closer to what was to come.

* * *

About an hour later, Rosa and the others crested the top of the hill above Chianciano. The spa town spread out below, its swanky hotels glimmering in the midday sun.

'We should split up here,' the marchese announced. 'My daughter and I are heading for Montepulciano. If you're planning on going there, you're welcome to join us. But we've decided to make our way across country. The main road will be too dangerous as it's probably being shelled.'

Babbo consulted with Rosa, Mamma and Nonna, then said, 'We'll go with you, *padrone*.'

Although Chianciano was closer, it was infested with *tedeschi*. Montepulciano would be a safer bet.

About sixty members of the party chose likewise. They trudged onwards and, as soon as they'd put a ridge between them and the shelling, the marchese suggested they should take a break.

Dora and Rosa's siblings crumpled, exhausted, to the ground.

There was a murmur of conversation and those carrying bread and bottles of water shared them with their neighbours.

'We've left all our animals to the mercy of the *tedeschi*,' Babbo muttered. 'I doubt I'll see our precious oxen and donkey again.'

'The marchese is in the same boat.' Rosa touched her hand to her father's arm. 'The important thing is that we've succeeded in escaping.'

'Not everyone,' Mamma said. 'That old grandmother who arrived the other day was unable to walk. She stayed behind with her daughter. I hope they've found somewhere to shelter...'

Rosa glanced at Nonna. She'd managed to keep up thus far, but there was still a long way to go.

What would they do if she couldn't carry on?

It wasn't long before they set off again, scrambling along a rough track, up and down steep gullies through the forest.

The children were extremely tired, their footsteps faltering. The adults carried them when the trail became too difficult. And it wasn't only the children who were being carried. Some of the old folk too. Rosa took Dora from her father, and he lifted his mother onto his back.

'Mammina, when will we get there?' Dora asked.

'Soon, *cocca*. Soon.' It would still be many hours before they reached Montepulciano. Rosa sighed to herself. 'Why don't we play a game and count the birds we can see...'

The game kept the children occupied until they left the woods behind. But, when they arrived in the unforested open country-side, filled with wheat fields along the bluff above the main road, shells burst below them with a deafening noise.

'I'm scared,' Dora cried out.

'We have to go on, dearest. We'll be safe, I promise.'

Please, God, let my words be true.

Rosa startled as the rumble of an aeroplane engine drowned out the sound of crickets in the bushes by the sides of the road.

Mamma mia, a plane had dived down and was heading straight for them!

'Quick, everyone, run and hide in that field,' the marchese shouted.

Rosa grabbed Dora with one hand and Ines with the other, pulling them along with her.

They dropped to their bellies in between two rows of tall wheat, hoping the high stalks would hide them. All around them, others were doing the same.

Rosa's pulse pounded as she remembered being fired on by that Allied plane. The ricochet of the stones. The trumpets of mud. The cut on her cheek. She covered her face with her hands.

'Keep your head down, girls!' She could sense the panic in her voice.

'It's all right, Mammina, the plane is leaving.' Dora tugged at her skirts.

Rosa risked a peek between her fingers. Sure enough, the aircraft had tipped its wings and was heading back up into the sky. Her body sagged in relief.

The *padrone* gave the order for them to set off again. On and on they trudged, taking the unmetalled road to save time. The heat of the afternoon brought them out in a sweat, made worse by the biting insects so prevalent at that time of the day.

Nonna was faltering and spent more time on Babbo's back than off it. She'd lost weight lately, her frame sparrow-like, but even so she must have been a burden which Babbo was bearing stoically, kilometre after kilometre until finally, after about four hours, they arrived at the chapel of San Bagio, at the foot of the Montepulciano hill.

Sitting in a ditch for a breather with the rest of the party, Rosa gazed at the long line of cypresses climbing the slopes to the golden-hued city walls. A steep road cut through the trees, leading to the town perched on a ridge over six hundred metres above sea level. She exhaled a slow breath – it would be another exhausting hike.

'Look!' Dora nudged her.

Rosa squinted. A group of people were coming towards them. Followed by another group, and then another.

The marchese and his daughter went to greet them, and shortly returned to Rosa and the others with their faces wreathed in smiles.

'The citizens of Montepulciano have come to help us,' Emma said. 'They were watching our progress from the ramparts, saw how we were struggling. They've brought water and will give us a hand to get up the hill.'

Rosa's eyes were drawn to the final cohort of people approaching. There was something familiar about them. Her chest fluttered. Could they be men from Marco's formation of partisans?

Oh, my God. Yes!

Tom was coming towards her, and then Dora was running to him, and he was twirling her around, and Rosa was so overcome with emotion she found herself rooted to the spot.

He'd reached her before she knew it, put her daughter down and wrapped her in his strong arms.

'Dearest Rosa, thank God you are safe.' He kissed her.

'I've been so worried about you, Tom,' she said, her heart overflowing with love for him.

'I've been worried about you too. So very much.'

'When did you get out of prison?'

'I managed to escape a couple of days ago,' he said. 'I'll tell you about it later.'

'Where's Marco?' Rosa looked around for him.

Tom's expression turned sombre.

'He went with a group on a secret mission yesterday, but hasn't returned.'

'He'll be all right, won't he?' Her chest squeezed with worry.

'I hope so.' Tom bent and lifted Dora onto his shoulders. 'Come, you and your family can stay in the partisans' safe house. There's more than enough room for you all.'

28

After supper, when her younger siblings and Dora had been bathed and put to bed, Rosa sat with Tom and Babbo, sipping red wine at the wooden table in the partisans' safe house kitchen. Lucrezia, Mamma and Nonna had said they were exhausted and had opted for an early night, but Rosa wanted to spend more time with Tom and Babbo said he was curious about the Scotsman's imprisonment. Rose gazed at the copper pots on the walls and enjoyed the feel of the cool terracotta-tiled floor beneath the soles of her aching feet.

'Were you hurt when you fell as you were captured, Tom?' she asked.

'I only grazed my knee. But the Germans were on me before I could get to my feet.'

Rosa touched her hand to his. 'What was the prison like?'

'It was a horrible place, a military barracks on the outskirts of Chianciano. I noticed a honeycomb of small holes denting the bricks of a wall in the courtyard, which must have been made by bullets. It was probably the execution site for political prisoners.'

'*Mamma mia*,' Rosa gasped. 'How awful!'

'Indeed.' Tom nodded. 'I was dragged up a flight of stairs to a landing and a door labelled *Kapitän Hofmann*. The captain barked at me in Italian, asked who I was. I answered in English, said I was a POW.'

'Did the captain speak English?' The question came from Babbo.

'He insisted we spoke Italian. We had quite the conversation. He asked me how I came to be in civilian clothes, who helped, demanding names and so on.' Tom took a sip of his wine. 'I kept on giving ambiguous responses, not wanting to give any information that could incriminate my friends. Every time, Hofmann hit me a jolting blow under the base of my skull with the back of his hand.'

Rosa gave another gasp. 'What a cruel man!'

'You can say that again.' Tom squeezed her fingers.

'What happened next?' Babbo asked.

'The interrogation went on and on and my head was spinning from the blows, but I managed not to reveal anything. Eventually, Hofmann had me escorted to the cells. They locked me up in a dirty, dark, depressing chamber. A plank of wood had been attached to one wall, and there was only a bale of stinking straw and two torn blankets.'

It was Rosa's turn to squeeze Tom's fingers.

'My poor love,' she said. 'What happened next?'

'I managed to get some sleep. Morning came and I heard church bells ringing for early mass. A sergeant and two privates marched me to the toilet block, then to a water pump in the courtyard for a quick wash. I was hungry but, when I asked for some breakfast, they laughed contemptuously.'

'*Bastardi*,' Babbo muttered.

'Indeed. They took me back to Hofmann and, for about half an hour, he asked me the same questions as the day before,' Tom said. 'When I carried on answering in vague terms, Hofmann changed tack, told me he could have me shot as a spy, without trial and without delay, along with the hostages.

'It was then that I realised I had to say something. I couldn't let those innocent people die. But, before I could try and make up a story that wouldn't incriminate anyone, Hofmann laughed. It was a cruel laugh. He told me they'd actually released the hostages after the partisans had left the arms, that it was obvious I was one of them, and he wanted names.'

'*Caspita*.' Good heavens. Rosa widened her eyes. 'How did you respond?'

'I said that I didn't know any of them. I just happened to be in the wrong place at the wrong time. I'd found a comfortable stable in that village and fed myself by stealing chicken eggs and picking fruit off the trees.

'Hofmann raised his hand to hit me, but a sergeant entered. He spoke to the captain in German, of course, so I don't know what was said. Hofmann gave orders for me to be escorted back to my cell and, to my great relief, I never saw him again.'

'Did you find out why that was?' Babbo asked.

'Yes. A guard let slip that a colonel had arrived from the front, and Hofmann had been seconded to his staff and transferred to Montale.'

'So, those poor villagers are playing host to a contingent of Germans,' Rosa said, sighing. 'I hope treatment of you improved in the prison?'

'It did. My cell was swept out and I was provided with clean sheets and a pillow. I was told to work in the cookhouse and have my meals there. But it was rumoured I'd soon be sent by train to a camp in Germany, so I decided I had to attempt an escape.'

'Good for you!' Babbo exclaimed.

'The cook was a local man, Bruno, and after a few days had gone by, I found out he'd been approached by Marco, who'd bribed him to assist me.'

'And did he do so?' Rosa asked.

'Yes, but it had to be done in such a way that no finger of blame would be pointed at him. I remembered there was a door at the back of the kitchen storeroom and asked if it opened onto the road. When Bruno confirmed that it did so, we cooked up a plan, no pun intended.'

Rosa couldn't help laughing.

'What did you do then?' she asked.

Tom's eyes sparkled.

'Between us, we decided that I would tie him up, so it would look as if I'd jumped him and taken him prisoner. Then I would make good my escape. Which is what I did.'

'Had you managed to get a message to Marco?' Babbo asked.

'He'd spoken with Bruno, and was waiting for me on the pavement outside. We hid and then, under the cover of darkness, made our way to this safe house.'

'What an incredible story.' Rosa's face broke into a smile. 'I wish Marco was here, and I'm sure Emma wishes it too.'

'He'll be back before we know it, my darling. Don't worry!'

'Marco can look after himself,' Babbo said, yawning. He got to his feet. 'I think I'll go to bed now. *Buonanotte*, you two.'

Rosa wished her father goodnight in return. She was grateful to be alone with Tom at last.

He poured her another glass of red wine and she sipped it, mulling over how she and the others had climbed up to the town earlier in a triumphant procession, children on shoulders, old folk carried, while the Montepulcianesi contended with each other to offer hospitality. The marchese and his daughter had acted as billeting officers, assigning the 'refugees' to various hosts. Rosa had learnt that the *padrone*'s friends, the Brandinis, had taken them in, as well as Marco's parents.

Rosa had been with Tom when he'd told them about Marco. Emma's face had turned ashen, and Rosa's heart had wept for her. She wondered about the secret mission he'd gone on, but as it was 'secret' she couldn't ask about it.

'I couldn't bear it if I were parted from you again, Tom,' she said.

He took her hand and kissed it.

'There's something I need to tell you, my love. I found out that my old battalion is part of the Allied advance heading this way.'

'And?' Rosa gave an involuntary shiver. She could guess what was coming.

'If I can convince them that I tried desperately to break through German lines and reach them, that I did useful war work with the partisans, they might let me fight on with them.'

'Why would you want to do that?' Her voice trembled.

'Rosa, if I don't report to them, I'll be considered a deserter. I'm still a soldier, I haven't been discharged. Either I carry on fighting in Italy, or they send me back home and deploy me elsewhere. I could be sent to France, for instance...'

Her chest shrank with disappointment.

'I thought that, once the front had headed north, you would come back to the *podere* and help Babbo rebuild.'

'There's nothing I would have liked better, my darling.' He lifted her onto his lap and kissed her. 'But there's still a war on and I have to do my duty.'

'I see.' She nodded, making a desperate effort not to burst into tears.

She snuggled into him, breathed in his warm male scent. Desire flamed through her, hot and sweet.

'Please, make love to me, Tom.' She longed for him so much.

He kissed her again.

'Marco and I are sharing a room. I never thought I'd be glad he isn't back yet, and I'm not exactly, but we'll have some privacy if that's what you really want.'

'I do.' She got to her feet and held out her hand. 'But I need to wash first. It was a long, sweaty walk to get here.'

He took her to the bathroom and turned on the tap in the big iron tub.

'I'll join you,' he said.

She undressed and so did he, their eyes locked.

'I'll get in first.' She clambered into the bath.

He got in after her, sat behind with his legs stretched out on either side.

'Would you like me to wash your hair, Rosa?'

'That would be nice. *Grazie.*' She leant back while he reached for a bottle of shampoo someone had left on the rim of the tub.

'Relax, *amore.*' He lathered her long tresses, then massaged her scalp.

'Mmm. That feels wonderful.'

'Lean forward so I can rinse out the suds.'

She did as he asked, then manoeuvred herself around to face him, wrapping her legs around his waist. Smiling, she eased herself onto him.

He moaned with obvious satisfaction.

They rocked together, their pleasure building, until they both cried out their release.

Giggling like schoolchildren, they rinsed each other off and climbed out of the bath.

'Should I go to my room now?' She dried herself and reached for her clothes. They were dirty and she hoped to borrow some clean ones from someone tomorrow. She kept the bath towel wrapped around her and headed for the door.

'I can't let you go so soon,' Tom groaned. 'Stay with me for a while, please, my darling.'

'*Va bene.*' She smiled. All right.

His bed was narrow, so he spooned himself around her and soon they were making love again. Afterwards, she cuddled into him, caressing his strong shoulders and peppering kisses on his jaw.

'*Ti amo*, Tom.' She came right out with it. 'And, when the war is over, I'll marry you and move to Scotland with Dora, if that's what you still want.'

He let out a whoop and his face broke into the biggest of smiles.

'Of course I still want that. I love you and Dora to the depths of my soul. I'll give you a happy life, I promise.'

'I know you will.' She stroked his soft beard and gazed deep into his kind blue eyes. 'Remember you said we'd come back and visit Tuscany regularly? I hope that's what we'll do.'

'I'll do everything in my power to make that happen, my love.'

'*Grazie.*' She nestled into his warmth. He was a good man, and she loved him.

Tiredness threatened to overcome her – it had been such a long day.

'I should go to my room now. Dora might wake up and ask for me.'

Rosa and her daughter were sharing with her sisters, as usual.

Tom held her close, kissing her with such love that she almost cried.

'*Buonanotte*, Rosa. Good night. This war will end eventually, and we'll be together for the rest of our lives.'

There was certainty in his voice, and she prayed his confidence wasn't misplaced.

'*Buonanotte*, Tom. I'll see you in the morning.'

Of that, she was sure. The Allies were nowhere near Montepulciano, by all accounts. She'd still have time with him, before she had to let him go.

29

Emma rolled over and glanced at her watch on the bedside table. *Ten a.m.!* She'd slept for over twelve hours, despite her worry for Marco. When Tom had said he'd gone on a secret mission and hadn't returned, she'd waited for him to qualify his statement with the word 'yet'. His reassurances that Marco would be fine hadn't rung true.

Emma felt cold all over, notwithstanding the summer heat.

She got out of her bed in Agata and Edoardo Brandini's guest room, and took off the nightdress Agata had lent her. After a quick wash in the wall-mounted basin, she picked up the pretty cotton dress with puffed sleeves, left behind by the Brandinis' twenty-five-year-old daughter, Luisella, when she'd moved to Rome. Agata had given it to her last night. Emma slipped it on and headed downstairs.

In the dining room, she found her father drinking coffee and smoking.

'There you are! Did you sleep well, my darling?' He gave her a smile.

'I did, Papà. Like a log, actually.' She kept her worry about Marco to herself and pulled out a chair.

'I went for a stroll earlier,' Papà said. 'I talked to a few of the townspeople. All are afraid. Shops are closed. The Germans have helped themselves to practically all the food reserves...'

'When did they ever not do that?' She frowned.

A maid appeared with a pot to refill Papà's cup, then went to fetch another cup so that Emma could have some coffee too.

'Where is everyone?' She glanced around.

'Marco's parents have gone to ask for foodstuffs in nearby farms. Agata and Edoardo went to the town hall.'

The maid returned with a cup for Emma, and she poured herself a coffee.

'Have you managed to find out the latest news about the Allies?' she asked her father.

'Edoardo has a clandestine radio. Unfortunately, the Germans have retaken Chiusi, and fierce fighting is going on in the district.'

As if to confirm his statement, gunfire echoed in the distance. Emma's hand trembled as it was followed by a barrage from the German batteries lower down the Montepulciano hill.

She spent the morning trying to read Aldous Huxley's *Brave New World*, which she found in the Brandinis' library, but the book lay open on her lap while her thoughts flitted through myriad possibilities of where Marco could be and what he could be doing.

When his parents returned with milk and fresh vegetables – bell peppers, green beans and tomatoes – they said they were desperately worried about him too.

'I hope he hasn't gone back to the villa,' Orazio muttered. 'It would be just like him to take it into his head to try and help us. He wouldn't have known that we'd left.'

'If he's there, he'll be in desperate danger,' his mother said. 'It's right in the front line.'

'He'll know that, surely.' Emma tried to sound positive. 'I hope he's gone to ground somewhere and is waiting for the right moment to rejoin his men.'

Shortly before lunch, the Brandinis came back, saying they'd spent a frustrating morning dealing with requests from German officers for cars, tyres, bicycles – anything they could use in their upcoming retreat. Edoardo told Emma and her father that their lieutenant had laughed when Edoardo had dug his heels in.

'What's the point of hanging onto things? Your whole town will be flattened by the Allies in a few days' time,' the German had sneered.

'Rumours are spreading like wildfire,' Edoardo went on to say. 'Some believe the *tedeschi* will try and defend Montepulciano, that they'll knock down the houses on both sides of the main street so they can pass through with their tanks.' He shook his head. 'We might have to evacuate the entire place.'

Emma had no appetite for lunch when they sat down at the table. But she had to eat for the sake of her baby. She forced down a bowl of minestrone soup – the tinned spinach in it was a good source of iron – and then made the excuse that she was still tired from the gruelling walk yesterday. She went up to her room on the first floor of the palazzo. Her balcony overlooked the rolling green hills of the Val d'Orcia. In the distance, Monte Amiata punctuated the skyline.

Had Marco gone to meet up with the partisans there? Her father had said they were getting weapons drops from the Allies.

She lay down on her bed and tried to take a nap. But agitation worried at her and she couldn't settle. Despite her tiredness, she decided to go out for a stroll. It might relax her enough to rest properly when she returned.

Downstairs, it occurred to her that maybe she was being stupid going out on her own. She went to find Papà, searched for him in the living room, knocked on his bedroom door, but it appeared he'd gone out as well.

She stepped through the heavy oak door. Outside, the narrow cobblestoned street was eerily silent. *Where was everyone?*

She walked on until she came to the steps of a church. There, the road widened out a little.

The space was lined with people staring open-mouthed at something.

Oh, dear God, a body was hanging from a lamppost.

Bile rose in Emma's throat. The body was terribly mutilated, the face beaten to a pulp. Totally unrecognisable. Mangled flesh, purple bruises, blood-matted hair.

Marco's hair.

Horror crawled across Emma's skin.

A priest stood next to the man, giving the last rites.

He wasn't dead yet.

German soldiers prodded the cleric with their rifles, urging him to get a move on.

Emma found herself moving forward, her eyes searching for anything that would identify the poor soul.

The victim's eyes were staring blankly and his tongue had protruded from his mangled mouth.

Emma's stomach hurled, and she retched.

He had the same build as Marco.

Firm hands grabbed her.

'Come away from here, Emma,' her father said. 'This is not a place we want to be.'

'It's Marco,' she sobbed.

'What makes you think that?'

'His... his... hair. And his... his... figure.'

'It's not Marco. This man has been accused of shooting a German soldier in Chiusi. I doubt Marco could have gone there.'

'Are you sure?' She could hear the hysteria in her voice.

'Absolutely. Marco is safe. You'll see. This poor fellow is not him.'

She allowed her father to lead her away from the scene of horror, praying his reassurances were true.

'Where are Marco's parents?' she asked as they made their way back up the street.

'Someone took them to visit the Vaninis at the partisans' safe house.'

'Thank God they didn't see what I just saw. They might have thought the same thing that I did.'

'Indeed. I'm sorry you witnessed such horror, dear girl.' He handed her his handkerchief to wipe away her tears.

In bed that night, Emma mulled over the day's events. The horrific hanging had brought home to her that she'd done the right thing when she'd given herself to Hofmann. She placed her hands on her belly. Her sacrifice had saved lives; it had been worth it. Even if Marco reacted badly when she eventually told him.

Oh, Marco, where are you? Come back to me, my love.

The corpse was left to hang for over twenty-four hours as an 'example' to the population. The entire town appeared haunted by it. But Emma's spirits were lifted when news came through that the Allies had apparently retaken Chiusi. In the evening, the German batteries below Montepulciano fell silent, raising every-one's hopes.

Next day, at midday, the radio announced the capture of Sarteano. There was a lot of gunfire that night, which she learnt was directed at Chianciano. Despite her worry for Marco, she managed to sleep through it. The tiredness of pregnancy overcame her fear.

In the morning, she listened to the radio with the others. News from abroad was good. The Allies had occupied Cherbourg in France. But Emma's chest constricted when she learnt that their troops had been held up on the shores of Lake Trasimeno, twenty-five kilometres away from Montepulciano, and the Germans were back in Chiusi, battling the Allies in the streets of the town. She went to the balcony and stared into the distance. Smoke obscured the horizon. Men were dying out there. Her body tensed at the horror of it all.

That evening, she learnt that Castiglione and Rocca d'Orcia had fallen to the Allies and they had reached the Astrone Stream, between Chianciano and Chiusi. The roar of shelling hurt her ears as the fighting was getting ever closer. Would she and the others have to go down to the cellars?

They managed to sleep in their beds that night, but at breakfast the next morning everyone seemed nervous and mindful they might have to shelter underground before too long.

Emma dunked a piece of jam-covered bread in her coffee. She was chewing it when the Brandinis' maid appeared.

'There's a young man at the door,' she said. 'His name is Marco.'

Emma jumped to her feet so quickly her chair fell backwards.

'Show him in, please,' Edoardo Brandini said.

Marco's parents got to him before Emma did, hugging and kissing him.

She stood back, overcome with sudden reticence.

His clothes were torn and he was covered in dirt.

Emma almost forgot to breathe.

'Is everything all right?' she managed to ask.

'More than all right.' A wide grin spread across his face. 'Hofmann is dead.'

'Oh, my God.' Emma swayed slightly. *Could it be true?* 'How did it happen?' She sounded disbelieving to her own ears.

Her father picked up the chair and she lowered herself onto it.

Marco sat next to her, after accepting Agata Brandini's offer of a coffee.

Edoardo Brandini asked him to tell them all about Hofmann's demise, and everyone listened agog while Marco recounted the tale.

Apparently, a spy had told him that a squad of Germans had been examining an abandoned farmhouse on the ridge between Le Faggete and Chianciano. Intelligence had come through that they were searching for suitable gun emplacements.

Marco acted immediately, placing four partisans at the highest point of the ridge, and then deploying about twenty men in a defensive formation on the slope below, spacing them thirty metres or so apart and making sure each man hid himself well in the thickets.

He ordered them to keep as still and as quiet as they could, told them that in no circumstances must they open fire until he gave the signal. Marco's eyes glowed with excitement as he clarified that, in the meantime, they were to hold themselves '*pronti a scattare al mio cenno*', ready to spring at my nod.

He sent orders to the four men on top of the ridge to open spasmodic fire on the abandoned farmhouse. They did so, and it wasn't long before all the Germans began to head up the slope. They moved slowly and carefully, firing random rifle shots and machine-gun bursts as they went.

Marco's team fired back, but on his orders they did so at long intervals, to give the impression they were conserving ammunition.

Then he gave his signal – rapid machine-gun fire – and the rest of his men attacked, hurling grenades and killing several *tedeschi*.

Hofmann, who was leading the German advance, could do nothing to stem the confusion or bring order from the chaos.

Marco jumped from behind the bush where he was hiding and yelled, '*Partigiani all'assalto!*'

They charged the enemy, firing as fast as they could. Marco said he believed they killed about fifteen of them, including Hofmann, and more fell as they stumbled down through the forest.

A chill spread through Emma, and she rubbed at her arms.

'Are you sure he's dead?'

'Very sure, *amore*. I went up to him to check. He was riddled with bullets and his cold blue eyes were staring sightlessly up at the sky.' Marco leant across the space between them, took her hands. 'You won't need to worry about him any more, darling.'

Emma nodded. Marco didn't know the half of it.

'You did well, my boy,' her father said.

'I'm proud of you, son,' Orazio added, and Marco's mother echoed the sentiment.

'Afterwards, I went to the Bivio.' Marco smiled, then winked at Emma. 'It took me a couple of days to get there as I had to avoid German patrols. I realised I'd missed you when I snuck down to the cellars and found them empty.'

'So the *tedeschi* have gone?' Emma's father asked.

'Appears so. The villa is still standing, by the way. Shells have fallen in the gardens and on the stables, but so far the house is untouched.'

'Wonderful news.' Papà shook his hand. 'We've been worried about you, dear boy. I'm glad you've made it back to us safe and sound.'

Emma longed for Marco to hold her. Longed to have some time with him on their own, just the two of them.

'I can't stay long,' he said. 'There are still too many Germans in this town and I'm a wanted man.'

'Where will you go?' she asked.

'To the partisans' safe house. I'll have to stay there until the Allies get here.' He lowered his voice. 'I'll get someone to come and fetch you soon, *amore*. We can be together there.'

More hugs and kisses from his parents, and then, finally, he took her in his arms and kissed her. For a moment, she could believe there wasn't a war on. That it was just the two of them and she hadn't done what she'd done with Hofmann. But then reality bit, sinking its teeth into her like a viper. The man who could be the father of her baby was dead. But she felt nothing for him, not one iota of regret at his passing.

She melted into Marco. This was where she was meant to be. She wanted desperately for him to be her baby's father. Fate wouldn't be so cruel as to have it any other way, would it? Not after everything she'd been through. But fate was often cruel, she reminded herself.

And not to the people it should be cruel towards.

30

A massive explosion jolted Emma awake. Her heart pumped madly as the whole house shook. The terrifying crashing sound of falling glass, tiles and masonry rang in her ears. *Oh, my God, the palazzo is about to fall down!* She squeezed her eyes shut; there was nothing she could do. But then, miraculously, everything settled – like a broody hen that had ruffled its feathers before sitting back down on its eggs.

She checked the time – 4 a.m. – swung her legs from the bed, shrugged on her borrowed dressing gown, and ran out into the corridor. Her father, as well as Agata Brandini and Marco's parents, had got there beforehand.

'Edoardo has gone to find out if that explosion was the Germans blowing up the bridge,' Papà said, swiping a trembling hand across his forehead.

Emma exhaled a shaky breath.

The action had been on the cards the past couple of days. Wehrmacht soldiers had been arriving in Montepulciano in ever-greater numbers. They'd been swaggering around as if they owned the place, ordering that the shops be kept open to meet their demands – demands which they'd enforced at the point of a pistol. Their presence had made it too dangerous for Emma to be taken to visit Marco. More so, when they set about blowing up some of the townhouses, to obstruct the inner road. They'd also destroyed the magnificent gateway to the Medici fortress, and groups of Montepulcianesi had stood about, staring mournfully at the ruins before making their way to shelter in cellars for the night.

Emma startled as footsteps sounded on the stairs and Edoardo Brandini appeared.

'The *tedeschi* have indeed blasted the bridge to smithereens to delay the Allies. But the good news is that a large cohort of them have left the town.'

Emma hugged her father and then everyone was hugging everyone else and expressing the hope that the Germans really had gone at last.

'We should go back to bed, dear girl,' Papà said. 'We'll find out more in the morning.'

Emma did as he suggested. She slept deeply and didn't get up until nearly midday.

Downstairs in the dining room, she gasped with surprise. Marco was sitting drinking coffee with her father.

He got to his feet and hugged her.

'You'll never guess what we've been doing.' Excitement rippled in his voice.

'Marco and Tom came to fetch me earlier,' Emma's father chipped in. 'One of their sentries had come across a small patrol of Scots Guards, and their subaltern was asking for me.'

'Oh, my goodness.' Emma pulled out a chair.

'We took your father down to where they were waiting in a wheat field. They'd come from the Bivio, where they'd camped in the courtyard, and wanted to know if any Germans were still in Montepulciano.'

'I said I thought they'd all left, but couldn't be sure,' Papà said. 'They told me that our villa has been hit in two or three places, that the damage inside is considerable but not beyond repair.' He sighed. 'I can't wait to return and start sorting out the mess.'

'When will that be?' She looked from her father to Marco and back to her father again.

'They said the plan was for the regiment to occupy Montepulciano this afternoon.' A smile gleamed in Marco's eyes. 'We'll be able to head for home soon afterwards, I hope.'

'Where's Tom?' Emma asked, looking around for him.

'He went with the British. There are about twenty Germans who've stayed on here and they've gone to get rid of them.'

* * *

Emma spent the next four hours or so on tenterhooks until, at last, Edoardo rushed into the living room, where she was still attempting to read *Brave New World*.

'The Scots Guards are here,' he announced with a smile. 'Come outside and see!'

She put down her book and let herself be swept into the street with her father and Marco's parents.

In every doorway, beaming faces greeted the British, soon to be sent rushing back indoors when the whoosh of shells came from a German battery at the bottom of the hill.

Icy sweat beaded Emma's forehead.

Why haven't they given up and left with the other tedeschi?

'Come inside, darling,' her father said.

No sooner had she done so than a knock sounded at the door.

Two Allied officers were standing on the front step. They introduced themselves as Major Peters and Colonel Charles, and said they'd spent last night camped at the Bivio and wanted to meet Marchese Ginori.

Emma's father invited them in, and Edoardo and Agata soon appeared with a bottle of *Vino Nobile*.

They sat talking and drinking wine by the light of an oil lamp, the electricity having been cut a few days ago. Emma gathered her courage and asked about the terrible flying bombs she'd been told the Nazis had started launching against England. She was reassured when the officers said that the damage they caused, although extensive, was too erratic to be considered a military menace.

'Would you like us to drop you at your villa?' they asked when it was time to leave.

Emma's father accepted their offer without apparent hesitation, but she held back.

'I'd prefer to stay here with Marco's parents,' she said. 'If that's all right.'

She was hoping there would be an opportunity to tell Marco about the baby.

'Of course, dear girl.' Papà caught her eye. 'You'll be wanting to say goodbye to Tom, I expect.'

'Why? Is he going somewhere?'

'I must have forgotten to tell you. The Scots Guards who've arrived are from his old regiment, and they've agreed he can rejoin them.'

Emma stared down at her hands.

Poor Rosa. She'll be distraught.

31

It was Tom's last night and Rosa had been praying for the chance to spend it alone with him, but that was not to be. Shelling from the German battery below the town had increased, and everyone staying in the partisans' safe house had gone down to the cellar.

Rosa and Tom cuddled with Dora on a dilapidated sofa.

It wouldn't be long before the Allied military government took over. But would they be any better than the Germans? She expressed her concerns to Tom.

'I'm going to tell everyone about the kindness I've received here – and about the farmers who've risked their lives and homes to take me and other POWs in. That should convince them to play the game.'

'I hope so,' Rosa said.

She glanced at Marco and Babbo, who were sitting on rickety chairs opposite. They were discussing the harvest and hoping they would go home before too long so that the corn could be saved.

'As soon as we get back,' Marco was saying, 'the marchese wants every able-bodied man to be set to reaping.'

'But will we get back in time?' Babbo pondered.

'We can only hope.' Marco gave a sigh.

'Mammina, I feel sick,' Dora suddenly cried out.

Rosa took her hand and led her to the bucket in the corner of the cellar, where the child promptly threw up.

'There, there, *cocca*.' She smoothed the hair back from Dora's clammy brow. 'Let's go find you a drink of water.'

But Tom had known exactly what to do, and had appeared with a glass in his hand.

'Here, sip that,' he said.

In between sobs, Dora did as he suggested.

It had all become too much for her, Rosa realised. She picked her daughter up and carried her back to the sofa, where she soon fell asleep, snuggled between her and Tom.

'*Ti amo tanto*, Rosa,' he whispered. I love you so much.

'I wish you didn't have to go,' she said. 'I'm going to miss you terribly.'

'I'll miss you too, my darling. It won't be for long. We'll soon send the Germans packing.'

Rosa remembered how long it had taken the Allies to break through south of Rome. Was Tom being overly optimistic? The Germans wouldn't give up on Italy that easily. But she kept her pessimistic thoughts to herself.

Instead, she allowed herself to relish being with him, to enjoy breathing the same air as him, to feel his love for her vibrate between them.

She didn't expect to sleep. Mamma and Nonna were snoring fit to wake the dead. Her siblings were sleeping on mattresses placed on the floor. But Rosa was so tired, she eventually dropped off.

In the morning, they all went back upstairs for breakfast. Fulvio, the partisans' cook, had already managed to bake some bread and make barley coffee.

Rosa sat at the table next to Tom. She knew what was coming, and her stomach turned to lead.

'My regiment are expected to arrive any minute now,' he said. 'I've been told where to meet them.'

'So this is goodbye?' She met his eye.

'I'll try and visit before we leave this afternoon, my love,' he said.

She could only nod in response; her throat felt so tight.

* * *

Later, Mamma and Nonna said Rosa and Lucrezia could leave the little ones with them, so they could watch the Allied soldiers arrive.

Rosa accepted the offer gladly, to distract her from Tom's impending departure.

The steep, narrow roads of Montepulciano were filled with British troops, and all the population had come outdoors to greet them.

Rosa strolled arm in arm with Lucrezia.

Partisans, with tri-colour armbands and guns slung across their shoulders, stood at every street corner. Children crowded around the tanks, catching sweets thrown by the *inglesi*. Pretty girls had put on their best dresses, and were smiling flirtatiously at the soldiers.

'I wish I had something nice to wear,' Lucrezia said, frowning.

'Me too.' Rosa smoothed her skirt. A *stafetta* had lent it to her, along with some underclothes, but it would hardly be described as 'elegant'. She was grateful for them, though. And for the items of clothing the shopkeeper next door had given to the children.

She caught sight of Marco, strolling with Emma.

They approached and said they were heading for the safe house.

'I'll come with you,' Rosa said. 'Tom said he might get the chance to say goodbye before he leaves.'

'Oh, good.' Emma smiled. 'I'd like to wish him well.'

'I've said my goodbyes already,' Lucrezia chipped in. 'So I'll carry on out here a little longer.' She lowered her voice. 'I know you want to be alone with Tom, dear sister.'

Not much chance of that, Rosa thought as she set off with Emma and Marco down the narrow cobblestoned street.

Rosa's heart gladdened as she stepped into the front room. Tom was there already, sitting in the living room with Dora. He got to his feet and enveloped Rosa in his strong arms.

She stepped back and eyed him. He looked so handsome in his khaki Scots Guards sergeant's uniform.

'I'm glad I've caught you.' Emma came forward and gave Tom a hug. 'Stay safe, please. If you get any leave, you're always welcome at the Bivio.'

'We hope we'll push the Germans out of Italy sooner rather than later.' A smile quirked the corner of his mouth. 'I've promised Rosa that I'll visit.'

'Come, Emma,' Marco interjected. 'Let's give Rosa and Tom some privacy. We can go through to the kitchen.'

He clapped Tom on the back. '*Arrivederci, amico mio.*' Until we meet again, my friend.

Tom pulled him in for a bear hug. 'Bye, chum,' he said in English. 'I'll be back before you know it.'

And then, it was just the three of them. Rosa, Tom and Dora.

Tears streamed down Rosa's face, and Dora clung to his legs.

He lifted the child up and swung her around.

'Be good for your *mammina*, Dora. I know you will be, but I want her to tell me so when I return.'

'Will you be my new *babbo*?' she asked.

'Would you like that?'

'Yes.' She nodded vehemently. 'I would.'

'Good.' He put her down and wrapped his arms around Rosa. '*Arrivederci, amore mio.* As I said to Marco, I'll be back before you know it.'

She gave herself up to his kiss.

And the bittersweetness of it broke her heart.

32

Emma sat with Marco at the solid wood table in the partisans' kitchen with Rosa's parents and grandmother, drinking barley coffee. She steeled herself. She needed to talk to Marco and tell him about the baby. Get what she had to say over with to stop it festering like an infected sore. When Rosa's parents and nonna got up to go and say goodbye to Tom, Emma hung back.

'I'd like a word with you, Marco,' she said.

'Of course.' He led her up to the room he'd been sharing with Tom.

There, he sat her on his bed, pulled up a chair so he could sit opposite. He reached across the space between them and took her hand.

'You're looking very serious. Is anything wrong, *amore*?'

Her pulse thrummed and she took a deep breath. How would he react when she told him?

'I'm... I'm pregnant, Marco.'

A big smile spread across his face, and he pulled her in for a hug.

'I can't believe I'll be a father. That makes me so happy.' His voice vibrated with evident joy. 'We must ask the mayor to marry us as soon as possible.'

She shook her head, regret knotting in her belly. He must know the truth.

'You might not be the father, *tesoro*.'

'W... w... what do you mean?' He sagged back into his chair.

She told him. Told him haltingly about what had happened with Hofmann.

'I had to do it.' She looked him firmly in the eye. 'Otherwise he would have killed those innocent people.'

Marco said nothing. He stared at her, shaking his head in slow, back-and-forth sweeps of denial.

She spoke quickly now. If she didn't, she might not have the right words.

'It was horrific. He treated me like a whore. And maybe I whored myself in exchange for the lives of the Montaliani.'

'You're not a whore, Emma.' Marco seemed to choke on the words. 'You're the bravest girl I've ever met. I'm so sorry you went through that.'

'You're not angry?'

'I'm furious. But not with you. I'm glad that Nazi abomination is dead. I hope it was one of my bullets that finished him off.'

Marco perched on the bed next to Emma, his arm around her, and she nestled into him.

How Marco has grown up, she thought. The war had changed him. And his reaction showed that he truly loved her.

But then, he said, 'I know I'm the father. I was with you before that fucking German. The child is mine, you'll see, Emma.'

'But what if he or she isn't? How would you feel then?'

'He or she is your baby, *tesoro*. I'll love him or her as much as I love you.'

He brought his mouth to hers. Their kiss was gentle at first, filled with all the love they felt for each other. Then he kissed her more passionately, his tongue chasing hers.

She throbbed for him.

'Please, Marco, please make love to me...'

Tenderly, he undressed her, kissed the skin of her belly.

'Making love won't hurt the baby, will it?'

'Of course not.' She giggled.

He undressed himself, took her swollen breasts into his mouth, sucking on her nipples and applying pressure with his teeth and tongue.

She gave a soft moan.

'God, how I love you, *amore mio*,' he said.

His eyes smouldered as he eased into her.

She tensed, the memory of Hofmann making her freeze.

Marco kissed her lips.

'Relax, *tesoro*.'

She took a slow breath, released it, and took another.

'Brava. Well done.'

She held onto his shoulders, cradling him, her body moving with the same rhythm as his... until every vestige of her horrible experience with the German captain was replaced by the incredibly sensual, wonderful feeling of having Marco inside her.

They held each other tight while their breaths slowed. Then they turned towards each other, their foreheads touching.

Tears of happiness trickled down Emma's cheeks.

'I love you so much, Marco.'

He captured a tear with his thumb and brought it to his lips.

'I can't wait to be the father of our child. He or she *will* be our child, Emma. It doesn't matter how he or she was conceived.' He touched a finger to her mouth. 'It will be our secret, though. Neither of us can ever tell anyone.'

Overwhelmed with love for him, she trailed kisses down his face.

'I agree.' She sighed. 'I suppose I'll have to put my university studies on hold for a while...'

'Only until the baby is old enough for day care in an *asilo*.'

'You're already planning ahead.' She smiled. 'You really amaze me, my darling.'

He smiled back at her.

'Talking of plans. I'll walk you back to the Brandinis' and have a word with Edoardo. We should get married before we return to the Bivio.'

* * *

Edoardo, as Mayor of Montepulciano, issued a special licence. In the town hall that very afternoon, not long after the Scots Guards had been replaced by troops from a Coldstream regiment, Edoardo pronounced them husband and wife. Marco's parents were their happy witnesses.

Emma took Marco's hand as they walked through the city, luxuriating in the feeling of freedom, smiling at the soldiers who were being embraced by the townspeople and accepting glasses of wine from them. By then the German shelling had ceased. Emma presumed their battery had finally been annihilated.

Next morning, Edoardo arranged for a car to take Emma, Marco and his parents back to the Bivio. Rosa, her family, and the others would follow on as soon as transport could be organised.

A surreal feeling spread through Emma as their driver took them down the same way she'd walked just over a week ago. Shells and bomb-holes cratered the road and the fields. When they neared the Bivio, she gasped at the sight of the damage done to the fortress and the clinic, both of which had been badly hit. Further chaos met her eyes. A shell had made a huge hole in the garden façade of the villa, and another had fallen on the *fattoria*.

Emma descended from the vehicle, followed by Marco and his parents. Her father came to greet them, his expression grim.

But when Emma and Marco told him their happy news, not leaving out the fact that she was expecting a baby, a smile creased his face.

'You've cheered me up enormously.' He chuckled. 'Good thing I don't need a shotgun.'

He went on to say that the Germans had exploded a mine on the road below as a 'farewell gift'. Consequently, there were several holes in the villa's roof. When asked about the *fattoria*, he reassured Marco's parents that the house was liveable. Emma then said she would move in with them, according to the tradition that country brides lived with their husband's family.

'But only temporarily,' she added, having discussed the matter beforehand with Marco. 'When the baby is old enough, I'll study law in Florence. Marco will finish his architecture degree and we'll rent a flat. Our *bambino* or *bambina* will be looked after in an *asilo* when I have classes.'

Everyone trooped into the villa, aghast at the damage. In the dining room, the table was still laid, and there were traces of a drunken meal – empty wine bottles and smashed glasses. In the library, leather had been ripped off the armchairs, there were gaps in the shelves where books had once held pride of place, and more empty bottles lay in the fireplace. The toilets were filled to the brim with filth. Decaying meat had been left in the kitchen, the smell atrocious, and flies buzzed around. There was no water and still no electricity.

They went to inspect the *fattoria*. Marco's mother wept when she realised that the enemy had looted all her cooking utensils, her linen, most of her blankets, her dearly prized furniture –

bought one piece at a time, year after year. Orazio carried out an inspection, then said that about a third of the cattle, sheep and pigs were missing, not to mention all the chickens and other small animals, and many of the farm tools.

The task of clearing up was so monumental, Emma didn't know where they would start. But make a start they did. She helped sweep and clean until her back was aching.

Marco found a sack of beans and some sun-dried tomatoes, which his mother turned into a stew for their lunch.

They all had a rest in the afternoon heat. The bedrooms were the first to have received their attention, but they had to sleep on the floors, the mattresses all having been stolen.

Later, Emma went with Marco for a walk through the gardens. Sadness scratched in her throat at the sight of the shell-holes and machine-gun trenches. The Germans had stripped the pots off the lemon trees and azaleas, leaving the plants to die. The ground was strewn with mattress and furniture-stuffing, as well as many of Papà's private letters and personal documents.

Emma looped her arm around Marco's waist, and they went to stand by the parapet overlooking the valley. Slopes of cultivated land, golden with wheat and verdant with olives and vines, stretched below. From this distance, they appeared untouched by the war. She turned her gaze to the forested hills on one side and the *crete sinesi* clay knolls on the other, criss-crossed by the zig-zag road lined with tall black-green cypress trees. It was her home, and she loved it.

Marco tilted her chin and kissed her on the lips.

'Death and destruction have visited us,' he said between kisses. 'But this land has endured as it always has and always will.'

'I believe you're right, *tesoro*. The whirlwind has passed. We can hope for a better future for us and our child.'

33

ONE YEAR LATER

Rosa paced the platform at Montepulciano station, waiting for Tom to arrive. Marco had driven her here and the train from Florence was due at any moment. She prayed fervently he'd made his connection from Trieste, where his brigade had been posted in May. Disappointment had crushed her when she'd received the letter telling her about his posting – one of the many letters Emma had translated for her. Trieste was hundreds of miles from Tuscany and Tom didn't know when he'd get any leave.

A whole year had gone by since Rosa had last seen her Scotsman, a year of worrying intensely about him and missing him so much it had hurt. Sighing, she thought about his confident prediction that the Allies would rid Italy of the Germans in no time. How she'd wished that had been the case.

After leaving Montepulciano, Tom's unit had been assigned to the South Africans who'd been combating the Germans at Lake Trasimeno. They'd taken part in the British Eighth Army's battle for Florence and had subsequently been transferred to the US Fifth Army to help spearhead its advance on Bologna. Fierce fighting had ensued on the German Gothic Line in the Apennines to the south of that city. Thousands of troops had died on both sides. The weather and the terrain had been dreadful. There'd been a stand down during the harsh winter months, and Tom's brigade had been snowed in. His censored letters described his frustration at not being able to travel south and visit, and Rosa had been frantic with fear for his safety.

When spring had arrived, Tom's brigade had come under the command of the British once more. Again he'd been unable to get any time off. His unit took part in the liberation of Trieste after Germany had surrendered, but had been held up there while an intensive military–diplomatic struggle had been taking place between the Allies and the Yugoslav partisans, who'd also 'liberated' and occupied the area.

Now, happily, the situation had calmed down enough for Tom to be granted eight weeks' furlough prior to his demobilisation. He'd written to Rosa, asking if they could be married before he travelled to Britain to sort out the paperwork and get his old job back. She would then join him in Edinburgh with Dora. After months and months of waiting, Rosa would finally start her new life.

She gave a happy sigh – she might not be leaving her family without guilt if a miracle hadn't occurred. Her brother had come home. Her heart filled with gladness as she remembered his arrival three weeks ago. He'd turned up at the *podere* unannounced, with a remarkable story to tell.

After being left behind on the Russian border with Ukraine by the retreating Italian troops in February 1943, he and a friend – both with frostbitten feet – had slowly made their way across the snowbound plain. Every night they'd found a farmhouse, where they would sleep and where they were fed, lodged and treated with great kindness by the Ukrainians. When their feet got so bad that they could drag themselves no farther, a farmer took them to a small civilian hospital about 125 miles from Kiev. They'd come down with typhus and were cared for by the local doctor.

After they'd recovered, they walked to Kiev, which was in German hands. They were transferred to a military hospital in Warsaw, from where they were supposed to have been returned to Italy. But, when they heard about the Italian armistice with the Allies, the *tedeschi* turned against Maurizio and his friend, threatening to send them to a labour camp. So they escaped and joined the Polish resistance.

Rosa and her family had listened agog to Maurizio's tales of fighting the Nazis, how his friend had been killed, how the Soviets had betrayed the Polish partisans during the Warsaw uprising, and how the Red Army had gone on to capture and then detain Polish anti-communist fighters.

'That was when I decided to come home,' Maurizio had said.

He'd joined groups of displaced people, mainly Jewish survivors of the concentration camps, who were heading to Italy – where they were hoping to board ships that would take them to Palestine.

'The Nazis treated them worse than animals, Rosa,' Maurizio said to her. 'I won't elaborate, it's too distressful. When the truth comes out, the whole world will be truly shocked. I hope humanity will learn from it and that such evil will never be allowed to happen again.'

Mamma and Nonna were now feeding him up – he'd lost a lot of weight – and he was looking forward to helping with the harvest as soon as possible. Thank goodness things were more or less back to normal at home.

Rosa's breaths slowed as she remembered returning to the *podere* a year ago. The roof had been holed by a bomb, and the entire family had camped in the stable. Everything had been looted, but the marchese and Emma soon bought cooking pots and pans for their sharecroppers in Montepulciano – where the shopkeepers had buried them during the German occupation. The Allied military government provided help to the *padrone* by transporting lorryloads of building materials and all his farmers found themselves with a roof over their heads before the winter.

'Rosa, the train is arriving!' Marco's voice broke into her thoughts.

She bounced from foot to foot, and swallowed a shout of glee.

'Tom!' she called out.

He was climbing down from a carriage, and looked as handsome as ever in his khaki battledress uniform.

Catching sight of her, he spread out his arms. She ran straight into them, and he lifted her, kissing her and smiling widely.

'Rosa, you're even more beautiful than I remembered.' Another kiss, followed by a hug.

Tears of joy ran down her cheeks.

'*Grazie*. You're looking good too, Tom.'

'How's Dora?'

'Bubbling with excitement. She's so looking forward to being a bridesmaid with my little sisters.'

'And Lucrezia?'

'She's well. Extremely happy, in fact. She's met someone. A new teacher has arrived to run the school. He's from Bologna and appears to have fallen head over heels for her.'

'And the rest of your family?'

'Nonna is a little bit frail, but I suppose that's to be expected at her age. Everyone else is fine. Did you get the last letter I wrote, where I told you about Maurizio?'

'I did, indeed. Such wonderful news.'

Tom took her hand, and they walked up to where Marco was waiting for them.

The two men enveloped each other in a bear hug.

Before too long, Marco was driving them through the gates of the villa in his Fiat 1500. Emma came out to greet them, carrying her daughter, Ginevra, on her hip.

'My goodness, she's a beauty, Marco.' Tom chuckled. 'Which is surprising as she's the spitting image of you.' He clapped Marco on the back.

Rosa gazed at the child. Everyone remarked on how like Marco she was – she had his green eyes and dark, wavy hair.

Marco took the baby from Emma, and swung her up over his head.

Ginevra giggled and babbled, 'Pa. Pa. Pa.'

At barely six months old, she seemed very precocious.

'Come inside,' Emma said, leading them into the home farm-house. 'I'll show you to your room, Tom. And then Marco and I will leave you two lovebirds to become reacquainted.'

Alone with her fiancé, Rosa was suddenly overcome with shyness.

But then, Tom dropped down on one knee.

He stared up at her and her pulse raced.

'Rosa.' He cleared his throat. 'I know this is a bit late.' He took a diamond solitaire ring from his pocket and slid it onto her finger. 'I love you so much. You've made me the happiest man alive by agreeing to be my wife.'

Their love had endured through a year of separation. It was strong. They were strong. Whatever life threw at them, their love would prevail. Hope for the future flowed through her, and she smiled.

AUTHOR'S NOTE

Soon after I'd finished writing *The Tuscan Orphan*, I read Iris Origo's published diary, *War in Val d'Orcia*. I found the events described to be truly inspirational, and started imagining how fictional characters would have lived through those events.

For further inspiration, I decided to go on a research trip to the area. Situated in a relatively unknown part of southern Tuscany, the valley is named after the river which flows through it. The dusty clay knolls, known as *crete sinesi*, and the verdant woodlands, have now become a UNESCO world heritage site.

On a blustery September day, I visited *La Foce*, the villa which inspired the fictional *Bivio*. I went on a guided tour of the beautiful gardens, where I gazed out at the spectacular views towards Monte Amiata. My gaze also landed on the iconic avenue of zig-zagging cypress trees which the Origos had planted, and it occurred to me they could be a metaphor for humankind's everlasting journey on the uphill path towards a better world.

Many of the roads criss-crossing the valley are still unmetalled, but the fields are no longer farmed by sharecroppers.

Now, most of the *poderi* are being run as *agriturismi*, with first-class accommodation and swimming pools. The grandchildren of the original sharecroppers have restored the properties they inherited and many of them manufacture and export top-quality olive oil and wine.

Every year, hundreds of travellers enjoy the valley's rental homes and charming bed-and-breakfasts. I was fortunate to stay in one, but couldn't help wondering if other visitors knew about the rubble and human misery from which today's prosperity has emerged and that, in this peaceful Tuscan vale, human beings once ruthlessly bombed and shot at each other.

Further research led me to read *L'Ultimo Partigiano*, in which Roberto Pagliai records his interviews with several of the partisans who fought with the Resistance in the Val d'Orcia. My freedom fighters are an amalgam of these brave men.

The partisans' hideout, *Le Faggete*, is inspired by several of the locations used by the Resistance. And my fictional town of Montale is based on Montecchio, where a real-life battle took place between the *partigiani* and the fascists. The German wife of a local man interceded with the Nazis and managed to save the inhabitants from execution by firing squad. Emma's actions, however, are entirely fictional.

ACKNOWLEDGEMENTS

I continue to be hugely grateful for all the support I receive from the entire team at Boldwood Books and for their help in the publication of *Daughters of Tuscany*. In particular, I'd like to thank my lovely editor Emily Yau, whose editorial comments and suggestions have made this a better novel, I'm sure.

Thank you, Joy Wood and Nico Maeckelberghe, for beta reading the book as I wrote it.

Special thanks to JH, for his input.

Also, I'd like to thank my readers. It makes my author's heart so happy that you enjoy my books. And I mustn't forget the bloggers who've been such staunch supporters of my work. I'm truly thankful.

Last, but not least, I'd like to thank my husband, Victor, for his love and encouragement as I write my books, and for helping me on research trips. I'm looking forward to our next adventure in Sicily.

ABOUT THE AUTHOR

Siobhan Daiko writes powerful and sweeping historical fiction set in Italy during the second World War, with strong women at its heart. She now lives near Venice, having been a teacher in Wales for many years.

Sign up to Siobhan Daiko's mailing list for news, competitions and updates on future books.

Visit Siobhan's website: www.siobhandaiko.org

Follow Siobhan on social media here:

facebook.com/siobhan.daiko.author

x.com/siobhandaiko

instagram.com/siobhandaiko_books

ALSO BY SIOBHAN DAIKO

Letters from
the past

Discover page-turning
historical novels from
your favourite authors
and be transported
back in time

*Join our book club
Facebook group*

https://bit.ly/SixpenceGroup

*Sign up to our
newsletter*

https://bit.ly/LettersFrom
PastNews

Boldwood

Boldwood Books is an award-winning fiction publishing company seeking out the best stories from around the world.

Find out more at www.boldwoodbooks.com

Join our reader community for brilliant books, competitions and offers!

Follow us
@BoldwoodBooks
@TheBoldBookClub

Sign up to our weekly
deals newsletter

https://bit.ly/BoldwoodBNewsletter

Printed in Great Britain
by Amazon